AVOIDING EXTRAS

AVOIDING EXTRAS

K.A. LINDE

To Joel, I'm writing and dancing.

ALSO BY K. A. LINDE

AVOIDING SERIES

Avoiding Commitment ✦ *Avoiding Responsibility*

Avoiding Temptation ✦ *Avoiding Extras*

SEASONS

The Lying Season ✦ *The Hating Season*

The Breaking Season ✦ *The Faking Season*

CRUEL

One Cruel Night ✦ *Cruel Money*

Cruel Fortune ✦ *Cruel Legacy*

WRIGHTS

The Wright Brother ✦ *The Wright Boss*

The Wright Mistake ✦ *The Wright Secret*

The Wright Love ✦ *The Wright One*

RECORD SERIES

Off the Record ✦ *On the Record* ✦ *For the Record*

Struck from the Record ✦ *Broken Record*

DIAMOND GIRLS SERIES

Rock Hard ✦ *A Girl's Best Friend*

In the Rough ✦ *Shine Bright* ✦ *Under Pressure*

TAKE ME DUET

Take Me for Granted ✦ *Take Me with You*

STAND ALONE

Following Me

PARANORMAL ROMANCE

BLOOD TYPE SERIES

Blood Type ✦ Blood Match ✦ Blood Cure

YOUNG ADULT FANTASY

ASCENSION SERIES

The Affiliate ✦ The Bound

The Consort ✦ The Society

The Domina

AVOIDING DECISIONS

JACK'S POV
THE FIRST TIME JACK MEETS LEXI

1

CORNER CAFE

Jack sat in the coffee shop, drumming his fingers against the counter. His coffee rested half-empty next to him, a vestige of the mad after-class rush that wore on his nerves.

He was thankful for the reprieve, so he could chill and listen to the underground Seattle rock music he favored. There was a pretty new band that he liked even if they were small and local and no one else had heard of them before. Maybe one day, they would get picked up and be popular, but he kind of hoped not. He'd prefer to keep their sound original and not have them sell out

He was just ready to get off work. He had a few more hours left to deal with customers, and then he was planning to grab a beer and watch last weekend's college football games with Seth. He had some intro accounting homework to wrestle with, but after the day he'd had, that was the last thing on his mind.

"Large coffee, please."

"Yeah, coming right up," he said, turning around to complete the order. "Cream or sugar?"

"No, thank you," she said.

Jack glanced over his shoulder, a smirk crossing his face. He quickly tried to school his features into order as he turned around. It was that girl again. Almost every day he'd worked recently, she had been here, studying at a table adjacent to the counter.

He didn't know who she was. It didn't seem right to ask while he was working, and he hadn't found a way to bring it up during the short conversations they had when she ordered her coffee—always a large, always black. She might actually drink more coffee than him, which was a feat, considering he worked here.

"Here you go," Jack said, setting the steaming cup on the counter.

The girl was wearing soft pink lip gloss, accentuating her full lips, as she smiled up at him beneath thick black lashes. Under those lashes were deep, dark chocolate brown eyes as big as saucers that made him feel like he was sinking through quicksand. Her curly brown hair cascaded out around her shoulders and over the curves of her breasts, giving her a wild look.

His cock twitched as he leaned forward on the counter. He sure as hell didn't want anyone to notice his reaction. Christ, he was at work!

"Thanks." She handed him her credit card.

He promptly swiped it and handed it back to her along with a receipt.

She smiled up at him once more, a big grin showing all her teeth, like she had remembered her confidence after all. She quickly turned around and headed to her table where she immediately removed stacks and stacks of papers.

Blowing out a breath, Jack straightened and adjusted himself. Maybe he shouldn't get her name.

He fished his phone out of his pocket and hid it behind the register. His manager didn't like employees to be on their phones, but she wasn't in today. If he didn't have any customers, then he didn't see why it was a big deal.

He sighed when he saw that he had missed a text message from his girlfriend, Danielle.

Hey! Really missing you right now. Ugh, I wish I would have transferred in, but now, it's too late...

Ugh was right. He was really glad she hadn't transferred.

Since school had started a couple weeks ago, Danielle was hovering even more than normal. Somehow, they had survived freshman year with her attending community college in Savannah while he was in Athens. He knew he had kind of been an ass to her lately, but they had been dating forever, so Danielle was used to it.

Then came the summer. This summer had been brutal. He wasn't used to her being around all the time anymore. He wasn't used to her being in his space, taking up all his time, and forcing herself into everything he did. He had just forgotten what it was like to have a girlfriend around.

Seth had made fun of him all summer about it. Seth's affectionate term for him was *pussy-whipped*. He could take Seth's jokes when they were alone, but when Seth would say it around Danielle, Jack would get in a few good punches. Danielle thought it was cute and funny, and Jack thought it sounded like a slow, painful death.

After a summer of agonizing torture, he had really thought it was over. He couldn't take it anymore. Two weeks before school started, he had tried to break up with her, but she had looked at him with her coy smile and determined gaze right before she dropped down to her knees. How could he even argue with that?

Since then, that had pretty much been the staple of their relationship—Jack thinking he wanted to break up with her, and Danielle convincing him rather thoroughly that he didn't.

Still, he had moved back to Athens with Seth the first weekend he could. He was ready to have his own life back. Yeah, he probably should have manned up and just told her to fuck off, but it wasn't like he was getting it from anywhere else right now. Plus, he had the benefit of being four hours away from her. Maybe he would do it over fall break...or sometime when he knew he wouldn't be going home for a long time.

He ignored the message from Danielle. He might call her later or something—if he remembered.

As Jack rang up the next customer, he found his eyes drifting to that girl again. She had a friend with her, which was new. With a bleached out pixie cut and tight-ass pants, she was cute, but not hot like her friend. The new girl kept looking up in his direction, her breasts falling out of her low-cut top. Jack quickly turned away, not wanting to draw unnecessary attention, but he could still feel her eyes on him.

His phone beeped again, and he groaned, wondering when the messages would ever stop.

Can we Skype tonight? I'm really missing you. ;)

Oh, how the wink face wasn't necessary.

"You busy there?" a girl chirped happily.

Jack hastily put his phone away and stared up at the blonde girl with the big tits. Seriously, if her shirt were any lower, he would be able to see her nipples. Did she expect him to look at her face?

"How can I help you?" Jack asked.

The girl leaned forward on the counter as if he couldn't already see straight down her shirt.

"I'd like a caramel macchiato with a double shot of espresso and lots of whipped cream," she said in a seductive tone.

"Sure thing," Jack replied.

"So...what are you doing tonight?" the girl asked.

Jack sighed. In a way, he had expected it. Before this job, he hadn't known girls could actually be assertive enough to ask him out point-blank like that. He had always been polite about it, but they had never been his type, not that he really had a type. Blonde, blue eyes, nice ass, put together—that was Danielle. He didn't know if it was a type, but none of the girls who had approached him were ever it.

"Ah, you know, just hanging out with friends," Jack said with a shrug.

He placed the drink on the counter in front of her as she slid a purple slip of paper toward him.

"Do you see my friend over there?" She nodded her head in the girl's direction.

Jack glanced over at the girl. Her head was buried in her books like she might never look up again. She was chewing on her bottom lip and pushing a lock of hair behind her ear reflexively before it fell back into her face again.

"She's coming to this concert tonight."

The blonde pushed the paper into his hands.

Glancing down at it, Jack saw that it was an advertisement for a show at the Theatre. He had never heard of the group, but they were described as an original DJ-rap duo. Not really his thing.

"And?"

"You should be there," the girl said, raising her eyebrows.

He folded the paper. "I'll think about it."

"If you're smart, you'll show." She straightened abruptly and took her drink. "Thanks for the coffee."

The girl winked at him before she departed.

That hadn't gone as expected. Jack was surprised that he had been wrong. Nonetheless, he was glad he didn't have to turn the blonde girl down. It tended to hurt business.

Jack's eyes fell to the purple flyer in his hand. He knew he was a sucker for even contemplating the possibility of meeting her. Really, what could he accomplish by following those big brown eyes anywhere? He had been dating Danielle for three years now, and though he kept saying he was going to break up with her, he didn't really even believe himself.

He took one last look at the girl seated at the table across from him. When he stared her, he felt that same stirring in his body that he'd had when she had been at the counter. He didn't know what it was. She was hot, but it was more than that. It was just something about *her*.

Fuck. He was going to that concert.

2

THAT GIRL

"You want us to go to what?" Seth asked. He leaned back in the dingy brown recliner and reaching out for his beer.

"There's a concert at the Theatre tonight."

Jack ran his hand back through his dark hair as he waited for some smartass comment from his best friend. He knew it was coming.

"Dude, no one goes to the Theatre in the middle of the week unless they're chasing townie pussy. I don't recommend it," Seth said.

"You're such an asshole." Jack shook his head and plopped down on the couch. "You know that, right?"

"That's why the ladies love me." Seth raised his eyebrows suggestively.

"You're delusional."

Seth chugged the rest of his beer, set the empty aluminum can on the table, and belched. He wiped his mouth with the back of his hand and smiled at Jack.

"Seriously, how *do* the girls resist you?" Jack asked sarcastically.

"Can't keep them off me."

Jack hated to admit how true that was. His friend had the weirdest game Jack had ever seen. It was like the less Seth tried, the more girls threw themselves at him. Since they had started college together, Jack couldn't remember a single time when Seth didn't have at least two or three girls around the apartment, vying for his attention.

"So, why do you really want to go to the Theatre?" Seth asked, returning his attention to the football game on the screen.

Jack was silent for a minute. It wasn't that he couldn't tell Seth about the hot girl he had seen at work. He had told Seth about hundreds of hot girls he'd met while working. He didn't know why he wanted to hide it, especially after just asking Seth to go to the concert with him. It just...something about this felt different. Why was he making a big deal out of this? After all, it was just a girl, and it was just a concert.

"I was invited." Jack took out the purple piece of paper from his pocket and unfolded it before handing it to Seth.

He looked at it briefly and scoffed. "DJ-rap duo Nick and Neal? Dude, are you serious right now?"

"What the fuck else do you have better to do besides work on finishing off that case of beer?"

"Anything sounds better. I don't have time for wannabe rappers when I have free booze sitting at home."

"If it's any consolation, a blonde with huge tits gave this to me," Jack said.

Seth's ears perked up. "Now I'm listening."

Jack chuckled to himself and grabbed the paper. "She and her friend are going to the show, and she gave me the paper while leaning against the counter and showed me her nipples."

Seth walked into the kitchen and grabbed another beer. "Wait, are you into her? Because you know how I love girls who show off their nipples in the middle of the day," Seth called out.

"She's all yours," Jack offered. He hoped he sounded generous and not just like he was giving in too easily.

Seth crashed back into the recliner, tossed Jack a beer, which was caught in midair with one hand, and then he popped open his own.

"So, it's the other girl then," Seth said intuitively.

Damn! Seth knew him too well. Even when he tried, Jack couldn't hide anything from Seth. That was the problem with staying friends with people Jack had known all his life. Sometimes, he thought Seth knew him better than he knew himself.

"I mean, she's hot," he said casually.

Seth stopped mid-drink and set his beer down. "Whoa."

"What?"

"I don't know, dude," he said, staring at Jack. "First, you hesitated, which means she drew your attention. Most girls really don't for some reason. Second, you answered me like you didn't care, which immediately makes me think you do. So, who is this chick?"

Jack shrugged and turned away. "Just a girl who comes into the coffee house. I don't know her name or anything."

"Dude, you've got it bad."

"Fuck off. You don't know what you're talking about," Jack said gruffly.

"Remember when you first started dating Danielle, and I told you it was a terrible fucking idea?"

Jack slung his arm across the back of the sofa and threw his head into the cushion. He knew where this was going.

"Well, it was a terrible fucking idea. She's a fucking doormat. I mean, I didn't blame you for getting laid all the time in high school, but now, you can get way better ass than that, man," Seth said. He shook his head like he couldn't believe that Jack was still with Danielle.

"Whatever."

Great comeback.

"I'm totally going to this concert with you, and I'm bringing the guys," Seth said with a crooked smile. "I hope you fuck her until your dick falls off."

3

———————

THE THEATRE

The guy sitting behind the desk was about as townie as it came in this city. He was tall and lanky. No, he was more like skinny or even scrawny. Jack was sure the guy had never heard of a gym before. He had tattoos running up and down his arms and peeking out from beneath his perfectly rumpled ironic T-shirt. Jack liked to keep his hair long enough to fall into his eyes, but this guy's hair was just too long and stringy. Hygiene was lacking all around.

"ID?" The guy thrust out his hand while looking at Jack in disdain.

At least the feeling was mutual.

Jack handed him his fake ID, which was a duplicate of a friend of his. He didn't think it looked much like him, but in Athens, it didn't matter. If it said he was twenty-one, and it wasn't just a flimsy piece of paper, then no one gave a shit.

"Great," the guy said.

He barely glanced at it before handing it back to Jack. He placed a giant black turtle stamp on Jack's hand and let him pass.

Jack pulled open the door to the Theatre and walked into

the music venue. The room was cool as if to make up for the Georgia heat, and he was glad he had worn his dark jeans and black button-up with the sleeves rolled to three-quarter length. His trusty navy Chuck Taylors were on his feet.

His roommates, Seth, Luke, and Michael, had come with him to the show. The conversation to get all his roommates to come out with him had been about as embarrassing as Seth could manage, and he had a talent in such things. His friends, Clark and Hunter, had been over to witness the spectacle, too. None of them liked Danielle, and they were more than happy to help Jack find someone else, so he would grow some balls and dump her. Clark was the only one who had been hesitant, but peer pressure had won him over in the end. Clark and Hunter were going to meet them out for drinks later since they had an intramural soccer game.

"So, which one is she?" Seth asked as he walked in behind Jack.

Jack made a quick sweep of the room. "I don't see her."

He had only been here a handful of times to see some pretty popular bands or to catch a couple local bands that had a strong following in Athens. Last October, he and all the guys had come here for a Halloween blowout full of angels, devils, cowgirls, and every other variety of slutty costume imaginable. People were crushed wall-to-wall while a DJ blared club music. This was nothing like that. The venue was actually quite sad on a weekday.

About two-dozen people were standing in the center of the room, bobbing up and down to the college rap music some guy was spitting into the microphone. A handful of townies sat around the perimeter of the room on cheap couches and bar stools, drinking PBR, and ignoring the music.

And then, there she was. She was wearing a short black dress and heels that accentuated her toned legs and butt. Jack had only ever seen her in the outfits she wore to study in at the coffee shop, which usually consisted of a loose T-shirt and jeans. She had gone from hot to off the charts in that dress.

"That one," Jack said, gesturing to the girl.

"And she's not even blonde," Seth said, elbowing Jack in the side.

"Ha-ha," he responded dryly.

"I'd fuck her."

"You'd fuck anything."

"Yeah. Anything that hot."

"That's the girl with the big tits." Jack pointed out the girl who was jamming out to the music at the front of the stage.

"She's actually into this music?" Seth looked contemptuous about the girl's lack of taste. "I'm going to pass. If Chasity is working at Chamber, I'll see if she'll give me a blow job in the bathroom."

"Good luck with that."

"Anyway, go talk to your girl. I'll take the guys to the bar." Seth walked away with the rest of their entourage, leaving Jack alone to determine his course of action.

She was here, swinging her hips side to side as if in invitation. Her lips were moving along with the music, and he could see the shine of that damn pink lip gloss teasing him from a distance. He had come to the show with the intention of meeting that girl. He was too committed to back out now.

Taking a deep breath, Jack walked across the empty room and stood next to the girl. She was so enthralled with the music that she didn't even notice him. Her eyes were glued to the duet on stage, and she was yelling out all the words she knew.

"You're not bad. Maybe you should show them how it's done," Jack said, leaning over to her.

When she giggled, her curls bounced all around her face. One strand was stuck to her pink lip gloss, and he had to fight back the urge to brush it away. What had gotten into him?

The girl turned toward him, and the look of shock on her

face was about as obvious as her friend's flirtation had been earlier that day. She tried to recover, and damn, was it cute to watch her try.

"You think so?"

"Honestly, no," Jack teased.

She was good, but he kind of liked to see her all flustered.

"Well, thanks. I'm very offended right now."

Her hand fell to her heart as if she was wounded, and Jack took the opportunity to let his eyes drop to her chest. Yeah, she had a pretty nice rack.

"So...do I know you or do you always just insult people when you first meet them?" she asked.

He snapped his eyes back to her face. He could drown in those dark eyes.

She was so tiny that he had to bend down to avoid yelling over the music. He cleared his throat softly before he responded. "I think you study at the coffee shop where I work."

He breathed the smell of her in. How did girls always smell so good? He didn't even know how to describe it, except that it could have been edible.

"I think you might be right." She shot him a smile that could kill.

She removed the tiny piece of hair still stuck to her pink lip gloss and then tucked the loose strand behind her ear. They never broke eye contact, and he wondered if she knew what she was doing to him.

"Are you much into college boy rap?" she asked abruptly.

He laughed at the turn in conversation. "No, not really, but this guy's not bad. Is he a friend of yours?"

"Yeah, he lives in my dorm."

So, she was a freshman. He wouldn't have guessed that. Something about her confidence and the sexuality she exuded had made him think that she was his age or older, not that he minded the age difference in the slightest.

"Nice. Those guys over there." Jack pointed at the bar where his roommates were sitting. "They lived on my hall last year in the dorms. Which one are you in?"

"Um...Russell."

"That's where we were. Fifth floor east. You?"

"Five north," she told him.

Fuck. If she were a year older, they would have lived on the same floor together.

"Small world."

"Yeah, it is," she said, tucking another lock of hair behind her ear. "How exactly did you hear about the band? I mean, if you don't really listen to the music."

Jack reached into his back pocket and pulled out the folded piece of paper. "I believe a friend of yours gave this to me." He pointed the girl out in the crowd.

Her eyes were brimming with happiness as she became all giggly. "Well, yeah, that's Olivia for you," she said, shrugging. "Oh, I'm Lexi, by the way." She extended her hand to him.

"Lexi...hmm...I like that," he said, taking her outstretched hand firmly in his. "Jack. It's nice to meet you."

Jack let the silence stretch between them as all hope of conversation died with the increasing volume of the hip-hop beats. When the duo's set ended, everyone started to leave the venue. Lexi filed out of the room with the rest of her friends, and he followed. He caught Seth's eye and nodded his head toward the door.

They made it outside and past the townie that had stamped his hand. As Lexi's friends all turned and started walking to the backstage door, she stood with Jack off to the side and waited. His friends stood on the sidewalk a short distance away.

Now, he had to figure out what the fuck he was going to do. The show was over. He knew her name. Wasn't that all he had come for?

Her friend, Olivia, exited last. She was swaying on her feet, humming loudly to herself. "Hey, sweetie." She kissed Lexi on the cheek, and without another word, she stumbled along after the rest of the group.

"I guess she's a bit drunk," Lexi said to him.

"A bit?" he questioned with a smirk. "Hold on one second." Jack walked over to his friends standing in a clump on the sidewalk. "Hey guys, I'll meet you at Chamber. I think Chasity said she was working."

Seth winked at him, and the other guys chuckled like they thought he might bang the girl right then and there. They departed down the street, happily leaving him alone with Lexi.

When he turned back to Lexi, she was glancing around the corner toward her friends. "I'm not sure what my friends are doing. But by the look of things, I'm going to have to carry half of them home."

Even in her high heels she was more than a handbreadth shorter than him. It would have been interesting to see her try.

"I should go catch up with them before they get into any trouble."

He didn't know if she was actually interested and playing it off or if she was just ready to be rid of him.

"My friends are probably lost without me, too," Jack said. It surprised him that he wasn't ready for her to leave.

"Are you working tomorrow?" she asked.

"Are you studying tomorrow?"

"Yeah."

"Then, I should be there."

"Guess I'll see you there."

"Sounds good," he said, knowing she was going to leave and he wouldn't see her again until the next time he worked.

She turned and started down the alley.

He should let her leave. He should. Honestly, he really, *really* should.

What good could come from him stopping her? He had a

girlfriend back at home. Sure, he could become friends with Lexi. She could hang out with Seth and the guys. Maybe even meet Danielle sometime. That might be feasible...maybe.

He knew that letting her go was the smart thing to do. If he wanted anything from this, then he needed to be smart about it. Leave her alone...watch her walk away...figure things out with Danielle...

That was what he should have done.

But he couldn't.

They got along, and they had some kind of connection. He would be an idiot to not do anything about it. Even if absolutely nothing came from it and they just became friends that would be okay with him. Her leaving without him knowing if he would ever see her again...that wasn't okay with him. He couldn't see that ever being okay with him.

"Lexi!" Jack called, jogging down the street to catch up with her.

She turned to face him, those big brown eyes swallowing him whole. He had to see her again.

"I know you have to study tomorrow, but what are you doing Friday?"

She didn't respond right away, as she seemed to be thinking about her schedule. He waited impatiently, wondering what she could be doing.

"I don't have any plans," she finally responded.

Jack blew out a breath. *Good.* "Do you want to hang out?"

Lexi nodded. "I thought you'd never ask."

4

THE DATE

He should call the whole thing off.

Jack stared down at his phone, wavering back and forth. He knew that if he broke off the date right before the event, he would look like a total dick. Not a good first impression. But if he didn't call it off and it ended up being a real date...then he'd feel even more like a dick.

In the end, it was this backward way of arguing with himself that led to his decision. If he were going to look like a dick either way, then he would rather spend time with Lexi. He was probably overanalyzing this anyway. This probably wasn't even a date.

Seth, Luke, and Michael had left to pick up Hunter and Clark. Jack knew that Seth was trying to get out of his hair. Despite the fact that he and Seth had gone to dozens of parties, bought drinks for girls, and then danced and flirted, Jack had *never* done anything like this before. There was always a point where he was like...well, time to get back to Danielle. Seth would bring a girl or two home, and Jack would go to bed alone. There wasn't even a moment when he'd thought it would be any other way. He was pretty sure that

Seth believed that would change tonight, so he had left Jack alone.

Jack was happy for the reprieve, but he couldn't let anything happen.

"Fuck it."

He shook his head and shoved his phone in his pocket.

He had already made up his mind. He wasn't going to go back on it.

Jack walked out to his car and revved the engine. He shot off a text message to Lexi, saying he was on the way. He didn't live too far from the dorms, so it was a quick commute. Soon enough, he was driving up to the front of Russell Hall. He pulled over, turned on his hazard lights, and called Lexi to let her know he was here.

She answered on the second ring. "Hello?"

"Hey, do you want me to come upstairs?" Jack asked.

"Nah. No point in making you try to get past security. I'll be right down."

Jack hung up the phone and waited for her to leave the dorm. A few minutes later, he saw a girl racing down the steep hill to where his car was parked. Her dark hair had been tamed and slicked back into a high ponytail. Her curls bounced up and down as she jogged down the hill. She looked great in dark skinny jeans and a green tank top that hugged her in all the right places.

She reached his car, opened the door, and slid into the black leather seat. He stared at her just long enough to see that she had on that same damn pink lip gloss. For a split second, he wanted to lean over and kiss those plump lips, but then he recovered himself. Letting off the clutch, he flew down the road.

Jack took a breath, already relaxing in her presence. All the anxiety from worrying about whether or not this was the right idea fell away from him.

"So, where are we going?" Lexi asked.

She leaned back into the seat as he took a turn.

"It's a surprise."

"Hmm...I like surprises."

"I thought you might." Jack glanced at her briefly, taking in her slight smile.

He put his iPod on shuffle, and John Mayer's acoustic cover of *Free Fallin'* filtered through the speakers. He veered the car toward their destination, tapping his fingers against the steering wheel in time with the guitar chords.

"Do you play?" Lexi asked.

"A little."

"Oh yeah? What instruments?"

He chuckled softly, thinking about the answer to this question. He had been kind of a musical fiend when he was younger. He had picked up every instrument imaginable. He wasn't wonderful at any of them, but he was good at pretty much all of them.

"*Just* guitar, bass, piano, saxophone, and some drums, but I'm really rusty."

"Jesus!" Lexi cried. "All I can do is sing."

"Oh, and I sing." He smirked as he hit the brake at a red light.

"Well, don't you seem to be good at everything?" Lexi said, staring up at him through thick dark lashes.

Jack hastily returned his attention to the road, but he still watched her out of the corner of his eye. "You just wait and see."

"I look forward to it." She giggled, turning back around to face the front.

Jack's smirk grew with her laughter. Something about Lexi seemed to just fit. She was so easy to be around. There was no forcing the conversation. There were no awkward silences. There was only Jack and Lexi.

He took the last turn to their destination, and Lexi's eyes

widened considerably. Before them, on an expanse of university property that was typically just an empty field, stood a recently constructed carnival with university students flooding the park. A giant Ferris wheel with dozens of bright twirling carts rested at the center of the field with carnival rides and booths surrounding it.

"I didn't know a carnival was coming through town!" Lexi cried.

"One night only," Jack explained. "The university sets up celebrations like this throughout the year. Since you're new, I thought I'd take you to the first one of the year."

He was rewarded with a gorgeous smile that knocked him breathless. He was glad that she liked the surprise, but if she kept looking at him like that, she wouldn't have any pink lip gloss on by the end of the night.

A plump older man in an orange vest was waving a light stick to direct them into a makeshift parking spot on the lawn.

The couple trekked across the muddy terrain toward the vinyl ticket booth. After handing over their student identification cards, the student association representative slid the cards through a reader. The machine dinged each time, confirming their authenticity.

"Have a good time, and don't forget to grab a complimentary T-shirt on your way out," the woman said.

She handed them back their cards with one hand and used the other to gesture toward a display of boxes containing hundreds of bright green tees.

"Thanks," Jack said.

He grabbed Lexi's arm and raced through the entrance. She laughed completely and totally carefree as she rushed after him through the bright flashing carnival signs and booths. Jack pulled up short when he saw who was standing directly in front of them.

Damn! He thought he would have had more alone time with Lexi before he ran into his friends.

Between his five friends, they were counting out at least several hundred orange paper tickets, like little kids at Chuck E. Cheese. Each looked more excited than the next. Seth and Clark began trying to steal each other's tickets, and Jack shook his head, expecting a fight to break out any minute. He laughed at their behavior, not surprised in the least.

"Hey, guys," he said, casually approaching them with Lexi.

They all stared at her with knowing smiles on their faces.

He could have punched them, but instead, he just swept out his hand and said, "This is Lexi."

Thankfully, the guys gave their names and nodded hellos without completely embarrassing him. He hadn't known what to expect from his friends when they would inevitably meet her. Maybe Seth had talked some sense into them.

After introductions, they had to decide which ride to hit first. Seth took the lead as per usual, and he started to push them toward the bumper cars. When Luke put up a fight, claiming they always ganged up on him, he and Seth started arguing.

Jack laughed as they bickered, but his focus was on Lexi. She seemed completely relaxed with his friends. They were a lively bunch, and most girls didn't seem to fit in right away. He liked that she had no such problems.

Overriding Luke's complaints, the group got into the line for the bumper cars.

Jack moved closer to Lexi, taking a little too much pleasure in sidling up to her. He whispered in her ear, "We actually do gang up on Luke. Better make sure you join in on the fun. His reaction will be well worth it."

She nodded and even seemed anxious to mess with Luke.

Had Jack ever met a girl who immediately followed along with their joking?

As expected, Luke got rocked on the bumper cars. When he came off the ride, he started swinging at anything he could get his hands on. He even knocked over a tiny blonde in his angst. His friends' laughter only egged him on further.

Without thinking, Jack slung his arm across Lexi's shoulders as they laughed. As she turned into him, trying to catch her breath through giggles, he breathed in sharply. He needed to stop this. Why did she make that so hard?

"I cannot believe him," Lexi said, breaking contact, as she wiped away tears of laughter.

"He is a riot," Jack confirmed.

They watched Luke try to punch Seth, but Seth ducked under Luke's halfhearted blow easily.

"Why don't we get you something to rot your teeth?" Jack suggested.

He wanted her away from the walking comedy act, so he could have her all to himself again. He grabbed her hand and pulled her away toward a cotton candy machine. Her hand fit perfectly in his, and he quickly dropped it when he came to that realization.

Needing to change the subject, Jack asked, "So, tell me, Lex, what do you normally do on Friday nights?"

She shrugged. "I hang out with my roommate or Olivia, go downtown, see movies, game nights, dinners, fraternity parties."

She seemed to add the last part reluctantly.

"Cool. I like to do all of those things," Jack said with an easygoing smile.

"Fraternity parties?"

"Mike's in a fraternity," he told her. "So, yes, even fraternity parties. Probably not as often as my freshman year though."

After they ordered cotton candy, they made their way toward the Ferris wheel. When Jack offered the candy to Lexi, she snatched a piece of it and stuck it in her mouth. He stared down at her mouth where pink sugar had mingled with her lip gloss. He couldn't seem to pull his eyes away.

Lexi licked her lips, and Jack swallowed.

He would really like to know what that tasted like.

"You're such a mess," he said, trying to cover his inappropriate thoughts.

They stopped at the line for the Ferris wheel, which was wrapped around the ride. Jack popped some cotton candy into his mouth as she watched the machine transfixed. He didn't even see the giant ride when standing next to her.

He let the sugar dissolve in his mouth before speaking. "What's your major?"

"As of today, I'm undecided." She seemed happy about it.

"An indecisive one, I like it."

"I'm not indecisive. Just open minded."

"Same thing."

"Well, what's your major, Mr. Decisive?" She stuck one hand on her hip and gave him with a knowing look.

"I'm not decisive, just practical. I'm pre-business, likely going to the accounting route. Not so sure though."

Lexi wrinkled her nose. It was adorable.

"Ew. I'll forestall practical. Thank you!"

He found himself laughing at her forthrightness. She didn't seem to hold anything back.

"Yeah, it's what I'm good at."

"At least there are a lot of jobs out there for you. Not much a person can do while being undecided, and what I really want to do has only a few more jobs than that," she said, shrugging her shoulders.

"And what is that? What do you *really* want to do?" he asked. Despite the joking, he found that he was actually very interested in what she wanted to do with her life. It suddenly mattered a lot to him.

She paused before answering, "Gymnastics."

"That's awesome," he said, noticing all the wonderful muscles gymnastics had put on her small frame. And...she was probably flexible. He needed to stop that line of thinking or else it could get embarrassing.

He knew the gymnastics captain. He wondered if Lexi had been recruited or if she had tried walking on. "Have you talked to the gymnastics team here? If you like it so much, you should try out."

"No," she responded.

"Why not?

"You don't just try out for the gymnastics team here. They're amazing. If they don't recruit you, then you have no chance. No walk-ons. Nothing."

"How do you know that? Were you recruited?"

"No, I wasn't," she said sharply.

Oh, sore subject. He should introduce her to Krista. Maybe that would help.

"Oh, well, I know one of the gymnasts. I bet she could talk to the coach. Even if you can't be on the team, you could probably practice with them."

The glance she gave to him was as if she were approaching a Martian.

"Okay, maybe not," he said, raising his eyebrows. He took another bite of cotton candy to prevent himself from speaking again.

"Even if I could get to talk with the coach, there would be no way she would let me practice with them."

"Never know until you try," he said, swallowing the remaining bit.

She was hot when she got herself all riled up. Luckily, they were now at the front of the line, so he didn't have time to think about it again.

Jack handed the man four orange tickets, and then he ushered Lexi into a big swinging yellow bucket with the number twenty-five plastered against the back. He recognized the guy working, and as Lexi took a seat, he asked the guy to do him a favor. The guy laughed, called him an asshole, and told him to sit down.

Once Jack took his seat next to Lexi, the Ferris wheel began to rotate in an endless circle. Jack smirked at Lexi, and then started shaking their bucket back and forth. She grabbed on to the sides and squeaked. The girl in the bucket in front of them started threatening them, but he just laughed.

Lexi put her hand on his knee. "Calm down. We don't want to get kicked off!"

"I know the guy who's running it. No way we'll get kicked off," Jack said.

But he stopped anyway and used that moment to throw his arm across the back of the bucket seat. Lexi relaxed until she was almost leaning into him but not quite. He wondered what she was thinking.

As they made their final rotation, the ride crawled to a stop at the very top, looking out across the open fields. Jack smiled, silently thanking his friend, as the sun was setting low on the horizon, casting the last sliver of orange, pink, and red on the sky.

The world was lost to them in that moment, and without a second thought, he dropped his arm across her shoulders and drew her into him, her head falling into the crook of his neck. She fit into him like she was the missing puzzle piece. She sighed contentedly just as the sun dropped from the sky, leaving them to stare out at the twinkling white stars burning in the distance.

They spent the next several hours perusing the carnival life. He even won her a huge teddy bear from a dart game. She held it tightly as they made their way toward the exit with the rest of the crowd. An associate stuffed two green T-shirts into their hands as they stepped across the threshold.

Later that evening, Jack drove Lexi back to her dorm. The whole time he couldn't stop wishing that the night didn't have to end. He'd had a great time with her, and despite all the complications, he really wanted to see her again. It felt like only seconds before he was pulling up in front of her dorm again.

"Do you want me to park and walk you up?" Jack asked. He turned on his warning blinkers again.

"No, not necessary. Thanks," Lexi said, collecting her things to exit.

He couldn't let her just leave like that. He'd had too good of a time to let her just leave like that.

"Hey, wait," he said. He threw the car in park and ran around to the other side.

He had to say good night. Fuck everything else...he just *had* to. It was Lexi.

As soon as she was at arm's length, he reached out for her and pulled her into his arms. When she slid her arms up around his neck, he pushed their bodies flush together as he stood there, letting her legs dangle.

He couldn't help feeling like she belonged there. He didn't want her to go. He wanted to put her back in the car and take her to his place. He wanted to kiss her, explore her. He wanted to know everything about her little body. He wanted to know everything about her. Just her.

Fuck. What was he doing?

With her pressed into him, all he could think was that it didn't matter.

"I hope you don't mind, but I couldn't leave without a hug."

"Oh no," she said breathily, "I don't mind at all."

He had to restrain himself as he placed her back on her feet. He couldn't kiss her. No, he couldn't go that far. He wouldn't do that to Danielle—no matter how ready he was to break up with her, no matter how much he wanted Lexi, no matter how much Lexi was staring up at him like she would go back with him.

He bent down and placed a chaste kiss on her cheek. He'd give himself that much. But that was it. He needed to get out of there before he changed his mind.

Straightening abruptly, he turned and fled. He felt like a coward...even if he was doing the right thing.

5

CHOICES, CHOICES

Jack hadn't been able to stay away from Lexi. Something was wrong with him. What kind of dick keeps letting her show up when he couldn't find the right time to tell her about his girlfriend?

She kept appearing at the coffee shop, chatting with him in between studying for her tests. Then, he started bringing coffee to her at her classes. She began coming over to the apartment and playing video games with the guys.

Soon, she was always around, and he liked her being around all the time. And the more he liked her being around, the less he wanted to tell her about Danielle.

He tried to keep his distance. He would never be around her when he was drinking. He didn't trust himself to not do anything.

On the first game day, she had tailgated with friends on the other side of campus, which was a relief because Danielle had shown up. He'd had no idea how he would have explained that.

When he had gone home last weekend, he thought about breaking up with Danielle. Sure, a large part of the reason that he hadn't done it was probably due to the sex, but they had been together for so long that when he was with her, it was just different. He didn't know what he wanted to do.

Then, there was the time that he almost hadn't been able to hold it back. Lexi had come over for to watch a movie on Sunday night, and she had dressed up for him. She was all smiles and flirting. He had picked her up and carried her into his room, kicking himself the whole time but knowing that he wasn't going to stop.

He had tried to tell her. He'd tried to say what she was driving him to do, but then she had straddled him, and he was lost. If his phone hadn't rang in that moment—with fucking Danielle calling no less—he knew he wouldn't have stopped. And it scared him.

Lexi terrified him. How did she have such control over him? He'd never cheated on anyone before. That wasn't the kind of person he was! But when those big brown eyes stared up at him, begging and pleading, and she smiled up at him with her pouty lips coated in pink lip gloss...he fucking forgot who he was.

But he hadn't kissed her. And he wouldn't.

She was coming over later, and he was going to end it. He was going to tell her everything. That was the way it had to be.

Jack sighed and picked up his phone to call Danielle. Maybe if he heard her voice, it would remind him that he was making the right decision.

"Oh my God, is Jack Howard calling me?" Danielle asked snootily into the phone.

"Yeah." Jack scrunched up his eyebrows. What the fuck was her deal?

"Well, that's new. I thought I was the only one who called anymore," she snapped.

"Apparently not," he said, gritting his teeth. He didn't know how much of this conversation he could handle if she was going to act like a bitch.

"Are you going to come see me this weekend? Or do I have to drive to Athens *again*?"

The way she said the word again was like he had never driven down to see her, but he had just been there two weeks ago.

And suddenly, he realized...he didn't even want to see her this weekend. "Actually, I'm working all weekend. I can't come down to Savannah, and you'd just be stuck here all alone."

"So, now, you don't even want me in Athens!"

"Danielle, do you have something you want to say? Because I'm tired of this passive-aggressive shit," he barked, surprised by his anger bubbling up.

"I'm fine. Fine!"

"You're clearly not fine, so just spit it out."

"Fine! You know what? I'm tired of being the one putting all the effort into this relationship. I'm tired of traveling and calling and messaging and trying to spend every ounce of time with you when you only want to fuck me. I'm tired of you not acting like you used to. I'm still your girlfriend, and I don't even feel second-best...I feel last!" she said, her voice cracking. He heard the tears in her voice.

God, he hated crying.

"Stop crying, Jesus. You're not last in my life." Was she?

"Yes...yes, I am! You don't even know how you treat me!"

"How do I treat you?" he asked in frustration.

"Like I'm last! Work, school, the guys, parties...everything comes before me. How can we have a relationship if that's how you treat me, Jack?"

"I don't know." And he really didn't. Maybe...they couldn't.

"Well, if you don't know, then I certainly don't. So, maybe... maybe we should just take a break!" she chirped

"Fine," he responded immediately. "Whatever."

"Fine!"

The line went dead in his hand. She had hung up on him. They were on a break.

Whoa. What the hell had just happened? And how had it spiraled out of control so fast?

He flung his phone onto the couch and stormed into his bedroom. He needed to take a shower or do something to get his mind off of this. He couldn't believe she had just done that.

6

———————

THAT MOMENT

Jack heard a knock at the door. He grabbed a blue T-shirt from off the clean clothes pile and threw it over his head. His hair was still damp from the shower, but it had calmed him down and made him think more clearly. Whatever had just happened with Danielle…whatever break they were on was probably for the better.

When he opened the door, he saw Lexi standing on his front porch. She was the whole reason that this was for the better. She looked amazing in tight pants and a bright silky shirt. Her hair was down, her eyes lined, making them look even bigger than normal, and she was wearing that pink lip gloss. He was going to try that today and see if it tasted as good as he had thought for the past month.

"Hey," Lexi said with a smile, walking into his house.

"Hey, it's good to see you."

And it was.

He reached and drew her into a hug. She folded into him like she had been anticipating it as he slid his hands around her small frame. He didn't want to let her go, but he did.

"What are we doing tonight? Is Luke going to try to beat me

at Mario Kart again? Or would you prefer to study?" She continued without waiting for him to answer. "I've already had such a long week. I could seriously use a drink."

"Do you want me to make you one?" he asked.

"Oh, you don't have to!" She threw her hand up like she didn't care one way or another, and then she dropped her purse at the foot of the couch. Lexi kicked off her flip-flops and turned back to face him. "So, what are we doing?"

"Let's just relax. Maybe a movie?"

"Sure," she said, bending down and sorting through his collection.

She popped in *Pirates of the Caribbean*, and then she sat next to him. When he wrapped his arm around her shoulders, Lexi rested back against him.

He had seen the movie a hundred times, but he couldn't have told anyone a thing about it this time. All he could think about was the feel of Lexi in his arms, the touch of her breast against him as she adjusted in her seat, the feel of her fingers caressing his hand. His mind was set solely on the woman lying next to him, and it all felt right. He didn't feel rushed or unsure about what to do next or where to go from here. It just felt right.

Too soon, the movie ended.

"I think I have to go home and study. I'd like to stay, but I think that philosophy paper is calling my name," she said, standing and stretching.

"That's all right. Maybe you can come over tomorrow?" he asked.

"Sure. Sounds good."

She put her shoes back on and grabbed her purse, and he followed her to the door.

"I'll see you tomorrow then," she said. She had a smile on her face when she turned back to him for their obligatory good-bye hug.

When she moved forward to wrap her arms around him, his hand found the smooth shape of her jawline. She stopped when he touched her and stared up into his eyes. He was sure that he saw surprise written on her face. The last time she had tried to kiss him, he had backed off.

"Jack," she said, her voice coming out breathy and needy.

It was addicting. He wanted to keep leaving her breathless.

He pushed his fingers up into her hair, and her eyes closed of their own accord. His other hand moved to circle her waist.

"Lex," he whispered, hearing the urgency in his voice.

Tilting her head up to him, he bent down and kissed her mouth. She tasted like strawberry lip gloss and every addictive substance on the planet. He couldn't get enough.

He pulled her hard against him and angled his mouth, so he could trace his tongue across her lips. She moaned into him and opened her mouth. As their tongues connected, he wondered why he had waited this long. Their kisses were urgent, like they had both been waiting too long for this. Still they weren't rushed as their lips melded together and moved in uninterrupted unison.

Lexi drew his bottom lip in with her teeth, and he nearly lost it. In that moment, he was using every ounce of self-control to stop himself from just grabbing her, throwing her back against the wall, and taking her right then and there.

He kissed her deeply, hungrily, like how a starved man devours food. He could never and would never get enough of the way she tasted and felt.

How he pulled back, he didn't even know.

When he kissed her now swollen lips one last time, she was putty in his hands. She wrapped her arms around his middle as much to steady herself as to hug him good-bye...and he really, very seriously considered keeping her here. She didn't really need to study today...did she?

"Jack," she whispered.

"Yeah, Lex?"

She sighed pleasantly like there was nowhere else in the world she wanted to be. "I like when you call me that."

"Then, I'll never stop."

Jack smiled and drew her in closer. He didn't care if everything seemed to be spinning off axis. He only cared that he was hopelessly falling for her. And all he wanted was to stay exactly where they were with his arms wrapped around his girl. Because when he was with her, there was nothing and no one else.

"I think...I think I have to really go this time," Lexi muttered.

She hugged him tighter and then released him. He kissed her one more time on the lips, and then she opened the door.

With a sad smile, he watched his Lex walk out the door. He had this strange feeling creeping through his chest. It started at there and blossomed out to his extremities. She had ignited something in his body that he would never forget—just like he would never forget the way her hand fit perfectly in his, those soul-searching brown eyes, the taste of her pink lip gloss, the intoxicating nature of her presence.

It reminded him of his parents, and it scared him shitless. Fuck. Fuck. Fuck. He couldn't let himself feel this. He couldn't let it sweep him away. But she swept him away.

His phone buzzed in his pocket, and he reluctantly shut the front door before he answered. "Hello?"

"Jack?" Danielle called into the phone. Her voice was shaky and cracked when she had said his name.

He could hear her tears through the line. She sounded like she had been crying for a while. He wanted to be angry with her. She had been bitchy after all, but just the way she had said his name sounded pitiful.

"Yeah, I'm here."

"Jack, baby, oh my God, what did we just do? I'm so, so, so

sorry. I'm so sorry. I didn't mean to say anything like that to you. I never want a break. I love you. I love you so much." She broke down into tears again, and he waited for her to recover herself. "I'm so sorry. Please forgive me. You're my world. I can't live without you."

"Danielle..." he said awkwardly, thinking about Lex's lips on him all over again.

"Please, please, please, Jack! I could never live without you. Ever. I'll come up this weekend and visit. I don't care if I have to be all alone most of the time. It will all be as it was. Don't force this break for no reason!" she blubbered. Her tears came heavier, and he sighed. "At least, let me talk to you in person. You owe me that much, Jack."

"Danielle..."

"I'll come up on Friday. We should talk about it. Please, Jack!" she gasped out.

"All right. All right. We'll talk," he groaned, hating this whole thing.

He hated when girls cried. Danielle knew he hated it, and she was using the waterworks to her advantage.

Danielle continued to talk in his ear, but he barely heard her. What was he doing?

He was pretty sure his future had just walked out that door.

———

RAMSEY'S POV

THE FIRST TIME RAMSEY MEETS LEXI

1

GET OUT

"Bek, come on. I know who I am looking for," Ramsey said impatiently into the phone.

He was ready to be back in Atlanta now that his vacation was practically over. He had business he needed to take care of with his clubs. In particular, a certain Valentine that he had just hired.

"You just can't fuck this up for me. Daddy wanted me to do the interview, but you were already in New York. It made more sense," Bekah said.

"I got it," he grumbled, running his hand across the rumpled hotel sheets. The cleaning crew better come to his room before tonight. It would be awkward if he brought a girl here, and it still smelled like the last. "Anything else?"

"No. But will you please pay more attention to the interview than your next conquest? I know the company matters to you so much," she drawled sarcastically, "but you'll be surprised to find out that it still matters to some people. Me, mostly."

"And we all know what really matters," he said, walking across the room, sitting in a chair that looked out across Central Park, and crossing his leg over his knee at the ankle.

"Oh, shut up," she snapped.

Ramsey smiled. He could practically see Bekah rolling her eyes on the other end of the line. She was so easy to rile up.

Bekah continued when he didn't say anything else. "I can't believe you're insisting on doing this in a club, as if you don't spend enough time in them." The disdain was apparent.

"It's where I'm most comfortable." Which was true. He spent more time in his clubs now than anywhere. After Parker had left, there hadn't been anything for him. Now he had the clubs, and most of the time they were the only thing that mattered.

Bekah scoffed. "Then so be it. Just remember call me later to tell me how the interview went. I have to go," she responded, clicking off of the line without waiting for his response.

Typical Bekah.

"How lovely," he said, stuffing his Blackberry into his suit coat pocket.

Ramsey picked up the drink he had left forgotten on the table after Bekah called. The ice sloshed through the whiskey and clinked against the edge of the glass as he twirled it in his hand. He tipped the glass up to his lips and tilted the liquor into his mouth. The whiskey slid easily down his throat, and he wished for at least the fifth time tonight that he had gotten something a little smoother. He didn't always care for finest things in life, despite how he had been raised, but whiskey was a resounding exception. He wasn't even sure why he had ordered this drink from room service, when he was going out soon. Maybe it just helped him drown out everything else in his life. Drown out her.

"Who were you talking to, darling?" a voice crooned from the bathroom.

"Really none of your business," he responded sharply. He took another drink and as he took a look at the woman standing before him, he remembered all over again why he had ordered it.

"Was it your wife?"

A tall, leggy blonde in nothing but a towel peered around the corner of the bathroom. She had flawless milky skin, long lean legs that didn't even touch at the tops of her thighs, and full fake breasts that peeked out of the top of the towel. Her lips were pouty and eyes wide and a light blue almost grey color.

"Wouldn't you like it if it was?" he drawled.

He had to refrain from rolling his eyes. This type of woman kind of disgusted him, and he wasn't sure what that said about himself.

"Oh, so you are married," she said, as if it didn't surprise her in the least.

"Hardly."

The girl shrugged. She actually didn't care one way or another. "Suit yourself. Are we going out?"

"I have work. *We* aren't going anywhere," he said curtly, staring at her with a blank expression on his face.

"What do you do anyway?" she asked.

Her blonde hair flopped to one side, and she managed to look completely incompetent. She had clearly spent her entire life using her giant boobs to get her way. Well, it had worked on him for a solid afternoon. Good enough.

"Please, get out," he said, pointing at the door.

"What?"

"Out. Get out of my hotel room."

"But...I don't understand," she said, her eyes wide.

"I'm sure you understand very little, but I think get out is in your vocabulary."

"Asshole," she said, dropping her towel shamelessly to the floor.

She strode casually across the room and reached ever so slowly for her clothes piled neatly on a chair. She changed back into the dress and heels she had been wearing that afternoon, when Ramsey had picked her up all too easy at the bar in the restaurant down the block. With how slow she was moving and the way she was twisting her body so that he had full view of all of her finer assets, she obviously thought he would change his mind or something. Not very bright indeed.

The woman took her time walking across the room, and Ramsey managed to control himself enough not to stand and force her out. She opened the door and looked over her shoulder at him. Her hair fanned around her face seductively.

"Are you sure you don't want another round, baby?" she purred.

"I'd rather use my own hand then have you remain in this hotel room."

Her shocked face was enough to make him smile as she stormed out of his hotel room and slammed the door to his suite. He finished his drink, and then stood and phoned downstairs for a town car.

2

———

PIE

Ramsey had a friend from Atlanta working at a club nearby, and it seemed like the ideal place for the interview that he was doing for his father's company, Bridges Enterprise. Ever since he had acquired his own clubs, he had become a complete and total night owl and frequently grew anxious as daylight dragged on. He loved his job working and managing the nightclubs and strip clubs that he had forced into prominence in the Atlanta nightlife.

Primarily, he had decided to come to New York because his longtime friend, Matt Hammond, was in the city from Las Vegas for the weekend. He hadn't seen him in about six months and Ramsey found it easier to fly to New York than to visit him in Vegas regularly.

Then he had got suckered into helping Bekah out. How did she always manage to do that?

The lobby was bustling as patrons filtered in and out of the massive extravagant hotel. Ignoring the crowd, Ramsey passed through the mass. He caught the eye of an attractive brunette talking to the bellhop and smiled like she was going to be

dessert. She noticed him, looking him up and down apprecia-
tively, and smiled back. Yep, Armani had been a good choice.

The drive to the club wasn't that bad. He had wanted to be
there early for the interview anyway so that he could meet up
with his friend, Lacy. He hadn't seen her in a couple months,
and the woman knew how to pour drinks. He had been sad to
see her leave Atlanta, but bartenders came and went.

A line had already formed in front of the club, which was a
good sign for Ramsey. His name was already on the list as well
as the guy that he was supposed to be meeting to interview. He
approached the bouncer confidently, ignoring the long line of
annoyed people staring him down.

"Ramsey Bridges," he offered.

The guy ran his hand down a list, checked his name off, and
then let him inside. The Bridges name held weight everywhere
that he went.

His eyes easily adjusted to the flashes of light ricocheting off
of the mirrored walls. The club was intricate and he took note
of some easy adjustments he could make in his own place. He
assessed the room with an eye for detail, paying little attention
to the crowd or the noise. He was used to both.

The winding set of stairs dropped him off at the VIP
section. He told the bouncer his name again. He was really
getting tired of this. New York didn't belong to him the same
way that Atlanta did. It was a mild irritation, but an irritation
nonetheless. After clearing him, the bouncer pulled back the
rope and allowed him into the exclusive upstairs bar.

He hated being impressed, but this place was high end. The
next one he purchased would have this flare. It managed sleek,
modern, and classy without going over the top in any of them.
Bottle service was provided at client's requests, but a full-length
bar was still accessible on the far wall.

That's where he saw her.

A charming smile broke out on his face, and he crossed the

room. He leaned forward against the bar and snapped his fingers twice in the most annoying manner. "How do I get good service around here?"

"Sir, I give good service to anyone who doesn't snap at me," the woman responded cattily, never turning around.

He tried to keep the smirk from his face. She had always been a petite girl with straight hair down to her shoulders. He nearly angled his head to appreciate the tiny ass hidden behind her too short shorts.

"If you snap at me one more time," she said, turning around angrily. Her mouth dropped open. "Holy shit!"

"Hey Lace," he said, letting that easy smirk fall on his lips.

"Ramsey fucking Bridges! You didn't tell me you were going to be here!" Lacy said, leaning forward on the bar and ignoring her clients. Her purchased breasts fell forward out of the black corset top she was wearing as she smiled up at him.

"I like surprises," he said with a shrug.

"I like your kind of surprises."

She immediately grabbed a bottle off of the back wall and started pouring into two shot glasses. Pushing one across the bar, she raised it for him to toast.

"Can you drink on the clock?" he asked.

"Nope." She clicked her glass against his and downed it in one clean sweep.

He followed suit appreciating the top shelf tequila. He set the glass back down and smiled at Lacy. "When do you get off?"

"Is that a trick question, Mr. Bridges?" she asked, waving her hand in the air. He shrugged. He would let her come to her own conclusions. "Oh fine. Probably four. If I'd known you were going to be here, I could have been done earlier."

"Four works for me. I have some work to do anyway," he told her. Lacy handed him another drink, remembering his preferences like a pro. "You know a good pie place around here?"

"Sure. Pie at four in the morning? Only in New York," she said, rolling her eyes and moving on to help her other needy customers.

Ramsey checked his watch. Perfect timing. His interview should be here any minute. He pulled up the guy's resume on his cell phone and scrolled through it absentmindedly. Pretty impressive until the company he had been working for had gone under, and he was originally from Georgia. That was always a positive in hiring new people from out of state. Hopefully this guy had some people skills; Ramsey was easily bored.

He sipped on his drink, waited on his interview, and watched the VIP section fill up. Geez, where was this guy? It was really bad to show up late to an interview. Even the strippers showed up on time.

Impatient, Ramsey stood from his seat at the bar and made a quick sweep of the perimeter. He wanted to give it his best chance of finding the guy. He had a picture of who he was supposed to interview, but didn't see anyone yet that looked like him.

What kind of wild goose hunt had Bekah sent him on? This was the last time he was ever doing her a favor again. Okay, probably not, but still...

His drink now empty, he returned to the bar and took over a seat that someone else had just vacated. Setting his empty glass on the bar, he waited for Lacy to pour him another one amidst the chaos, letting his eyes skim the crowd again. As they traveled over one of the couches, he stopped and was glad he was sitting down.

What the hell was Parker doing here?

3

ONE WAY TICKET

Ramsey couldn't help himself. He just stared at Parker. Holy shit, she was beautiful!

His heart was beating wildly in his chest, and it was hard to swallow. Why did she have to be here? He was trying to forget her. Why wouldn't she just let him forget her?

Tonight was not the night for all of this, and yet he couldn't push the feelings aside. He wanted her—not just physically either. He had never wanted anyone else more—anyone else at all.

It had been three years since the breakup, since their fuck up, and she still managed to grip his heart. She kept him from feeling anything for anyone. How could he? Why would he feel, when she was out there somewhere?

And yet he had never tried to make it right. They couldn't mend the crack that had shattered their love. It was irreparable. No matter how much he wanted to fix it, to make it better, he couldn't. They couldn't.

His heartbreak ate away at him beneath his confident façade.

Parker turned her gaze in his direction, and he quickly

diverted his eyes. He didn't want her to see him. It would be too much. She was dating someone else. She didn't love him anymore. It was over. It had been for a long time. Seeing her here, now, would just be another reminder of how much he had lost...how much he had given up.

Out of his peripheral vision, he took a closer look. Parker was blatantly staring at him now. He could almost see the clock working inside her brain as she eyed him, registering who he was. Would she come closer? Would she say anything? Or would she avoid him, just like he was avoiding her?

And then he saw it even in the dimness, and his heart contracted. She was not his Parker. She looked a whole hell of a lot like her, but she wasn't her. No one else could ever be her.

He sagged in his seat, hating himself for the disappointment that settled in his gut.

Oh, God, she was getting up and walking directly toward him. It was now or never. It was his call. If he turned away, she might leave him alone. She might not come after what her walk was suggesting she wanted. But he couldn't do it. Christ, she looked like Parker. And those hips were coming his way, and he wanted what they were screaming.

She tripped just as she neared him, her heel catching in some unknown crack in the floor, and she yelled out, "Oh!"

His move.

He caught her body, as light as a feather, in his arms. She was tiny, but all toned muscle underneath her scat clothing. It wasn't something he normally saw in women like this. He always expected them to be soft and pliable not to be fit. He liked fit.

The girl's hand reached out and rested on his chest. Once she realized that she was safe, she still didn't move it immediately. He righted her, keeping his hand firmly planted on her slender hips.

Getting a better look at her, he was just as shocked by her

resemblance to Parker. Same dark hair, same dark chocolate eyes, same goddamn height! But he had to force himself to see the differences. This girl was much tanner than his Parker, who was alabaster pale in the hottest of summers with soft freckles across the bridge of her nose. This girl was a different build too. Parker had an athletic build from various sports—soccer, mostly. So, her thighs and calves were solid. Whoever this was had a much lither figure, less to hold onto. And now that he was looking, her face was slightly different shaped. Parker had a circular face, which her waves covered half the time, but this girl had a heart-shaped face and almond seductive eyes. It worked for her.

"I am so sorry. I just can't seem to keep my balance in these things," she purred and he glanced down at her heels.

He slowly dragged his eyes back up her body and into her face. Still all he saw was Parker. Her voice was more musical, but it was easy to ignore the difference. He was about to earn his one-way ticket to hell. At least it was all done with good intentions. Maybe.

"It's no problem," he finally said, still holding onto her hips. "Did you twist your ankle or anything? Did you need to sit down?"

She paused, sucking her bottom lip in between her teeth and giving him a doe-eyed expression as if she were contemplating the question. It was damn sexy, and the last fleeting thought of his interview left his mind.

"I'm not sure," she conceded.

"Here. Take my seat. Do you need ice or something?" he asked, not taking his eyes off of her as she slid past him and occupied his stool. Damn, she was making this easy.

"Oh no, I think if I just sit a minute, I should be fine."

"At least let me get you a drink," he said, flashing her an award-winning smile. That always worked. He didn't even need to use it. She was already pretty drunk and clearly on the prowl.

It wouldn't be wrong if he let her use him as much as he was about to use her, right?

She giggled as if she had been expecting that. She probably had been. Parker always got offered drinks when they had gone out too.

"That'd be great," she drawled, crossing her hurt leg over the other.

"What's your guilty pleasure? You seem like a Sex on the Beach kind of girl." She blanched at his words. All right. Guess not. He would change tactics. "Or are you more of a whiskey girl. I hear a Southern accent in there. Did you want a SoCo or a Jack and Coke?"

He waited for her response. He wasn't sure what nerve he had touched on, but she fidgeted at the suggestions. But he knew a Southern accent when he heard one especially up here. He hoped he hadn't offended her, because now that he had started, he wanted to see this through.

Ramsey tilted his head and studied her as he waited for a response. Why was she trying to make this difficult? Her body language was an open book, and all she was screaming was *read me*.

And he intended to.

"Shots," she yelled over the music.

Finally, she made up her mind. At least it didn't mean that she was backing out. They had a bargain. Well, she didn't know about the bargain, but it was a bargain nonetheless. "Do you care what of?"

"Anything *but* Jack," she stated firmly.

He smirked at her answer, and then nodded his head. He leaned over the bar and smiled at Lacy. She sauntered over immediately and he ordered the shots.

Lacy looked at him incredulously. "Really?" she asked, glaring at him. "Two?"

"Don't be difficult," he said.

She started pouring the drinks. "Don't forget about pie."

"Never." He added a smirk for good measure.

Ramsey snatched the two shots off the bar and handed one to the girl. They downed them happily. He liked a woman who could hold her liquor, and she was a tiny little thing. He ordered another round, more replaced that round, and then another round after that. She melted into him, and he let her. With his hand around her waist, he could almost close his eyes and picture another.

His eyes snapped back open and brought him back to reality. Could he really do this? The alcohol was taking a toll on her tiny body and her breast brushed up against his hand. She seemed very pleased to be past the point of intoxication. Yeah, he could do this.

4

———

TRUST

"So," she slurred, "what do you do?"

He looked at her glazed eyes wondering if he could answer that question. Deliberating was futile in the long run. She was in the VIP section of a high-end club. There was no way that she wanted to *actually* know what he did. She just wanted to know whether or not he had money. And he did.

He leaned in closer to answer her. "Live off a trust right now," he said, giving her the answer she wanted to hear.

"Oh?" she asked dryly, clearly unimpressed.

He was thrown off. What did she want if not for him to have money to take care of her? Wasn't that why girls came to these places dressed like that in the first place? He didn't understand. He had used that line dozens of times...more than that probably, and it had worked every time. The girl was putty in his hands. They tried to tell you that money didn't matter, that they cared for you regardless, but it was a lie. They wouldn't have cared half as much if he'd been broke. He knew. He had tried that too.

So what made this one different?

"Yeah," he said, trying to recover from her obvious distaste. "Not really my thing, but it helped me when I was in a pinch."

He shrugged, trying to push aside the discomfort of having to backpedal.

"Well, what are you doing here, Mr. Trust?" she asked, giggling. It was adorable.

"Daddy's work," he said coldly. Why was he telling her this? She didn't need to know anything about him. "Just trying to get a feel on a guy they're interviewing for a job, and he's in New York. I happened to already be in New York. It was a win-win for them."

"Oh," she said, nodding along as if she cared.

He doubted that she did. He didn't even care about his father's stupid interview. He was already trying to forget that guy.

"Where are you supposed to be meeting this guy?"

He smiled, wanting nothing more than to get the subject back on her. He didn't talk about himself. All women talked about themselves. Begrudgingly, he answered her questions, "Here, actually. I tend to feel more comfortable in clubs, but he hasn't showed yet." His eyes left her for the first time to scan the VIP area once more. Might as well make sure he wasn't going to miss the guy now that he had already invested in this girl. "Guess he got caught up."

She reached forward, pulled his blue and white striped tie between her fingers, and tugged lightly. This was more like it. "Well, then it's your lucky day, isn't it?"

He smiled wide. "I suppose it is. How's your ankle? Can you dance on it?"

She nodded. "It's just fine."

Ramsey pulled her out onto the dance floor. She was a good dancer, clearly trained in some way. It would account for the way her body was built, and right now he was getting a pretty good grasp on what her body was like. They moved together really well, and soon even he was forgetting what he was going to do later.

As the music changed, he guided her hips to match his and she followed easily. He liked that. Meant good things for later. Or now.

"Do you want to get out of here?" he questioned into her ear.

She leaned her head back against his chest and swayed to the music. "I'm here with a friend. I can't leave without her."

He sighed. Seriously? She was going to pull that?

Suddenly she was going to get all guilty on him. He hadn't heard of any friend up until now. Seemed a bit suspicious…like she was trying to find a way out. Not sure why. She had been throwing herself at him all night.

The girl started describing her friend, who apparently was gorgeous. He could appreciate exotic beauty, but he was really just ready to take this one home and have his way with her.

Now he had to ditch her friend, who he hadn't seen all night. It would be easier to just pick someone else up, but this girl had him intrigued. She looked like Parker and didn't care about his trust fund. He had never met anyone else like that. He had wanted to sleep with her with only the first criteria. The second was a fucking bonus.

Ramsey located her friend much more quickly than she would have been capable of alone. His height gave him a distinct advantage.

"Chyna, time to go," she commanded, peeling her friend, Chyna, off of some guy she had locked lips with. Whoever he was didn't look too pleased, but after seeing Ramsey, he quickly backed off and vacated the premises.

"Alexa," she shrieked, "the love of my life!"

Alexa giggled as Chyna tackled her, forcing them both back into his hard chest. He could appreciate this. The friend *was* pretty fucking gorgeous. She was probably a model though and self-absorbed. Now that he had what he was looking for, he had no interest in the other. A threesome would have been icing on the cake, but he kind of wanted this Alexa to himself. And she probably wouldn't be up for it.

"Oh, excuse us," Chyna trilled, batting her long lustrous eyelashes.

He nearly rolled his eyes. This was what he had been expecting. "It's not a problem. I was just helping, Alexa, find you."

"Ohhhh," she said. Her eyes moved from Alexa back to him. "Well, thank you for that. She's hardly ever able to find me on her own."

"So, she told me," he said, glancing back over at Alexa.

"It is time for me to go," Chyna said, faking a yawn. Yes, go! "I guess I should check out. I'm sure you can find your own way home, right chica?"

Alexa glared at her friend, and Ramsey wondered why. They *were* going home together. It was time to leave.

"Can you excuse us for a minute?" Alexa asked him.

As he nodded reluctantly, she yanked Chyna out of earshot from him. God, he hoped she was telling her to get the fuck out and quickly. His place at the Plaza was calling his name, and he was pretty much ready to fuck her in every room in his suite. Maybe multiple times in one room. After all he had the bed and the floor in the bedroom, there were two chairs in the den, a shower and bath...

He wasn't sure how long their conversation lasted as he envisioned what he had planned for her, but they soon returned. Alexa looked sheepish. What was that about?

"Sorry, we have to get out of here," she said as she turned toward him.

"We?" he asked incredulously. She pointed between her and Chyna, and his face transformed at the realization that she was going to leave without him.

Fuck! She had to be joking! He had put in all the effort. He had done all the right things. Okay, so maybe wanting to fuck her because she looked like Parker wasn't *exactly* the right thing, but she had been after him anyway. It wasn't like she was all sweet and innocent. And now she was going to leave him hanging? What the fuck!

"Sorry. I know you have that meeting," she added quickly. He knew she was lying. She didn't care about his meeting and neither had he. "Maybe we can meet up some other time."

"I'm leaving the city tomorrow," he told her, trying to keep the sexual frustration out of his voice.

He couldn't push her. She was pretty set even if she did look sorry. He didn't need her regret. He needed her in his hotel room. He responded warmly anyway, "But maybe I could get your number and the next time I'm in town we can meet up."

Chyna grumbled something in her ear, but she swatted her away. She clearly didn't want to hear a voice of reason. "Sure. Here's my number."

She quickly punched her digits into his Blackberry and then dragged Chyna to the door. He watched her walk out of the club in a state of shock.

How did he keep letting Parker just walk out of his life without a fight?

5

STARVING

Ramsey had to remind himself that whoever that girl was, that Alexa, she wasn't Parker. She just happened to look like her. And he had been about to use her. Man, he was fucked up.

He glanced down at the screen, where she had put her phone number under just the name Alexa. He smirked as he recognized the Georgia area code. She did have a Southern accent.

He should probably delete the number. He wasn't going to call her anyway. When he sobered up, he would realize how big of a mistake this all was. If he was already recognizing it now, then it would be ten times worse tomorrow. Or maybe he wouldn't care. He didn't normally care about anything, especially not some girl who had refused him a one night stand.

Ramsey sighed, running his hand back through his blonde hair, and walked back to the bar.

"You look like you got hit with a ton of bricks," Lacy said, pushing a drink toward him, "and you probably need that."

He nodded not acknowledging her statement.

"Did that girl actually turn you down?"

Lacy sounded disbelieving, and he didn't want her to think that. He very rarely was turned down. Actually, when was the last time that had happened? He couldn't remember. Maybe it hadn't happened. Not until Alexa.

"I could go for that pie," he said, swirling the drink around, but not indulging.

Lacy turned and looked at the clock. "It's only two."

"So, get out of it."

"It's Saturday, and it's swamped," she told him. "I'll make another couple hundred in tips alone tonight. No chance."

"Lace, the money. Really?" he asked, raising an eyebrow.

"I'm not letting *you* pay."

"I'll be buying the pie."

"You have such a way with words," she said, rolling her eyes.

He smirked wishing he could put more effort into it, but he was glad he didn't have to with Lacy.

"Fine," she said, giving in. "I'll meet you out front."

Ramsey nodded, relieved that at least something was going as planned, and left the club. It was surprisingly nice to leave the ever-present din behind him. After Alexa's departure, all he wanted was to forget ever thinking about Parker. Thinking about Parker only stirred up old feelings and old memories. It brought up why he had bought the clubs in the first place, and didn't let him escape in them as easily. After what had happened tonight, he needed a bigger distraction than that.

Since he figured he had awhile to wait for Lacy, he pulled out his phone and dialed Bekah's number. He wasn't sure if she would be awake at this hour, but he might as well let her know about the interview...or lack thereof.

She answered on the first ring as if she hadn't even been sleeping. Strange. "Hey," she said, her sugary sweetness melting through the phone.

"Hey, your interview never showed," Ramsey told her.

"Yeah, he called and said he had to cancel. Something came up," Bekah told him. "Did I not mention that?"

"No, you didn't," Ramsey said through gritted teeth.

"I hope you didn't wait long for him," Bekah said in her sugar sweet voice.

"I didn't. Is he rescheduling? I'm only here until tomorrow."

"No. I think I'll make him wait. He has promise, but he's going to have to come to Atlanta if he wants the interview this time. Maybe I'll give him a month," she said with a giggle.

"It gives you some sick pleasure torturing this guy, doesn't it? You don't even know if you want him for the company, and yet you're going to make him wait a whole month before another interview."

He wasn't sure why he was bothering with Bekah. She never listened to him. And he didn't want to be a part of the company. Sometimes he just wanted to shake some sense into her.

"If he wants it bad enough, then he can wait. It's not like we're dying to fill the position anyway," she said.

"Then why did you have me take time out of my vacation to do this?"

"Because I knew you would," she said.

He could almost see that characteristic smile cross her face. Her mask of innocence attempting to conceal her controlling ways. He was so tired of it all.

"Can you try to keep me out of your plans next time, Bek?" he asked, knowing it was futile.

"Sure, Ramsey," she said. "I'll try."

Bekah hung up again without another word and he sighed. She needed to quit doing that.

He ran a hand back through his hair, frustrated about everything that had happened tonight. He had been so...cheery earlier. This Alexa girl had fucked him up.

Luckily, Lacy rounded the corner at that moment. A thankful reprieve from his thoughts.

"Hey, you ready to go?" Lacy asked, stubbing out a cigarette with her high heel and walking up to him.

"Very ready," he said, helping her into a waiting cab and sliding in next to her.

"Still hungry?"

"Starving," he told her, resting a hand on her thigh.

AVOIDING INTIMACY

PRESENT

Chyna lounged back in her chaise, soaking up the remaining afternoon rays from the hot Italian sun. Her olive-toned skin was at home in its natural habitat and had darkened considerably over the course of the last month and a half. Milan had treated her well, and she adored it here. She had grown up in New York City—fashion week, the MET, the Upper East Side, Central Park—but even she had to admit that as much as she loved the city, Milan was just something else.

Her Italian tour was nearing an end, and soon the designer label she had been modeling for all summer would no longer need her services. She was reluctant to move from the penthouse they had provided overlooking the Via Montenapoleone, Milan's most illustrious shopping district. She would miss the private beach in Genoa where she would take jaunts to the coast with Giovanna, Ravenna, and Brigitte. Most of all, what really surprised her was that she would miss the work.

Modeling ran through her veins. Most believed that all you needed were long legs and a pretty face to be an effective model, but there was so much more to it than that. It was truly an art form that she had mastered. Who knew all those years of getting plastered at her mother's shoots would pay off in the long run?

"Chyna, the sun is almost down," Brigitte whined.

So, maybe she wouldn't miss her.

"I know, Bridge." Chyna used the nickname just to annoy her. She was so French sometimes.

Brigitte wrinkled up her tiny nose at the comment and swung her honey blonde hair over her shoulder. "Fine. You do your own hair and makeup for the Glam Ball. Marco will not be kept waiting."

Chyna sighed as Brigitte walked away. Marco was yet another reason she should stay in Italy, and he was also the biggest reason to leave. Marco was...everything. As the head proprietor of Camera Nazionale della Moda Italiana, the nonprofit organization in charge of Milan Fashion Week, he practically owned the city, which meant that he owned her, too.

Stretching out her long lean legs, Chyna picked up her dirty martini and downed the remaining contents. She plucked the string of olives out of the glass and carried them with her to the exit. Tonight was going to be an interesting night to say the least.

***

Glam Ball was an annual event for Milan's high-end fashion clientele, and Marco had played host to the event for the past four years. As his lucky number five rolled around, in true Marco fashion, he had way overdone himself. Chyna had stumbled across a bill for the French-imported champagne alone and had cringed. The number had actually made her cringe.

The pièce de résistance of the entire glorious occasion though had to be utter perfection. He needed something better and more spectacular than he had ever had before. And, he had never had Chyna before.

When she had found out that Marco was using her, an American, as the centerpiece for the ball, she could barely contain her excitement. She had never wanted anything more in her life. He had picked her out single-handedly in front of the entire group of exhibition models, and it had taken all of her self-control to not burst into tears right there in front of him. She hadn't had the same self-control when she had returned to the penthouse. After only two weeks of modeling for him, he had chosen her. It had almost seemed too good to be true. Almost.

She and Marco began private lessons and photo shoots shortly thereafter. The amount of time she put into her modeling that next month would have made her mother proud, if she did that sort of thing. Chyna didn't care about the other girls' jealousy. The business wasn't built on friendship; it was built on taking advantage of the opportunity that lay in front of you.

So, she spent hour after hour locked in a room with him, his camera, and his favorite piano composition. She practiced pouting her lips just so, making her eyes give off five-hundred different meanings with a glance, swishing her hips, adjusting her hands to perfection, fluffing and blowing out her long black hair. He knew exactly what he wanted and how to extract it out of her through the camera lens.

She should have expected the turn it took. She should have seen it all for what it really was.

Chyna shook her head as she entered her closet and stripped down out of her bathing suit. It hardly mattered what she wore to the Ball itself. The models would change at the venue into the handcrafted outfits designed for the event. A limo would be here soon enough to whisk them to La Scala Theatre, the world-renowned opera house in the heart of Milan. Chyna didn't even want to know the lengths he had gone to in order to acquire the sixteenth-century Italian theatre for the evening.

"Chyna," Giovanna cooed in her thick Italian accent, "the limo has arrived."

Chyna certainly wouldn't miss this about Milan. She had never had a roommate in her life and certainly not three. The fact that they could just waltz into her room at any given time—like right now when she was completely naked—irritated the shit out of her. Didn't they have any common decency? As it turned out, no, they didn't. Apparently, walking around nude was commonplace for models, especially European models. She didn't particularly have anything against it, but she preferred to *choose* when people saw her naked.

"Coming," Chyna told her. She picked out a pair of fit dark-wash jeans and a plain, white, V-cut T-shirt with four-inch pumps. She would be dolled up soon enough.

Giovanna was the polar opposite of Chyna. She was blonde, blue-eyed, and pale with the quintessential sweet and innocent vibe. She did, however, manage to look like a complete and total hooker any time she dressed herself. She wore a pleated miniskirt that failed to cover her ass, a black lace bustier, and six-inch heeled booties. A white blazer hung from her finger, but Chyna knew she would never cover herself up that much.

Brigitte had gone for simple as well with a white tank tucked into high-waist shorts and Hermès sandals. It had been rumored that she would be the spokesmodel for their next collection.

On the other hand, Ravenna just looked fierce no matter what she wore. As much as Chyna liked Ravenna, she was a certified bitch, who was technically too big to be one of Marco's girls. But, she had been a favorite two years ago, and she was so spectacular on camera. With her fiery, dark red hair, deep compelling eyes, and uncontrollable curves, it was hard to resist her.

The foursome exited the penthouse, and they were whisked away in the black stretch limo. As they approached La Scala Theatre, Chyna realized how much she was dreading the coming evening. She had wanted to be the centerpiece of the show so desperately, and now that it was here, she was reconsidering. She wasn't nervous exactly, but everything had evolved so quickly that it was completely out of her control. She wasn't sure how to get it all back without doing something drastic, and that wasn't a particularly appealing option.

The drive was shorter than she would have liked, and soon, they were before the grand structure. Chyna had been here once before as a child. Her parents had been together then, and the ballet had been stunning. She had tried her hand at ballet when she returned home, but she became easily bored when she didn't look like the prima ballerinas overnight. Staring up at the gorgeous castle-like building, her memories made her wish that she had stuck with it.

Chyna followed the other girls out of the limo, and in an instant, Giselle, Marco's personal assistant, was before them. She was all legs with sky-high heels and a too short dress accentuating her very best feature. Diamonds glittered everywhere on her—strings of them around her neck, giant round ones in her ears, rings covering her fingers, and some even peeked out of her hair piece that was placed carefully in her dark brown hair. It appeared diamonds had actually been sewn into the glittering bodice of her dress. The rules about moderation had never applied to her.

"Come along. Come along," she said, not halting to see if they followed.

The girls kept up with her easy pace, following her to an enormous door leading into the building. A flurry of activity was already underway when they found the dressing area.

Two dozen models were being fit into an array of clothing sets for the fashion show. A few models were walking around in flowing designer gowns. Several were wearing glittering lingerie, tastefully constructed for the evening. Still others were helped into animal print bodysuits and barely there bathing suits. Makeup artists were painting faces to match, accent, and highlight the garments. Blow dryers went off around the room as hairstylists brushed and sprayed their locks into submission. If Chyna didn't know better, she would have thought it was all chaos.

"Brigitte, Ravenna, Giovanna, go to hair and makeup," Giselle snapped. "Chyna, Marco would like to see you in his office."

The girls were already eyeing her suspiciously, but Chyna ignored them and followed Giselle. It wasn't uncommon for her to be called into private sessions with Marco, and they knew it. Still, after three weeks of one-on-one attention, her stomach still clenched at the possibilities. Powerful men hardly unnerved her—she had grown up with one after all—but Marco was different somehow. He had the authority to give her everything she wanted, but more importantly, he had the power to take it all away.

"Marco had your costume moved back here," Giselle explained as soon as they were out of earshot.

"Wonderful," she said dryly.

"Are you not grateful?" Giselle snapped.

Chyna should have known better than to act like this around Giselle. She would have killed for the opportunity to model for Marco, but Giselle just didn't have *it*.

"More than grateful," Chyna said, keeping the lilt out of her voice.

Giselle sneered anyway. Chyna wanted to tell her how unattractive that was. She would have been able to do that if it had been Alexa.

"Shit," she muttered under her breath.

"Yes?" Giselle asked, raising her eyebrows at the profanity.

"Nothing."

Chyna hadn't called Alexa in over a week. What a shitty best friend. She had been so wrapped up in her modeling and Milan and Marco that it had slipped her mind. She would be sure to call her soon. What was the time difference to Atlanta again? She scrunched up her nose. She was bad at these kinds of things. Whatever. She would make it work.

"Hey, do I have time for a phone call?"

"What?" Giselle demanded.

"Do I have time?"

"Certainly not. You're late as it is."

Chyna sighed. Another time then. She felt bad, but she pushed the thoughts aside. She would call her when she could. Alexa had never expected more than that. Plus, she was probably in a la-la land with her Ramsey. She just hoped that Alexa was avoiding his bitch sister and Jack—well, that was a given. Though, at least Chyna understood that maddening obsession...kind of.

"Here you are, darling," Giselle said, pointing at a door labeled *Director*.

"*Grazie*." Chyna thanked her gratefully.

Giselle's smile quirked at Chyna's clipped Italian accent, but she acknowledged her no less before departing, "*Prego*."

Chyna turned toward the rustic door with a solid gold placard and knocked.

"Come in," Marco called in a beautiful Italian accent.

His voice was out of this world. Chyna's body warmed at the sound.

She opened the door to the director's office and found Marco sitting among a collage of tutus, sequins, and fabrics.

Her eyes darted to the massive hardwood desk, and she smirked. A long black costume bag hung against the back wall with a shiny gold imprint marked on the top. She would recognize Marco's handiwork anywhere, even without being able to read his glossy name from a distance.

Finally, her eyes returned to the man behind the desk. He was staring at her with those deep chocolaty eyes like a predator feasting its gaze upon its prey. He stood, almost regally, from the desk upon her entrance. His square jaw, those broad shoulders, and cut waistline were perfection. He could have modeled, but he was just as talented in design, business, and behind the camera. He had shaved his ever present five o'clock shadow, and his brown hair was slicked back so it wouldn't fall into his eyes like she was so accustomed to. It had been cropped much shorter when she had first arrived. He was way past due for a haircut, but she thought the longer look suited him.

"My star," Marco muttered.

He had begun calling her that after their first late night photo shoot, centered near a large, open window in his apartment. He had told her that she outshined the stars in the background of the photos. As far as he was concerned, she would be his brightest star. He had been calling her his star often enough that it was now her pet name.

"Marco," Chyna said huskily, closing the door behind her.

As conflicted as she was away from him, when she was in his presence, he was like a heady perfume. The sweetest aroma in the world.

"You're late," he said sternly, with a glimmer in his eye.

"Marginally," she volleyed, walking toward him while he still stood imposingly behind the desk.

Oh God, that desk.

"You haven't even seen hair and makeup, and you smell like sunscreen," he chided.

"Can you smell me from all the way over there?" she asked, walking a slow catwalk toward him.

"Don't think I don't know all."

"I'd never entertain the idea," she murmured.

She focused on the lessons he had given her about her runway walk—one foot in front of the other, relax your hands, move your body naturally, smooth out that step, smile through your eyes.

"That one," he pointed crassly, pointing out the second step on her left foot. "That's the step you rush every time."

"After four weeks of detailed scrutiny, don't you think I know which step I falter?" Chyna snapped instinctively. She chewed on her bottom lip as his eyes hardened perceptively.

"What was that?" he asked sharply.

"Nothing. Never mind," she said quickly, realizing her fuck up.

She was always so brash with everyone. Having a boss was not something she was used to, especially when it was someone like Marco.

"Get your ass over here," he demanded, pointing at the desk.

Chyna tried not to smile. It would only set him off more. God, did she enjoy doing that. She trailed her hand along the fine piece of carpentry, wondering how old the desk was and if she could acquire it for her penthouse at home. Frederick would freak over it.

"By all means, take your time," Marco growled.

As she slowly rounded the desk, he reached out and gripped her arm, lurching her forward into him. She swallowed hard.

This was his favorite part—taking control.

2

———————

PRESENT

"Were you talking back to me?" he asked into her ear, nipping her earlobe.

Chyna melted. She would do anything for a domineering guy. It was *so* her type.

"Yes," she whispered into his chest. She loved that he towered over her, even when she wore heels.

"That's what I thought. You never learn your lesson. I almost think you like it," he said, his hand fisting softly into her hair. "Do you like it?"

She was having trouble remembering what she was supposed to say as her body pressed up against him. "Yes."

"You enjoy infuriating me?" he questioned, pulling harder on her hair.

"Oh no! No, Marco. That's not what I meant." She nearly groaned. He was so fucking sexy.

"Bend over the desk," he told her.

"Marco," she murmured shaking her head. We have no time for this.

"Bend over the fucking desk," he repeated slowly.

"The Ball—"

"Do you want me to force you?"

Did she ever!

Chyna couldn't hold the smirk back, and it set him off like it always did. His left hand tightened in her hair, and he used that as leverage to grab her hip with his right hand, turning her around to bend her face first into the desk. Her breathing was heavy, and her lower half was pulsing. She felt the walls of her sex tightening in anticipation.

He released her hair and ran his hands down her sides, across her taut ass, and between her inner thighs. His touch was intoxicating as his hands splayed her legs farther and farther apart. She thought about reminding him how little time they really had, but she wanted nothing but his hands on her at the moment.

"Don't worry," Marco spoke softly as he returned to a standing position. "I won't leave marks, not when you'll be wearing that costume."

She could hear the need in his voice, and she was sure he could feel her body revving up at his touch. She wanted to ask to feel him, even if only through her jeans, but he wouldn't want her to just yet. Later, he'd make her beg. He'd make her *want* to beg.

The first blow was always the worst. He didn't like to warm her up to it, and he never told her when it was coming. The smack across her ass wasn't the hardest she had ever received, but she still released a small yelp as her body went forward onto the desk. Marco was already making it better, rubbing the site of his hand mark, easing her discomfort. She would be feeling that one later.

The second and third came together nearly equal in force to the first, and they were just as unexpected. She clenched her jaw to keep from yelling out again.

That hurt like a bitch, but she was so turned on.

He was attentive to her pain, rubbing the area again, while

his right hand traveled between her legs. She moaned at the blending of pleasure and pain from his experienced touch.

He slapped her ass again, harder than before. She whimpered, never knowing if she wanted him to stop or continue.

"You're my little star."

She nodded her head. She was seeing stars.

"Just the way I fucking like her—that nice piece of ass high in the air and pussy screaming my name," he said, stroking her more demandingly before landing another blow. "Star?"

"Uh huh?" she all but moaned in anticipation as his hand came down another time. God, yes!

"You were a bad girl. You like me fucking punishing you? Do you like this?" he asked, his hand coming down hard and quick.

Chyna wondered if it really would leave a mark, but at this point, she couldn't care less. She had other things on her mind.

His hand fisted in her hair, tugging on it hard enough to pull her head back, her back arching. He teased her, smacked her lightly, as he pressed against her just like she had wanted. She felt his erection against her ass, and she gyrated her hips.

"You like when I show you how bad you are?"

She responded by grinding her ass harder against him.

"Star?" he cooed, slapping her ass until she stopped moving. "You clearly like me punishing you. Do you like being punished or teased?"

She bit her lip hard and waited for the spanking she knew she deserved when she didn't answer. It was an exhilarating feeling, knowing how much he was enjoying himself while he aroused her growing climax.

Marco's hand returned to play between her legs, and she gasped as her head was released back to the desk. Another smack hit her ass hard. "Answer me. Do you like to be punished or teased?"

"Both," she managed to get out. God, he did things to her

that were unbelievable. Her body was on fire. She would have pleaded for release if he would give it to her.

"That's right. You like both, and I like both," he said, rubbing her ass between both of his hands. He moved them to her hips and forced her back against his dick.

"Please," she sputtered out, losing control and begging.

He ran himself up and down the crease of her jeans and across her covered opening. "I love to hear you beg. You want me to fuck you?"

"God, yes, please! Marco," Chyna moaned, "fuck me."

"I'm not sure you want me enough," he said, pressing harder and hitting her ass again.

"Marco, please, make me come. Please, God!" she cried as he massaged the area.

He sighed, almost resigned to giving her what she wanted, as he knelt behind her. He trailed kisses across her butt and down between her legs. Breathing hot between her legs, he made her tremble with desire, and she fought desperately to not take control of the situation. Slowly, painfully slow, Marco backed away from Chyna, who was still lying out across the desk. A shiver ran up her spine from his absence. He landed one more blow before walking away.

"See how good you're being. I wish I could finish you. I fucking want you on this desk, but I have a show to run," he said in a low guttural tone. "Now, don't move that tight ass until I leave. I like to see it up in the air. However, you do need to get dressed. I'd prefer you wear nothing and show off your real beauty, but there's something to be said for a little mystery. Don't you think, my gorgeous star?"

She whimpered. "Yes."

"You better not get yourself off when I leave." Leaning down over her from the other side of the desk, he growled into her ear, "I'm coming for you after the show."

Chyna waited a few seconds after the door clicked shut before righting herself.

The bastard! Leaving her there all alone and desperate for an orgasm. She wanted to go find the first guy she could and fuck him senseless, just for payback. No one left her wanting. No one!

She made it halfway across the room before she changed her mind. Yes, she wanted to kill him, but now wasn't the time. As much as she wanted to forget her obligations, she was still the centerpiece of the Glam Ball. If she ever wanted to keep modeling, she needed the Ball, and she needed Marco. She turned around angrily and stomped back to the big fucking desk. What a big fucking asshole!

Chyna opened her clutch and fished out her cell phone while she waited for help. No way could she get into that outfit alone.

"Chyna?" Lexi asked, yawning into the phone. "What time is it over there?"

"Hey, chica." Chyna breathed. See, she's a good friend. "Not sure, like ten or eleven."

"Jesus." She yawned again. "And, you're not drunk?" Lexi giggled.

"Bitch."

"You love me."

"I miss you."

"I won't miss seven-thirty wake-up calls," Lexi said, yawning again.

"Sorry."

"When do you come home? I need your ass in New York."

At the mention of her ass, Chyna cringed and rubbed her sore backside. "Not sure on that either. Soon? Wait!" she cried. "What are you doing in New York? I thought you moved in with Ramsey."

"Uh..." Lexi hesitated.

Oh fuck! What had she missed?

"I moved back. We broke up," she explained.

"What?" Chyna asked in a shrill tone. See what happened when she didn't call for a week. "Why the fuck did you break up? You were cookie-cutter perfect a week ago."

"Um...well, my dad had a heart attack, and I found out that Ramsey is a compulsive liar."

"Oh God, is your dad okay? Are you okay?" Chyna asked quickly.

"Yeah, my dad's fine. I don't know if I am though. Ramsey dated Parker. They almost got married in college, Chyna."

"Hold up. Let's back this shit up. I thought he'd never had a girlfriend."

"Me too."

"Bastard!" Chyna was using the word a lot lately.

"Also, he got me the job in Atlanta and never told me he pulled strings. I don't know, C. Just seems pretty fucked-up when Jack is the one comforting me."

Chyna groaned. Did she say she understood that obsession? "At least you have one constant," she replied sarcastically.

Lexi laughed at the statement. "He's getting married, Chyna. He's not my constant anymore."

"Uh huh. Don't sound so sad about it."

"Oh, shut up. It's Jack."

"Don't I know it?"

"Anyway," Lexi drawled out, "how is Milan? Anything new?"

Besides her aching backside? "I'm about to change into my outfit for Glam Ball. It starts in an hour or so," Chyna told her.

"Are you still the focus or whatever? That's a pretty killer opportunity."

"Yeah. I am."

"And..." Lexi prompted.

Damn, she knew her too well.

"There's this fashion designer—"

Lexi immediately started laughing. "Of course there is."

"Whatever, chica. I don't know what to do about him." Chyna hated admitting it. As furious as she was with Marco, she wasn't sure she actually wanted to give up whatever they had.

"Give him up and come home." Chyna wished it was that easy. "New York is where you're meant to be. You own New York City," Lexi reminded her. "I didn't think any guy would change that."

"It's not that he's changing that." Man, it was weird for Alexa to be the one giving advice. "He's just a complication."

"Speaking of complicated—" Lexi began.

"What else have you gotten yourself into?"

"Not me! I'm talking about your complicated. I've been hanging out with Adam lately…"

The sentence hung in the silence. Chyna tried to push Adam out of her brain. She didn't need to think about him. They had made the right choice in breaking it off before she left. She wasn't a good girlfriend in New York, so she would be a terrible one halfway across the world. Why was she even still thinking about Adam?

She couldn't help it though. "How is he doing?"

"He's all right, C. We've been an interesting pair this past week—two heart-torn lovers and all," she said with a giggle. Chyna couldn't miss it, not from Alexa.

"Sorry I couldn't be there. I'd totally watch you veg on pot after pot of black coffee and gallons of double chocolate, chocolate chip ice cream."

"While you ate carrots and complained about being fat?"

"Only when I am fat," she told her, knowing full well that she was *far* from fat.

"Miss you, C," Lexi said softly. "I miss my no-nonsense best friend."

Was that her? Then, why did she take nonsense from every guy she actually thought she wanted?

A knock on the door brought her back to reality. Tonight was Glam. "I miss you, too, Alexa. I'll be home before you know it, and I'll let you drag me to Serendipity despite the calories. But, right now, I have a show to put on."

3

___

PAST

"Frederick, darling, don't you love this?" Chyna asked, pointing at a crystal-cut vase.

"Don't you have one like that already?" he asked, placing a hand on his hip.

God, why did he have to be gay?

"Don't act like you know my entire collection."

"Honey, I fucking picked out your collection. Remember who has the good taste in the relationship. If I leave you alone, you'll probably strip down the black leather sofas again and add animal print and bamboo," he cried dramatically.

"Then, don't leave me again, fucker," she said, walking away from the crystal display.

"Don't be such a cunt then," he said as a matter-of-fact.

She loved him! Any man who used the c-word as a compliment was someone she could appreciate.

"I'll keep that in mind."

"Do you want to get lunch? I know this incredible vegan cuisine a block from here. To die for. I took my boyfriend, Dallas—"

Chyna groaned, interrupting his statement.

"—there last week. Also, shut up, hooker. And, he fell in love!"

"With you or the food?"

"Well, when I took him home and fucked his brains out...me."

"Well played."

"Thank you," he said with a knowing smirk. "So, lunch?"

"I can't. I have to meet my boyfriend, Adam—"

Frederick groaned, mimicking her.

"Adam. Also, groan all you want. Take me on a silver platter at your convenience," she said, spreading her arms wide.

"You couldn't handle it, sweetheart." He patted her arm sympathetically.

"Bring it," she challenged.

Frederick just laughed and followed her out of the boutique. They walked arm and arm down Madison Avenue. Chyna wrapped her cashmere scarf tighter around her neck, bracing against the winter temperatures. They both paused before the new store being constructed on their favorite stretch of Madison.

There was an endless amount of buzz about the new store. An up-and-coming Italian designer had broken Madison before he turned thirty years old. She had hardly been able to believe it until his one-of-a-kinds started circulating in her group of friends. She had been shocked by their style, elegance, and creativity. Today, they had unveiled the gorgeous, shiny gold sign that topped the Italian boutique— Marco's.

She practically salivated at the store. It was more than perfect. It was her—everything she loved and more.

"Fuck. I can't wait to get my hands on those clothes," she said.

"You and everyone else in the city, hun."

"Why haven't I requested him to commission something for

me yet?" she asked Frederick, reluctantly walking away from the display.

"Probably because he's not taking orders," he reminded her.

"Right. Damn. Bad timing for him to go pre-made on me," she complained.

"Yes, how inconsiderate of him to expand his career. Doesn't he know better?" Frederick asked with dripping sarcasm.

"I know, right?! Doesn't he know who I am?"

"I doubt men with that much drive care, sweetie."

"I'd make him care," she said with a knowing smirk.

"You'd just get your ass in trouble."

"Probably," she agreed with a giggle. "But, I like trouble."

"Don't we all?"

"Anyway, girlfriend duties to attend to. Got to go, lover." She kissed both of his cheeks before darting across the street to her waiting town car.

Chyna hopped in the backseat and rode off of Madison Avenue. She was supposed to meet Adam at the gym, and then they were going to go get lunch. She was a little early, but that was all right. She liked to see him all sweaty.

Rounding the corner toward the New York Sports Club, her driver pulled up in front of the building.

"You don't have to wait today, Carl. Adam likes to drive for some unknown reason. Take the rest of the night off."

"Thank you, Miss Chyna. Have a nice night."

"You, too, Carl."

Chyna exited the town car and rushed quickly into the empty gym. The attendant waved her through. She had been here enough that they all recognized her now.

"I think he's on the basketball courts," the young perky blonde directed.

She couldn't have been older than eighteen. Probably getting lost in the city, trying to pursue her dream. Chyna wondered what that was like. She had never loved anything enough to do that.

Pushing aside those thoughts, she opened the door to the courts and entered, slipping silently into the room. Adam was there with one other guy playing one-on-one ball. Both guys were covered in sweat, drenching through their cut-off shirts. Adam's longish hair was a mop, sticking to his forehead and slinging around as he attempted to maneuver around his opponent. He was so cute and aggressive when he didn't know she was watching.

Her eyes moved to his opponent just as he stole the ball from Adam. Her eyebrows rose when she got a closer look at him. Hello! Excuse me, who the hell was he? He was even in height with Adam but broader. Gah, those shoulders! His hair was very short brown, almost military cut, but it worked for him. And, tattoos—she was such a sucker for well-placed tattoos. She could see one etched into the inside of his left bicep, and when he raised his arms, another one was written across the side of his right ribs. Where else do you have those?

Tattoo Guy pulled a sharp pivot move on Adam, passed him, and did a layup, scoring. "Game," he said, raising his eyebrows and that lovely left arm into the air.

Hmm...what was written there?

"Fuck!" Adam cried. "I hate that move."

"Gets you every time," he said with a lazy smile.

Oh, this guy was used to winning. Interesting. She knew Adam was really, really good.

Breaking the confrontation, Chyna walked her heeled feet on the court. The clicking noise ground both of them to a halt. They turned to her at once. Adam smiled. The other guy's eyebrows lifted.

Yep, there it was—*interest.*

"Hey, baby," Adam said, rushing over to her with a big goofy grin on his face. He brushed a kiss across her lips, careful not to get her sweaty.

"Hey," she said, breaking into a smile. "Who's your friend?"

"Oh, I've been meaning to introduce you two, but there was never a good moment. This is my older brother, John."

Well, fuck.

"John, this is my girlfriend, Chyna."

"Nice to meet you," John said, sticking out his right hand.

She shook it, making eye contact. Well, it was still there. Perhaps, John was thinking *fuck*, too. Adam's brother was gorgeous. There were similarities between the two, but fucking hell if John wasn't exactly the kind of guy she normally went for. Just her type.

"You, too. I didn't realize you were in town."

"Yeah, I have the long weekend off before I have to fly to Japan on business."

"Oh, interesting. So glad Adam clued me in," she said, glancing at her boyfriend.

"Can't be mad at him. I never told him. I just never know when I'll be in the city."

"Ah," she said with a smile.

"Hey, we're going to go clean up, and then let's get lunch. We won't be long," Adam told her.

"All right. I'll just wait out front."

Chyna stole a glance at John once more before exiting. He was staring at her rather attentively, his eyes smoldering.

She made a hasty retreat. Not good.

Not good at all.

She walked off the court and back over to the front desk area. The blonde attendant was on the phone talking insistently to a girlfriend of hers rather loudly. Chyna tried to tune her out as her thoughts drifted to what had just happened.

She didn't want to be attracted to her boyfriend's brother. This had never been a problem before because...well, she had never had a boyfriend that she stuck with for more than a couple of weeks. There was something about Adam that she really liked. She wasn't sure what that was exactly, but she did like him. He wasn't the kind of guy that she normally went for by a long shot but damn if he wasn't so sincere. He liked her for who she was and had never cared about anything else—not her money, her family issues, or her illicit social life. He had helped her out in her time of need when he totally could have taken advantage of the situation, and he had asked for nothing in return. She knew labeling someone a *nice guy* was the kiss of death, but Adam brought nice guy into its own category.

Then, why was she swooning over his brother? Because he had broad shoulders with tattoos and a smirk? She really needed little else.

Why the fuck was Alexa at the beach with her boy toy this week? That was so inconvenient. She should have known that Chyna was going to have a hot guy melt-down.

Chyna whipped out her compact and reapplied a coat of lip gloss. She already knew that she looked good. Some guys had been checking her out while she was shopping with Frederick. Still, she wanted to double check. She didn't want to look sloppy the first time she hung out with her boyfriend's brother. That was all, right?

God, she couldn't do this. She couldn't be attracted to John. It was out of the question. She wasn't like her parents—she didn't cheat! Inside, she preferred to just not get attached. If she was going to be with Adam, then she was going to fucking be with him. It didn't mean she couldn't look at and admire his brother—what girl wouldn't?—but that was where the line was drawn. She could eye-fuck John and his goddamn tattoos but nothing else. This would be an exercise in self-control. Lord, help us all!

Chyna replaced her mirror into her purse and immediately

began chewing on her glossy bottom lip. She could do this. Yep. She could totally do this.

"Hey." She heard someone call behind her.

She turned away from the desk toward the entrance to the locker rooms.

Oh, holy hell! Fuck! Really? How could one man be so attractive? She couldn't get past that strong jaw, those hazel eyes, and those fucking shoulders. When did he have time to build that Adonis body? All she knew about him was that he worked *all* the time, and now, she wanted to know everything. Did he actually have that good of taste in clothing, or did he have a personal assistant? Those dark-wash jeans fit him a bit too well, and the green button-up shirt mostly hidden beneath the grey pea coat was outstanding. If he didn't have someone dress him and he actually had a fashion sense well enough to look like he had walked out of a Barneys catalog, she might die. She would take two, please!

Had she responded to his welcome? She just smiled, deciding it would only sound dumb at this point.

He ran a hand back through his still damp hair and returned her smile. "Adam takes forever to get ready. Thought I'd come out here, so you didn't have to wait alone," John said, walking over to where she was leaning against the desk.

"Thanks."

She hated her natural instincts right now. She knew she could take him home in a heartbeat. If this were anyone else in any other situation, he would already be in her penthouse, and her tongue would be tracing those tattoos.

"So, what do you do?" John asked, smiling warmly.

"Uh...I'm in between work right now," she said with an unapologetic shrug. "I try not to define my life by my career. Instead, I just enjoy living it."

"To define is to limit. I get that," he said with that smirk.

"Something like that. What do you do exactly that has you leaving for Japan?"

He shrugged as if this was the most boring subject, but he had brought it up.

"International business. I negotiate business transactions overseas for my clients who want to expand their enterprise globally."

"Huh, sounds like a lot of work," Chyna commented. She had never wanted to work that much in her life.

"Yeah, it can be. I'm good at languages though. I'd love to be stateside a little bit more, and I'm working on bringing some global companies to the states, but I can't really complain."

She wasn't complaining either. A successful businessman who spoke multiple languages and had tattoos? Where the fuck did he come from?

"Yeah, it must be hard to be away from your family and your girlfriend all the time," she said, looking up into his hazel eyes. She knew it was a bad line, and he might even see through it, but damn, she couldn't help herself. She was curious.

He chuckled softly, glancing away. Oh, he had picked up on it all right.

"No girlfriend for me. Not much time, and I'm picky," he said, returning his eyes to hers.

He could afford to be picky. She cleared her throat and broke eye contact. Keep it together.

"Adam's always been the girlfriend type anyway."

"I noticed," she said with a smile. Adam was an excellent boyfriend. So nice. Too nice. Too good for her. "I'm just getting used to it."

"To Adam or a boyfriend?"

"Yes," she said. "I'm more of a party girl myself."

"I can see that."

What did that mean? And why did it look like he could appreciate a party girl

"When you grow up in Manhattan, it's just a way of life."

"I can see that, too."

Adam jogged out of the locker room then. "So, where are we going?"

Chyna broke away from John. When had they gotten so close, and why did it feel like they gravitated to each other?

Somewhere with a bar," she answered immediately.

Adam laughed, pulling her close and kissing her lightly on the lips. "Whatever you want."

It was a promise.

4

———

PAST

They exited to the garage where Adam's hybrid sat waiting for them. She slid into the passenger seat, feeling all the more awkward. She'd had her town car for as long as she could remember. She didn't even know how to drive.

Adam veered into traffic as he directed them across town to a grill he swore by. He pulled into a line for a parking garage, and she tried not to roll her eyes. She hated waiting.

"Just valet the car," John said with a clear hint of impatience.

Finally, someone who understood!

"It costs more," Adam responded, not moving.

"But, it's faster."

"By only a few minutes," Adam said, still not budging.

She had never seen him so stubborn. Usually, he was relatively compliant.

"Come on, Adam," she said, reaching out and touching his arm. "I'll pay the fare."

John muttered, "You have only a few years in which to live really, perfectly, and fully...time is jealous of you."

"Always quoting Wilde," Adam said with a shake of his head.

This seemed pretty common between them, and for some reason, it got Adam to move the car.

"Always," John agreed. "The man knew what he was talking about."

"He was a philandering, flamboyant extremist who saw the world through rose-colored lenses of beauty," Adam quipped testily.

"Perhaps you should live no other way," John said with a smirk as Adam pulled in front of the valet.

"Wasn't he gay?" Chyna asked.

Both guys started laughing at once. Chyna missed the joke.

"Yeah, he was," John said.

Was she misreading the situation entire? Was John gay?

Chyna looked over her shoulder, turning around in the car to peek at John, who was still chuckling at her. Nope. No way. Not with that look. She could pick out desire like she had a fucking radar.

Adam handed the keys to the guy at the entrance and took a slip from him. The trio walked into the restaurant, and they were instantly ushered to a table. Chyna took off her long black pea coat and handed it to someone to hang for her. Both boys seemed to appreciate her figure, clad in a short V-cut sweater dress that hugged her curves like a glove. She couldn't have picked a much better outfit for the occasion.

"You look great," Adam said, kissing her cheek and running his hand across the small of her back before sitting.

"Thanks," she said, seating herself across from him.

John pulled out a chair and sat down between them.

"I wish I'd known you had the weekend off," Adam said, turning to his brother. "I would have taken some time off, too."

"They were impressed with my latest find, so they gave me the time. Wasn't expecting it to happen."

"I don't know why you don't take all those clients of yours and start your own company. You're too good to be where you are," Adam told him.

"I'm doing perfectly fine, and anyway, the Global International name is well-known."

"Wait, Global!" Chyna gasped.

"See," John said, gesturing to Chyna.

"My mother worked through Global for a while when they were negotiating the Corsa fashion line," she explained.

Global International was a huge conglomerate that demanded and received results. Her mother had worked with a partner, of course, but it was rumored that all of the representatives were incredible.

"My point exactly. Anyone who is anyone comes through Global. I'm good right where I am."

"Who knew a Harvard MBA would get you there?" Adam said with clear admiration in his voice.

Chyna's ears perked up. Harvard? Was this guy for real?

"God, you sound like Mom," John said, running a hand back through his hair.

"Someone's got to do it. You hardly see her."

"I hardly see anyone," John said, just as the waiter arrived.

They all ordered drinks, and Chyna couldn't wait to get her hands on her martini.

"Do you want me to be like Mom and tell you that you could have gone to Harvard too if you hadn't followed in Dad's footsteps to bum-fuck-nowhere liberal arts college?" John teased.

Chyna blushed for her boyfriend. She knew he was smart, and he probably could have a better job than where he worked at a small, private architectural company.

Adam just shrugged, unaffected on the outside. She wondered if he was seething on the inside. She would be.

"I still could, but then I'd have to take your claim as the perfect son. I'd hate to do that to you."

John laughed good-naturedly. "Touché. King's to you, Fernand."

Adam laughed even harder, but Chyna didn't have any clue what they were talking about. Who was Fernand?

They clearly spoke their own language. She didn't have any siblings and couldn't comprehend a connection like that. The closest thing she had found was with Alexa. Chyna wished she was here. Alexa was the smart one, even if she was terrible with relationships. She could clue her in on what the fuck they were talking about. Chyna chewed on her lip and prayed for her martini to arrive quickly.

"Do you like movies, Chyna?" John asked just as the drinks arrived.

She sucked down a large gulp before answering. "I go to premieres sometimes."

John quirked a smile at Adam. "Where did you find her?" He stuck his thumb out at Chyna.

Had she done something wrong?

"You'd never believe me if I told you," Adam said.

"Try me."

Adam shrugged, leaning one elbow on the table. He took a drink of his beer before answering. "She was drugged in a bar, and I kept some jerk from taking her home," Adam told him. "Her friend showed me to her car, and we made sure she was all right. Everything else is history."

He winked at her from across the table, and Chyna smiled. She liked the story. It was romantic in its own way.

"Our little knight in shining armor. What's your thing with saving chicks like that? Didn't that happen with Christina, too?" John asked.

Um...who was Christina?

"Yeah, it did," Adam replied, and then took another sip of his beer.

"Who's Christina?" Chyna piped up, raising her eyebrows.

"My ex-girlfriend," Adam responded slowly, looking at John, who was hiding a smile behind his own pint.

Chyna did not like that at all.

"And, the same thing happened to her?" she asked.

How come she didn't know this? Seemed like a pretty big misstep especially considering how they had met.

"Uh…yeah. Well, not the same thing. I didn't save her. I just took her home when I saw her getting sloppy." Adam was practically squirming.

Chyna would have liked it if she'd had any clue about this Christina before this moment.

"That's strange. When did you guys break up?" she asked, honestly curious.

"Chyna…" Adam said, reaching for her hand.

"It doesn't matter. It was couple of months before I met you," he continued.

"That's pretty soon," she observed. "Why did you break up?"

"Can we talk about this later?" Adam asked, glancing uncomfortably at John and the rest of the restaurant.

"It's not a big deal," she said with a shrug, trying to keep her cool. She didn't get the whole ex thing, and she was trying to understand it. She wasn't a rebound. She knew that at least.

"Fine," he agreed reluctantly. "She moved to D.C., for a job as a lobbyist and didn't want a long-distance relationship. It was mutual. Long distance doesn't work."

"Huh," Chyna muttered, trying to take another drink and then realizing she had finished the whole thing.

Yeah, long distance sucked, but she didn't think it was completely out of the realm of possibility. She had never considered it, but Alexa was making it work. It felt like a cop-out excuse.

"I'm going to get another," she muttered. "Do either of you need anything?"

John shook his head, and Adam just sighed. She took that as a *no* and walked to the bar. She knew that she could have flagged down a waiter, but she wanted to process.

Chyna waited for the bartender to notice her. It didn't take long. She had another martini in hand as quick as the bartender could shake it. She wasn't even sure why she was worried. This wasn't like her. He wasn't with Christina now, and that was all that mattered. But, her Italian roots were rearing their ugly jealous head at the most inopportune time. She just felt too unsettled with having just found out about the situation, and she couldn't regain her calm. So, she did what she always did. She drank.

With her back to the table, she didn't see Adam come up behind her, but she felt his strong, capable arms wrap around her waist, pulling her against him.

"What's gotten into you?" he murmured softly against her skin, kissing her bare neck.

"I don't like not knowing things," she told him, melting easily into his touch.

"Christina doesn't matter to me, Chyna. That's why it never came up. I'm not hiding things from you," he said turning her around.

God, he was so fucking sincere. How could you not believe that face?

He leaned down and brushed his nose against hers. "You look beautiful."

"Don't try and sweet talk me," she said, brushing back against his nose. "I'm too susceptible."

He chuckled, kissing her pouty lips. "Come back to the table. I'm starving."

"Caveman," she responded, slapping his arm lightly.

"Don't make me throw you over my shoulder."

"Oh, please do," she said, wiggling her eyebrows.

Adam laughed again, shaking his head at her. "Come on. I don't get to see my brother too much. I think you'll like him."

If he only knew.

5

PRESENT

After nearly an hour of detailed work on her hair and makeup, the artists working on her finally left. She stood in the office with that big fucking desk in nothing but sparkly nude pasties and a seamless nude thong. She felt completely exposed, and she loved every minute of it.

The makeup artists had brushed a fine glittery powder across her entire body, and it felt silky smooth to the touch. Her long black hair was hanging down her back, framing her face in big swooping supermodel curls. The makeup was totally natural, but it made her innate beauty shine. It was a look only a true expert could have extracted out of various bottles, tubes, and containers. All that remained was what hung inside the black garment bag.

Giselle sauntered into the room.

"What are you doing here?" Chyna asked her. She was sure that Giselle would have been trying to help Marco run the show.

"Marco," she told her, walking to the black bag. Chyna rolled her eyes needing no further explanation.

"Where are my assistants? I can't get into my dress alone," Chyna asked.

"I am your assistant."

Chyna's mouth fell open. Giselle was so proud. She only worked for Marco specifically. That damn man!

"Well, get your ass over here!" Giselle snapped her fingers twice.

Chyna hurried over to her. Why would Marco have Giselle help her into the dress? It wasn't his style.

As Chyna was about to ask, Giselle unzipped the bag, and Chyna's mouth dropped open. That was *not* her dress. Her dress was long with flowing shades of purple sequins that draped artfully across her body in a pattern resembling waves crashing in the ocean. It was a one-of-a-kind designed just for her by Marco himself. It was crafted specifically for her body. She had practiced in it and completed a full photo shoot in the dress. She had never seen this one.

"I hope Marco knows what he's doing," Giselle whispered.

It was the first time Chyna had ever heard her doubt him.

Fifteen minutes later, when Chyna was secure in Marco's new creation, she made it to the backstage area. Her dress was pinned and hidden beneath a long white robe that was embroidered with her monogram beneath Marco's logo. Brigitte, Giovanna, and Ravenna flitted around her, anxious to begin the show. She couldn't even address them. She was too nervous. She had never been afraid of anything, but she had never been put into a dress like this with no forewarning and no practice for a production that was imperative to her career.

Marco's introductory words rang through the speakers. It was immediately followed by a thunder of applause. He was a raw talent with a booming voice that was as soothing, seductive, and stimulating as a Siren. He was in his natural element, charming an audience. She could see him in her mind's eye, gorgeous and tall. Intoxicating with a smile, he could cast a spell with those dark, dreamy eyes.

Assistants lined up models in order while a famous American singer began her latest number-one hit to open the show. Marco appeared backstage an instant later, pushing people into place, adjusting hair, and demanding overall perfection.

Chyna's green eyes bored into his back from a distance. She knew he could feel it, and then he pivoted around, quirking a smile at her. She continued to shoot daggers at him, which just seemed to amuse him further. He turned away from her then, finished off the last model, and disappeared back behind the curtain to watch the show.

"That man is insufferable," Chyna groaned.

"He is a genius," Giselle said in a voice that sounded like she agreed.

Chyna couldn't help continuing. "I want to rip off his head and post it on a stake sometime."

"But, most of the time, just his clothes, so he can work his genius on you, no?" Giselle responded.

Chyna gaped at Giselle. She was always so incredibly prudish.

Giselle broke out into laughter. "I'd try not to look that shocked on stage," she suggested.

Models were already being ushered back offstage to be escorted into the party to be put on display immediately. Time was moving fast, and Chyna wasn't prepared to step onto that stage. The room emptied more and more until even Brigitte, Giovanna, and Ravenna were kissing her cheeks and wishing her luck before they disappeared.

As soon as the very last model left backstage, Giselle stripped Chyna out of her robe and began unbuttoning the train of her dress and letting it loose behind her. When she was finished, Giselle admired her handiwork, her top lip turned up as she scrutinized with intense, hard blue eyes. "Are you prepared?"

No! Hell no! She couldn't do this. Marco was insane to even pull this shit on her, but she nodded, certain her face showed every evident concern.

"You'll do fine," Giselle reassured her. "I'm certain Marco wouldn't do something he thought would ruin the show."

"Let's hope."

"Chin up. Watch that step," Giselle reminded her.

Not that she needed the reminder. She almost rubbed her ass at the thought. "I can do this," Chyna said confidently, walking carefully up the steps.

She waited for her cue, her intro, the music—anything that would let her know when to begin, but nothing came. A hushed silence passed over the crowd, and suddenly, the lights were extinguished. A soft whisper, no louder than a hum, filled the room at the abrupt darkness, but it too died down. Was this her cue? She was' supposed to have music and lights! Where was her cue?

She was terrified to walk onto a fully lit stage in this dress, so the thought of doing it blindly in the dark was atrocious. When nothing else happened, she took it upon herself to make the decision. Her six-inch sparkly nude platforms created the only noise in the room as she clicked slowly across the black stage. What was the point? No one could see her, and it was dangerous. Marco better have something up his sleeve.

Chyna had obsessively counted steps all summer. Marco had some small fascination with knowing the length of every stage. He wanted his model to know where she was going and what she was doing. Then, she would have no excuse if she messed up because he had given a warning. She silently prayed that all that instruction was for this moment. She finished walking to where she anticipated center stage to be, and then she turned to face the darkened audience. She wasn't foolish enough to begin walking down the runway in the pitch black, even if she had been training for it.

So, she waited.

Then, it happened.

That damn man!

Candles flared to life on both sides of the stage at the end of the runway. They slowly traveled up the length of the platform as more and more lit up. Chyna's eyes rose to the perimeter of the enormous auditorium where more and more candles started glowing along the wall, in vases, and in the hands of models and patrons alike. The darkness faded, and soon she was awash with gorgeous, soft, ambient light.

She would have laughed if she could have. Instead, she stayed in character, producing a brilliant smile. Her dress was coming to life. She had thought it was gorgeous but plain when it had been hanging in that black garment bag. How could she have ever doubted Marco?

This was more than a Marco original, more than a one-of-a-kind. It was the culmination of all of his genius, and it was covering her body. The sheer nude base he had used for the design wrapped up in to a sweetheart shape across her breasts, stretched over her tight stomach, and ran down to her mid-thigh before it parted and fanned out behind her into a feathery light train. All of the edges were beaded by hand and dipped in some glassy shimmer to match. The glossy beading continued across the bodice in an intricate interpretation of a blossoming lotus flower.

The most stunning part was that it all shined at once—the dress, the shoes, her makeup, her entire body—like a star. In fact, she now realized that what she had thought was glitter being dusted on her body was actually finely shaved crystal. It caught the light in a way that glitter never could. That same crystal seemed to be embedded into the sheer material, so she did not appear to be nearly nude on stage.

She was simply Marco's creation.

When it seemed like not another candle could be lit in the entire place, a piano's soothing chords flowed through the hall. Up until that moment, Chyna had felt like she had been living through a dream. It all could have happened in a matter of seconds, minutes, or hours. She couldn't have told you the amount of time that had passed, but when that first chord struck, her body collided back with reality.

How could he possibly choose this song? She searched for his face out in the crowd, feeling the seconds creep by, as she stood trapped in the candlelight's glow. Then, he materialized at the end of the runway, his arms crossed and face smug. He had created her cue without ever telling her. How many times had this song played in his bedroom while he had photographed her, when he had trained her, when they had been rolling around in his silk sheets?

Her smile never faltered while everyone oohed and aahed about her dress reflecting the flickering light. When the piano really began picking up, she knew it was time. Then, she owned that runway. The dress moved flawlessly with her as she made her way toward Marco. She broke eye contact long enough to send dazzling smiles to people as she passed. Cameras snapped from all directions as Marco's clever creation traipsed across the floor.

As the piano hit the crescendo, Chyna reached the end of the stage and found Marco walking up the makeshift stairs to meet her. He reached out for her hand, and she obliged him. He turned to face the captive audience, smiling all the while, knowing that he had done it. He had won.

"Thank you so much for attending the thirty-seventh annual Glam Ball. I am pleased to present our newest model, Chyna Van der Wal, in my latest gown. I hope you all enjoyed my little star," Marco said, gesturing toward Chyna.

She almost cringed—almost. How dare he call her that in front of all these people!

Marco continued, "We'll all be seeing a lot more from her later."

She heard the double meaning in his words loud and clear, remembering the last thing he had said to her. *I'm coming for you after the show*. The audience might believe he meant her modeling skills or her body modeling his designs, but she knew better. Marco very briefly smirked at her only once. There was her man.

"Enjoy the remainder of the party!" Marco cheered, returning his attention to his audience. "Until Fashion Week," he said, holding his and Chyna's hands above their heads.

Dim lights filled the room at the end of his speech, and the crowd began milling around, discussing the exhibition. Marco dropped Chyna's hand back to her side, but he still didn't let go. She gulped, wondering if this was the time he had in mind.

He seemed to know exactly what she was thinking and shook his head side to side slowly. "Later," he whispered just loud enough for her to hear. "I know you're still ready for me, but it'll happen soon."

Chyna swallowed, wanting nothing more than to spit out every angry diatribe she had in her drama-laden body. But, damn it, she was still on stage! This whole thing meant something to her. "I'd still be ready, even if you had finished me earlier."

"I know how a performance turns you on," he said, gingerly leading her down the stairs. A halo of people surrounded them as they waited to get a closer examination of Marco's new star in the beautiful dress.

"I'm not the only one," she murmured, keeping her voice as soft and airy as she could. It was hard keeping the bite out of it, but she tried to avoid any negative attention. These people were like vultures, hanging onto every fleeting fashion and every juicy piece of gossip.

"No, you're not," he said, slowly twirling her for display.

She had to be extra careful in her shoes as the train swirled around her ankles.

He pulled her in close to steady her, and then he whispered into her ear, "But, you're the one holding on to all that built-up tension, and I can't wait to be the one to release it."

He chuckled in a way that only Marco could make sound so sexy.

She would show him built-up tension with a sharp kick to the ass. Chyna broke away from him now that she was steady on her feet again. She began to walk away, but he still held her hand in his.

He bent forward at the waist in a sweeping bow, drawing her hand to his lips and planting a possessive kiss on the soft crystal-dusted skin. She forced a smile on to her face, and a few surrounding individuals applauded at the display.

His responding smile was a promise.

6

———

PRESENT

Thankful to be out of Marco's clutches, Chyna made a beeline for the nearest waiter. He offered her a glass of Champagne with a curt smile.

"Anything stronger?" she asked, arching an eyebrow.

The guy did his best not to look surprised. "How much stronger?"

"Tequila?" she requested conspiratorially.

"We have wine."

Chyna rolled her eyes. "Seriously?"

"It's vintage," he offered apologetically.

"You've got to be kidding," she groaned, taking the Champagne out of his hand.

"*Mi dispiace*," he said actually apologizing.

Chyna waved away the apology. "*Va bene.*"

She sipped, okay, gulped down her champagne, finishing the first glass before her waiter even departed. He raised an eyebrow, but he handed her another glass before walking away as if he didn't want to be responsible for the centerpiece's alcoholism. She actually sipped this one because she was terrified of walking around in this thing drunk.

Her eyes instinctually found Marco in the crowd. The reporters were hovering over him like moths to a flame, trying desperately to get the next interview. He was engaged with a particularly attractive blonde at the moment. Chyna wasn't even surprised that the woman was basically molesting him or that he was letting her. They weren't together. Their arrangement had nothing to do with that. It was only about lust, need, hate, and passion, and she liked to keep it at that.

Still, there was some kind of draw she felt to him—that she had always felt to him. It was strangely magnetic. It made her want to claw her way out of her clothes one minute and then slap him clear across the face the next minute...before letting him tie her to the bed and tease her until he forgave her. It was a never-ending cycle—lusting after a man who had the power to break her and knowing half of the time she wanted him to.

"He is extraordinary, isn't he?" someone asked from behind her.

Chyna made the mistake of swiveling in place, twisting the train up around her ankles and nearly sloshing her Champagne on the priceless one-of-a-kind dress. She teetered in place, rearranging the skirt in her mile-high shoes before glancing up at the woman who stood before her.

She was plain in a way that made Chyna wonder if she had modeled when she was younger. Makeup, smiling eyes, and a camera could cover up plainness real quick. Wearing a molded burgundy mermaid gown tapered to a deep V in the back, she had the taste of someone accustomed to high fashion. Her only accessory besides her shimmery gold clutch was one long strand of white pearls that hung from her slender neck. Chyna would recognize the swirly Corsa logo on the clasp anywhere; after all, her mother had worked for them.

"Who?" Chyna asked, smiling sweetly at the woman.

"You know who," she said, slinking forward slightly.

Chyna glanced back at Marco who was speaking confidently into a tiny microphone.

"He is," Chyna answered her initial question.

"With, if I might add, impeccable taste," she said with a smile that didn't quite match her face.

"Why, thank you," Chyna said, wondering who the hell this woman was. She recognized quite a few of the faces in here, at least all the ones that really mattered. Yet, this was not a familiar face.

"Excuse me, I'm being rude. Cassandra," the woman said, holding out her hand.

"Pleasure," Chyna responded.

"You're American," Cassandra commented.

Chyna didn't know if it was a negative or positive feature. The woman's expression gave away nothing. Chyna never knew how people did that.

"Very." She smiled wider and took a sip of her Champagne.

Cassandra chuckled softly, eyeing her flute of champagne but not taking a sip of it. "However did he find you? Have you ever even modeled before? You seem like a natural. Maybe he didn't even need much time to mold you."

It was a bit presumptuous. All right, it was very presumptuous, but Chyna could appreciate that. In fact, it was a breath of fresh air in the crashing sea she had been wading through all summer.

"Forgive me," the woman said in a way that made it seem as if she had no reason to be forgiven. "I continue with my rude behavior."

"Seemed all right to me. Did you want something?" Chyna asked, trying to get to the point.

"I believe so," she said, surveying Chyna. "Yes, I believe I do."

All Chyna wanted to say was that she wasn't all that into

chicks because this woman was looking at her like she was deciding whether or not to take her home. Chyna didn't know what to make of it. Was she flirting with her or just being odd?

"I'd like to offer you a job," Cassandra told her finally.

"Excuse me?" Chyna asked, staring back at the woman as if she were a martian. She hadn't decided on what she was going to do now that her summer endeavor with Marco was coming to its conclusion. For the most part, she had been waiting for him to come to terms with the fact that he needed to keep her. He needed a model for his line, and she was his model. He had all but created her. It seemed a waste to let all that go after only a few short weeks.

She flipped back and forth about Marco every other minute, but she couldn't deny his genius. He was the most successful talent that had arisen in the fashion industry during this generation, and she was a part of that. She thrived under his influence like she never had before. Her whole world moved too fast and out of control. It seemed to have a life of its own. The entire experience was an adrenaline rush on steroids. She hadn't had that feeling from anything other than partying in a long, long time.

Partying used to be that escape for her. She could escape into the dancing, nightlife, alcohol, and men that floated through her existence like a traveling circus. It was a world within a world—a world where she felt more at home than in reality. She became addicted to it—not the alcohol but the feeling of release.

She was as much afraid of that feeling as she reveled in it. What if she went back to her life and it all felt lifeless in comparison? How would she ever be able to escape?

So, she was waiting, waiting for him to make up his mind. She wanted to choose for him, but when it came right down to it, she didn't know if she would choose him or not. She didn't know if she would choose this life for herself. Perhaps in the end, it was only a novelty that would wear off with the passing of time like everything else had.

With conflicted thoughts, Chyna turned her attention back to Cassandra.

"I would like to offer you a job," Cassandra repeated slowly.

"Oh."

"You are very good, and you don't even quite know it yet. I think you would fit nicely into our collection," she told her confidently.

After headlining Glam Ball, this woman wanted her to go be just another girl in her collection. Was she mad? She wanted...no, she needed to be showcased. Chyna craved it now. Marco had spoiled her, and at that moment, she knew it.

"I'm sure it doesn't sound like much to you," Cassandra continued eyeing her as if she had dealt with a thousand other divas. "However, I believe if you'd consider it, you'd realize it's a wonderful opportunity."

"Um...yes...well, thanks," she said, finishing off her Champagne. "I appreciate the offer, but I'm not sure what I'm going to be doing this fall...if I'll even be modeling."

"You'll be modeling," Cassandra said as a matter-of-fact.

Chyna didn't even bother asking her how she knew. She hardly stuck with anything long enough, even when she had loved many, many things. Perhaps modeling would die out for her as well. Though, the thought felt like a lie even when she was thinking it.

"I appreciate your confidence, but I just haven't decided about this fall yet."

Cassandra tilted her head to the side as if she didn't understand. She looked half like she wanted to laugh and the other half like she was taken aback. Her reaction was perplexing to say the least. Chyna had been modeling for all of a month and a half, but she had been around it her entire life. She had never heard of a Cassandra in the fashion industry. It didn't mean that she didn't exist. It just meant that she wasn't important.

"Well, I can't say I'll save a spot for you, but if you change your mind, do give me a call," Cassandra finally told her.

"I'll do that," Chyna said dryly.

Cassandra did laugh this time. At what, Chyna had no clue. Cassandra turned on her heel then and slowly began to slink back to where she came from.

"Wait!" Chyna called, glancing around to make sure she wasn't disturbing anyone. "You didn't tell me how to reach you."

Cassandra turned back to face Chyna without a trace of laughter left in her eyes. "Just ask Marco."

"Great," she muttered under her breath as Cassandra walked away. She had all but turned down a job offer without a consolation prize from Marco, and the only way she knew how to get in contact with this odd Cassandra woman was through the one person who would want to keep her away from anyone else. Not that she had any intention of taking some lame collection-modeling gig. She could do better than that, and she would.

When she glanced back up, she found Marco striding in her direction. She placed her empty Champagne glass on the tray of a passing waiter and braced herself for impact.

"My little star," he murmured softly as soon as he reached her. "You've been gone much too long."

"Hardly any time at all," she corrected.

"You had company," he stated plainly.

Somehow, she heard the threat in his voice.

"Everyone wants to marvel at your genius. It seems you have had another successful event," she said, playing to his ego when all she wanted to do was bruise it.

"Of course it was, but what were you doing talking to her?"

he asked, grabbing her arm and pulling her out of the center of the dance floor. He leaned in closer, so they wouldn't be overheard.

"She was talking to me," Chyna said, trying to pull out of his grasp.

"Why would she talk to you in the first place?" he growled, his brown eyes boring into her.

Chyna glared back at him, wanting none of this attitude right now. "What does it even matter? No one can talk to me?"

Marco laughed lightly at her. "Don't be ridiculous."

"I'm not being ridiculous," she said, turning her chin and facing the other direction. She was tired of the game, and she just wanted to know what was going to become of all of this. Was he going to offer her the job or not? If only she could just ask him.

"You're getting all worked up. While I like that, it is entirely unnecessary in this situation, and you should maybe hold on to that energy for later. You're going to need it," he said, running a hand down her arm.

"I'm not the only one getting worked up," Chyna responded.

"Nor will you be later."

"So, why shouldn't she be talking to me?" she asked, arching an eyebrow.

Marco laughed again at her ignorance. "Don't you know who that is?"

Chyna hated admitting her lack of knowledge, but she shook her head.

"She kept her maiden name despite her marital status," he said, clearly enjoying drawing this out for her. "Cassandra Corsa."

Cassandra Corsa. Chyna was floored, destroyed, and totally dumbfounded.

"She is Clarice Corsa's granddaughter and the owner of the

Corsa fashion line. She's one of the wealthiest women in the world."

And, Chyna just turned her down for a job.

Fuck!

7

———————

PAST

"Why? I don't understand Mr. Whatever-His-Name-Is at all," Chyna repeated for what felt like the tenth time.

"Does this have to happen every time I get called into work late?" Adam demanded, pushing his hands into his pockets deeper and deeper.

She knew he was frustrated. He had it written all over him, but she couldn't stop. Why was he always the one who had to go in? And, what did they need him to do at ten o'clock at night at an architectural company? Wouldn't the buildings still be standing the next day?

"Because you *always* have to go to work late," she reminded him. "Why don't you ask someone else to go for you?"

"It's a small company. I'm the only other person working on this building, and there's a deadline. Mr. Anderson is an old man. He doesn't get the graphic architectural design aspect as well as he should, and he trusts me," he said, looking down at the ground, shuffling his feet. "What would you say?"

She knew what she would say! The same thing she had been saying to him all along: Why even bother with this company? Why bother with an old senile man and a company going nowhere in today's market? It was a dead-end job with shit hours. She wished he could see that, but she couldn't say that to him. Not today. He looked too heartbroken to even consider turning down Mr. Whatever-His-Name-Is, and she figured he liked his job. Why else would he keep going back when he could do better? She wondered that about a lot of things with him.

"I'd tell him that I couldn't work tonight," she finally answered.

It was the best she could do. It wouldn't work. He would still go in, but she couldn't hold it back. She couldn't lie to him.

Adam sighed and looked off across the room, not meeting her eye. He looked as if he knew that she was going to say that. "Do you want me to call him back?" Adam asked dejectedly.

Chyna looked at him very closely. Was he serious? Would he actually try to get out of work for her? God, he looked like he actually would. She groaned. "Noooo," she sighed, annoyed. "I don't want you to call him back."

"Are you sure?" he asked, his hazel eyes meeting hers. "I would, you know."

She hmphed. "I know."

"Chyna," he said, looking up at her.

"No, it's fine. Go into work," she told him.

"Hey," he said, pulling his hands out of his pockets, reaching for her. "You're not going to be angry, are you?"

"No," she said sullenly, playing the part of the upset girlfriend wonderfully.

"I told you I would call in," he said, uncrossing her arms and pulling her into him.

"I know," she began.

"But?"

"But, you're only doing it because I asked you to."

Adam looked at her baffled. "Of course, I'm doing it because you asked me to."

"Do you think I should have to ask?" she questioned him, frustrated. They had plans tonight. She wanted to spend time with him. Why did it feel like she had to fight her way into that time?

"Chyna, I don't get you sometimes," he said, releasing her. "You tell me you don't want me to go into work, so I tell you I'm going to get out of work. Then, you get angry with me for deciding to get out of work. I can't win. How do I win?"

She sighed. He had already won.

"I don't know," she conceded. She looked down at the ground, hating this conversation as much as he did.

"Well, when you figure it out, will you let me know?" he asked quietly, reaching for his jacket.

"Are you leaving?" she asked, her voice raising an octave.

"I have work," he reminded her.

"But, you're leaving now? After we just fought?"

Adam closed his eyes and shook his head. "Did I miss something?"

"You're not going to have make-up sex with me?" she demanded with a giggle. She was so getting gypped in this situation.

He burst out laughing. "Am I supposed to?"

She nodded her head adamantly. "Of course."

"I'll keep that in mind next time," he said, still laughing softly to himself. "You astound me sometimes."

"At least I'm good for something," she murmured.

"You're good for everything," he said, pulling her close again. "And, I'd have make-up sex with you if I had time."

"Right here? Right now?" she asked, shimmying against him in the middle of the kitchen.

"I like the bedroom. A bit more spacious, don't you think?" he asked with a goofy grin.

Chyna rolled her eyes. "How romantic. Do you want me to close the door and turn off the lights, too?"

Adam leaned forward and brushed a kiss on her lips. "Shut up," he murmured softly. "I never hear any complaining when that door is closed."

She smiled against his lips. "So, let's go then."

"When I get home...or tomorrow," he amended, clearly thinking it would be a late night.

"Fine," she groaned before he kissed her again.

"I'll text you when I'm done," he said, grabbing his big sketchbook and walking toward the door. "Are you still going out?"

Chyna shrugged as if it was an actual question. She had nothing better to do, and she and Adam had been planning to go out that night anyway. She might as well hit a club while the night was young. Maybe when she was thoroughly sloshed, Adam would be home, and she could jump his bones. It sounded appealing.

"I figured," he said, wrenching the door open. "Maybe you can meet up with John later tonight. I know he was supposed to be hanging out with some friends from work, but I'm sure he'd like the company."

"Have you always babied him?" Chyna asked with a smirk. Really, she wouldn't mind hanging out with John.

"He's too busy for many friends, Chyna, and you have all of New York City."

She shrugged. Point taken. "How will I find this brother of yours?"

"I'll give him your number. Maybe you can pick him up, so he'll actually loosen up a bit," Adam told her.

"Sounds like a plan. I'll just wait for his call," she said, pushing down any and every thought she had about his brother.

"Please be safe. I wouldn't want anything to happen to you. You're far too precious."

She smiled warmly at his telltale good-bye. "I'll be as safe as always."

His smile caught her right in the gut at his exit, and she remembered why she had fallen so hard for him.

As soon as the door closed, she retreated to her bedroom to change. She stripped out of the navy skirt and sweater she had been wearing all day and pulled on a black minidress over her head. It was sleek and form-fitting. She knew it would draw attention, especially when paired with her favorite leather Manolos.

She didn't know who was going to be out tonight. It was still too early to find her friends, if she even wanted to call them that. They rarely frequented the clubs until well past midnight. She didn't care though because she was certain to know someone wherever she went. Either way, she just wished Adam was going with her. He wasn't the biggest party animal, but sometimes when she was with him, she didn't even need it. She could stay home, wrapped up in his arms, watching a movie, and just be.

Throwing her black hair out of her face, she took a deep breath and shut down her brain. This had always been her thing. She had always been the party girl, and she liked that. She wanted to keep it that way.

Chyna continued to shake that feeling as she grabbed her long black wool, belted coat and exited her apartment. She had Carl drive her across town and entered the nightclub. As the pulsing beats hit her full force, she eased back into her persona. The flashing lights and loud music coursed through her veins, and she closed her eyes as she soaked in the sensation of freedom.

A gentleman swept her up to the VIP section a moment later. Soon, she was surrounded by high-end clientele gyrating against one another, and she quickly moved through the mass to the bar.

When she approached, the bartender nodded at her and had two shots of tequila poured before she even had a chance to ask him. She smirked and downed them one after another. How refreshing...

A dirty martini landed on the bar next, and she smiled back in thanks. She had earned her bartender's manners by tipping handsomely. They all appreciated her here, and she appreciated how strong they poured the drinks.

She would have spotted the guy inching toward her a mile off. He was attractive. By all means, he was very attractive, but her taste buds were dull after having just met Adam's insanely hot brother. Plus, this guy looked like the type that thought his drink meant he should get something in return. She wasn't up for that anymore, not when she had Adam. It felt kind of nice actually.

"Nice choice," the guy said, finally moving close enough to her to brave speaking.

Chyna smiled sweetly up at him and tried to imagine what he would look like sweating in gym shorts. Yeah, no, not even close. He wasn't fat exactly, but he could afford to lose some weight around the waistline and bulk up those shoulders. God, could shoulders get much better?

Stop!

She wanted to kick herself. She couldn't think about John like that, and she certainly couldn't start comparing people to him. Just because he was hot and built and nice and—

Stop!

Okay, calm down! Breathe in, breathe out. This was stupid. She clearly needed to drink more. Her mind was all fucked-up.

"You...uh, come here often?" he asked next.

Chyna almost snorted at him, but she was too busy trying to down her martini to drown away her vision of John's tattoos. She had Adam, and Adam was sexy in his own right. Plus, she was dating him. No one else was able to handle her shit.

"I guess that's a yes," he responded, answering for her.

"Yes." She put down the martini and then glanced at her bartender.

"I can get the next round," he offered.

"That's really quite all right," she said, turning him down with a smile.

"You here with a boyfriend or something?" he asked as if that was the only reason it would make sense that she would be turning him down.

"Not tonight," she said as a dismissal, taking the next martini placed on the bar.

"I'll have whatever she's drinking," the guy said to the bartender, laying down a hundred dollar bill.

She almost rolled her eyes. *Was that supposed to impress me?*

Chyna sipped on her martini, wanting any excuse to get away from this guy. Why did he think he even had the right to be in her presence? Guys were so fucking irritating. Couldn't they take a hint?

She was off in her own world when the guy's hand trailed down the side of her arm. She glared up at him. "What are you doing?" she asked, pulling her arm back. She did not want him touching her.

"You want to get out of here?" he asked, looking ridiculous as he took a sip of his martini. "I have a suite at the Plaza right now. It's got your name written all over it."

"No," Chyna said exasperated. "What could possibly give you that thought? You don't even know my name."

"Come on, baby," he slurred.

Ah! He was wasted. He hid it well. "I'm not your baby, and I've politely told you no. I'm not generally polite," she said, raising her eyebrows.

"You'll have a good time," he continued.

"Of that I'm certain," she said sarcastically. She dropped her half-finished martini back on the bar and motioned to her bartender that she was through. She had a circling tab at the bar, so if she had to leave, they could just bill her. It was her favorite thing about this place.

"Where are you going?" the guy asked when she started walking away.

"Get a clue!" she yelled over her shoulder.

Chyna pulled her touch screen cell phone out of her purse to shoot off a text to her driver. She was sick of this place and needed a change in venue. If she stayed, she was sure that drunken asshole would press his luck. She was supposed to be safe tonight.

She hit Send on the phone and was about to put it away when the screen lit up with a strange number. Because she had reached the edge of the club and was already pushing through the double doors into the silence, she answered the call. "Hello?"

"Hey, Chyna, it's John."

Chyna stumbled in her high heels, knocking into the bouncer. She actually stumbled. She had been wearing high heels since she was twelve. She could be rip-roaring drunk and didn't miss a step in these things. The bouncer caught her easily, giving her a look like she needed to get her shit together before he released her.

"Adam gave me your number and said you might be out tonight," he continued.

"Uh...yeah, hi," she muttered. "He mentioned that."

"So, Adam's working late and can't hang out. You doing anything?"

"I'm just leaving a bar. Did you want to meet somewhere?" she asked.

Yes, Adam had told her to hang out with him, but what was she doing? She couldn't be alone with this guy. Hello? Bad idea? Yeah, nice to hear from you.

"I'm not meeting friends until later," he said.

"Me either," Chyna said, sliding into the backseat of her town car as soon as the door opened. "Adam said you might need a ride. I'm already in my car. Do you want me to pick you up?"

"Is he trying to get me drunk?" John asked with a laugh at the end.

"Sounds like him," she responded, waiting in her car.

"Sly bastard. All right, yeah, sounds perfect. I'll text you the address."

"Great."

"It'll take me a minute to get ready. You can have the attendant let you up to the top floor."

She shouldn't head that way. She really shouldn't.

And still she handed the address to her driver.

8

PAST

John's apartment building was in a nice part of town. He lived on the top floor. Global had to be paying him crazy money for him to afford a penthouse. She stared up at it in dismay because...fuck, she just wanted to fuck Adam's brother.

She would have laughed if it weren't so messed up. She couldn't go over to John's apartment. There were beds there... and counters...and she was horny. *Fuck.* She was also clearly teetering toward drunk. How fast had she downed those martinis?

Anyway. She pushed her mind back to the matter at hand —fucking John. Wait, no. Maybe she didn't even want to fuck him. Well, all she knew was that after only a few short hours, she had already completely pegged him as a bad boy—the kind of guy she would have fucked in an instant before Adam.

Before Adam.

Right. Why hadn't he fucked her before leaving again? That would have helped. Then, she wouldn't be so goddamn horny... and drunk. Had she mentioned that she was getting drunk?

No. No. No. Wait, this was probably a bad idea. She

shouldn't be this drunk and horny at once. She should probably tell Carl to turn the car around and find another club or better yet take her home so she can get herself off before Adam came home. That sounded appealing.

Damn Adam. Since when had she turned into this person? Her drunken mind laughed at her. She had done it as soon as she and Adam had started dating, and it hadn't even been difficult. She had just stopped bringing people home. Her doorman, Bernard, was the only other person who seemed to appreciate the change.

Fortifying her demeanor, Chyna pushed back her drunken thoughts. This was her boyfriend's brother. He was only here for the rest of the weekend, and then it was back to business as usual. Anyway, how big of a douche did you have to be to go for *his* brother's girlfriend?

Carl dropped her off on the sidewalk in the brisk March evening. Trying to keep the cold from sinking into her bones, she jogged into the building, pulling her coat tightly around her shoulders. She walked quickly to the attendant.

"Hi. Excuse me," Chyna said, reaching the desk and rubbing her hands together. "I'm here for John Ward."

"Ah, yes, he just called down. I'll buzz you all the way up," he said with smile as he gestured toward the elevator to his right.

"Thank you," Chyna said, heading to the elevator.

She pressed the up button and entered the elevator when it opened. The top button was lit up when the doors closed behind her, but it didn't have a number on it like the other ones. It just had a tiny scanner next to the button. Strange.

She didn't have to wait long to be let out as the elevator traveled at great speeds. It spit her out on a small empty hallway with only one door. She glanced around to see if this could possibly be the right place. She figured she was only left with one option and walked to the end of the hall. Another small scanner was placed on the door next to the handle. She scrunched up her features to examine it, and as she got closer, she realized the door was propped open.

"Oh," she said surprised. Why would he leave his apartment door open?

She felt a little weird just walking in, but he had obviously left it open for a reason, and likely, that scanner function meant no one else could get inside. She shrugged, her confidence returning, and she pushed open the door.

What she found was not what she was expecting. Her green eyes scanned the massive glass-domed room with an impeccable three-hundred-and-sixty degree view of the New York City skyline. An Olympic-sized swimming pool covered the majority of the open space in the room. Two enormous hot tubs and a kiddie wading pool rested on both ends of the massive pool. The pool itself had waves breaking in a clear V across the surface.

Chyna's eyes followed the form of the man doing a perfect butterfly from one end to the other. He cut across the water cleaner than a shark fin and as fast as a dolphin. The water barely broke around him before he dove back under, his muscled shoulders pulling him effortlessly across the surface. Well, at least that explained the shoulders.

John reached the end of the pool, grasped the concrete end, and lifted his head out of the water. He took a few deep breaths as the water dripped down his soaking wet body. All Chyna could do was stare. It was like catching someone showering or jacking off. It was totally private, but somehow, it was kind of like they wanted you to see it.

She wasn't even nervous or anxious about the possibility of him catching her staring. She was just hot...and completely bothered in all the right ways. What the fuck were those tattoos exactly? From where she was standing at the moment, she could still only make out the two she saw at the basketball courts, but she was still too far away to read what they said.

John planted both hands down on the concrete ledge and gracefully lifted his body out of the water. Her eyebrows rose as she watched his back muscles ripple from the exertion, and then she noticed his tight ass was covered by smooth black swim shorts. *Turn around. Turn around. Turn around!* She wanted to know what those shorts looked like from the front.

Her heel shifted on the squishy mat she was standing on, and it made some atrocious sound that broke the silence. John's head swiveled around quickly, noticing her standing there, but he didn't turn his whole body to her.

"Chyna," he said, "you got here fast. I thought I'd be done before then."

Uh huh. She was glad he wasn't. How else was she going to get to see him this naked? Also, tattoos! She could not get over those damn tattoos. What did they say? Her tongue was ready to find out.

"I must have misjudged the time."

Uh huh.

"It's all right," she managed to get out. "I don't really have anywhere to be." Had she just said that? Yep. Why yes she had. And by. By the confident look on his face, he had been expecting it. Ass.

Just the way she liked them.

"You don't mind if I do a few more laps then, do you?" he asked with that same smile.

Oh, he was milking it.

"Of course not," she said. *A few more laps on her.* "I was just going to find another lame bar. My best friend is at the beach for the week and left me alone in this frigid weather. No one else is going out for another hour or two from what I've heard."

"Going out alone then?" he questioned, turning back toward the pool as if he was going to dive into its depths.

"Occupational hazard."

He chuckled as his hazel eyes found hers across the room. "Hard life."

"You've no idea," she said slowly, walking her heeled feet across the slightly slippery surface.

"You should take those off," he said, gesturing to her heels. "Don't want you breaking your ankle on my watch."

Chyna debated in her tipsy state. She was an expert at walking in heels. But, on a wet surface with her balance already a little thrown? Yeah, not a good idea. She slowly slipped out of one shoe and then the other, leaving them next to the door, before padding over to the side of the pool in her party dress and jacket. He straightened as she approached, and she tried to keep her mouth from hitting the floor. Hello, front of bathing suit! She preferred her men well endowed, and—*damn!*—just from a glance she knew that he wouldn't disappoint.

Trying to get her mind off of the present wrapped in shiny black polyester, her eyes landed on his ribcage. She was close enough now to read his tattoos and figured that was better than staring at his crotch.

"There are extra suits in the changing room," John told her.

"What?" she asked, glancing up into his eyes. Had he said something? She was trying to decipher a tattoo. Stop moving!

"Bathing suits. If you wanted to get in the pool," he offered.

"You want me to wear someone else's bathing suit?" she asked, crinkling her nose.

"They're clean," he reassured her. "They just have them for residents. I doubt they've ever been used. If I'm going to keep doing laps, then you should get in the pool or at least the hot tub."

Her eyes darted to the hot tub and back. Valid, valid point.

"All right," she agreed.

When she reluctantly turned her back on John, she heard him chuckle faintly before he dove seamlessly into the water.

John was right. There was a collection of bathing suit pieces in a drawer in the dressing room. More than three-quarters of them still had a price tag on them. The amount had been removed, but it appeared as if they wanted to let you know that they were new. That's nice.

She slid her jacket off of her shoulders and placed it on a hook against the wall. Her dress followed as she pulled it over her head in one sweeping motion. She hung it next to her jacket. She tossed the rest of her clothes into an empty wicker basket. Grabbing a hair tie out of her purse, she knotted her long black hair into a messy bun at the top of her head. Finally, she slid into a simple black bikini, tying the ends on the triangle top and bottoms.

When she walked back out of the changing room, John was sitting on the edge of the pool, breathing heavier than he had before. Actually, she had seen him swimming way faster than she ever could, and she hadn't even noticed his breathing. He must have been kicking his own ass in her short absence.

She didn't make a sound as she approached him. His head was hanging forward, nearly between his knees, as his legs dangled over the edge of the pool into the water. She dipped her little toe into the water next to him and splashed some up into his lap. He jumped, kicking more water up. Chyna took a few skittish steps backward, not wanting to get her hair wet under any circumstances. When she saw he wasn't going to reciprocate, she walked forward and sat on the ledge next to him.

The water was warm, warmer than she thought it would be. It wasn't quite bath water, but it was refreshing and was probably cool against your skin after a good workout. She wondered how much he had to exercise in here to keep that body the way it was. A friend of hers was a swimmer and had always tried to convince her that it was the most amazing, impact-free exercise she would ever do. Chyna had gone once and decided to never go back because it had taken three showers to get the smell of chlorine off of her body.

"I love it up here," he finally said, breaking the silence.

Chyna tried not to look at him. They were too close together, and the tequila was still too strong in her body. "I can see why. It's peaceful. Is it always this quiet?"

"Unfortunately, no. Why do you think I'm up here so late at night? This place is swarming with children after school," he groaned.

"Makes sense," she said with a shrug, kicking her feet lightly in the water. "So...Global, huh?"

"Yeah, it's a pretty nice gig. How did you say you knew about them?"

"Everyone knows about them," she said, rolling her eyes.

He laughed, mirroring her feet in the water. "You mentioned that your mom worked for Corsa?"

"What do you know about Corsa?" Chyna asked, turning her face up to his.

He met her gaze. "Enough. What did your mom do for them?"

"She was a model. I mean, a supermodel," she said, waving her hands in the air like it meant nothing.

"Wow. Impressive. I've never met a supermodel."

Chyna smirked. "I find that hard to believe."

"They don't often venture to Flint, Michigan."

"You never see them around Global?" she asked with a raised eyebrow.

"Maybe. Not much time to pay attention," he said casually. "So, is that what you want to do? I know you said you don't base your life on your career, but do you want to model like your mom?"

Chyna wavered on the topic. She hated the idea of following in someone's footsteps, but on the other hand, she really thought she would be good at it. "Yeah, I think I'd like to try it. Just need an in besides old Mommy Dearest. Kind of like to forge my own path, if you know what I mean."

"Well, you should go for it. Really nothing holding you back," he said, nudging her shoulder.

"Yeah, maybe I will," she agreed, not convincing herself and probably not him either.

Silence ensued, and they were content in that moment to sit on the edge of the swimming pool, kicking their feet back and forth in time together. It was calm and peaceful.

The moment passed, and Chyna ventured forward with the conversation. "Have you always swam?"

"I got into it in high school. I always played ball, and my coach saw me swim during P.E., freshman year. He called me over and introduced me to the swim coach. She was the hottest teacher in school, so I agreed to be all but naked around her after school on a regular basis. I think that's how she got so many talented athletes on the team. I ended up being pretty good, and I stuck it out all four years. Got more money in swimming scholarships than basketball or academics. It was an easy choice."

"You're such a dude," Chyna said, giggling and making the mistake of looking up at him and his all but naked body. "So, did you hook up with your swim coach?"

"No way," he said with a knowing smile. "She was married with two kids. Way out of my league."

"I find that hard to believe."

He laughed, reaching down and splashing water on her lap. She squealed and shielded herself from his attack.

"You don't even know me. Judgey, judgey!"

"I surrender," she said, raising her hands over her head now that she was wet from the waist down. "Waving a white flag!"

"That's better," he said, eyeing her mischievously.

She brought her arms down slowly. "But, come on," she said, inching away from him, "didn't you want to?"

"Want to?" he asked as if that was a stupid question. "Of course, I *wanted* to…" He paused.

"And?" she prompted.

He laughed again. "And, when I went home on winter break sophomore year, she was divorced from her husband, so I did."

Chyna cackled. She knew it! "Now, who's judgey, huh? I pegged you spot on," she said, punctuating her last three words with sharp pokes to his chest with her finger.

He reached out quicker than she had expected and snatched up her wrist, wrapping his long fingers all the way around it. He pulled her forward and threw part of her weight toward the water. She screamed, not having anticipated actually getting in the water, and reached out for him to save herself. Her hand came up and around his neck at the same time as he put his hand on her stomach, pressing her toward the swimming pool.

"Don't you dare!" she screamed, feeling her body edging farther and farther off of the ledge toward the water.

"Oh, don't dare me, babe," he said, his hazel eyes narrowing with the promise of a challenge.

"I will kill you," she said, making a real promise.

"You wouldn't," he said, gripping her wrist harder and tugging her just a little bit more into the pool.

"If my hair gets wet, you will feel lucky to be alive," she said, clutching her hand around his neck for dear life.

No way was he going to do this. It would be a complete dick move, but she was already losing her balance. She wasn't even sure how she was still out of the water. The only thing holding her up was her hand around his neck, one foot pressed into the edge of the pool, and his hand gripping her wrist.

"Okay," he said with a smirk.

Just then, his foot came out of nowhere and knocked her leg away from the edge of the pool, and she fell feet first toward the water. She grappled for support, any kind of support, holding onto his neck for dear life. She managed to pull him into the water with her or maybe he did it of his own accord. She wasn't sure.

Right before her feet hit the bottom, her head about to submerge, John jerked upward on the hand he was holding and grabbed her by the waist. He had effectively kept her hair from getting wet, but now, she found herself completely pressed against his chest. Holy shit that! That chest! He was totally ripped. Where do those muscles come from? She needed to check out more swimmers!

"You asshole!" she cried as he slowly eased her feet to the floor.

She stood on her tiptoes to keep her head above water and looked up at his laughing face. His smile was all straight white teeth. He had little crinkle lines around his eyes and dimples at the corners of his mouth. She loved his mouth. It was the perfect shade of pink on a plump bottom lip and shapely upper lip. She was too drunk for this!

"I said I wouldn't get your hair wet," he said as he slowly released her.

She splashed water into his too cute face before reaching out for the ledge again.

"Hey, don't be mad." He reached out for her again, yanking her back into the pool as she tried to climb out.

"You threw me in the pool like a little kid!" she reminded him.

Her mind was on his hand that was gripping her waist, trying to keep her in the pool. Her body was betraying her, and she wished she hadn't had that last martini...or the one before that...or the tequila shots. Because, damn, did that feel nice.

"You were acting like a little kid," he said as she looked up into his chiseled face.

She bit on her bottom lip and tried not to let her features betray her as much as her body was. His gaze flickered to her lips and back to her eyes, and she knew that she wasn't hiding anything.

Any other person

But not this situation.

She covered her mouth with a pretend cough and broke out of his embrace. "I guess we both were," she admitted. "I'm going to need to shower before we go out."

He stifled a laugh. "Me too."

Her eyes darted to his quickly and saw his meaning. She probably should have blushed or giggled or something equally girly, but all she did was smile, a slow devious smile. Her eyes flickered down to the water and then back into his hungry hazel eyes. He was making this difficult.

"You should probably do that then. I need to get out of these wet clothes."

"You should," he said, clearing his throat as he watched her pull herself out of the water, "probably do that then."

"Oh, I will," she said as she dripped across the concrete floor back to the changing area.

As soon as the door closed behind her, she leaned back against it and closed her eyes, breathing heavily. What the fuck was she doing?

9

PRESENT

"This place is a dream," Brigitte said, finishing her fourth flute of Champagne since Chyna had ventured into their midst.

"It's an opera house," Chyna said nonchalantly.

"I'm not an idiot!" Brigitte cried. "Stop treating me like one. Stupid American." The last bit was muttered under her breath.

"She didn't have to say you were an idiot, Bridge," Ravenna responded cattily.

Even though the woman was bitchy, she still stuck up for Chyna. Chyna wasn't sure why, but it had always been that way. If anyone else stepped out of line, Ravenna was certain to bite their head off without a second thought. She was a vicious opponent who didn't back down, and it didn't take much with many of the twits that circulated the modeling community.

"Don't start with me, Ravenna." Brigitte scowled.

"Ladies," Giovanna cooed, "can we not?"

"Yeah, Bridge," Ravenna spat her name out. "Keep it together."

Brigitte teetered forward in her dress as if she were going to lunge for Ravenna. Giovanna quickly stepped in between them.

"Will you two *please* just quit it? It is our last event together. We have been living together for nearly two months now. We have done everything together. Can we just savor our last evening together?"

"Fine," Brigitte agreed, stepping back and lounging against a cream chaise. Her blue dress slit open to her hip as she rested backward.

Ravenna just shrugged, leaning against the wall like a Greek goddess statue. Black feathers trimmed her low-cut gown and held back one side of her cascading red hair wrapping around and over her right shoulder.

"Thank you," Giovanna muttered, turning away from the girls, her dress sweeping out behind her in layer upon layer of yellow tulle.

Chyna hadn't moved from the large window ledge she had been sitting on throughout the entire confrontation. She had been too concerned with when Marco would come for her. The four of them had disappeared into a private room after spending an hour on their feet while designers examined their gowns, taking no interest in actually speaking to the models themselves. It was dreadfully boring, and they took solace in each other's company as soon as they could leave. They wouldn't be able to be gone for too long before someone noticed their absence.

"*Ay! Americano,*" Brigitte chirped, saying the name like it was a dirty word.

Chyna's head snapped up and found all three girls staring directly at her.

"Were you listening to anything we were saying?" Ravenna asked with a pointed smile.

"No," Chyna said with a shrug. Did they say something they said been important? She assumed they were still arguing as per usual. It gave her a lot of time to drift away.

"We were just asking," Giovanna began, glancing between her co-conspirators for support, "what Marco is like?"

Chyna stared between them, wondering where this was going. She was sure whatever it was would only mean trouble. "What do you mean?"

"Oh, you know!" Brigitte chimed in.

"I'm sure I don't."

"What's he like in bed?" Ravenna asked bluntly.

"None of you know?" Chyna asked, throwing it back in their face. Though, she was mildly curious. It's not like she spent all her time with Marco. He could have had the opportunity to fuck every one of them if he had wanted to.

"Oh, why are we even bothering to ask her?" Brigitte asked, throwing up her hands.

"I don't know what he's like," Giovanna answered, ignoring Brigitte. "I know Bridge has no idea."

Brigitte hmphed in frustration. She was the youngest of the bunch, and sometimes it really showed through.

"Ravenna?" Giovanna asked.

Ravenna smiled her biggest, most devious smile.

"Well?" Chyna asked, not buying her act for one minute.

Ravenna was not Marco's type. Far from it. She was gorgeous and curvy, but she was unable, or at least unwilling, to take direction. Chyna wasn't submissive by a long shot, but she knew when to give and when to take.

"Spit it out," Giovanna said, planting her hand on her hip.

"Fine!" Ravenna called. "I haven't slept with Marco, but Chyna has. So, you spit it out. What was he like?"

Chyna shrugged, looking back out the window. She didn't have any desire to parade her sex life before these girls. The only person she had ever shared details with was Alexa, and she wasn't here. She was in New York, probably where Chyna should be, making Alexa feel better. "What does it matter?"

"Oh, come on. Don't be shy," Ravenna continued.

"Yeah, I mean, we all knew what you were really doing all those days and nights trapped in his apartment," Brigitte pointed out.

"Do you, now?" Chyna asked, a smile playing across her features as she stared out at the darkened sky.

The moon was bright overlooking the city, but the stars weren't all that visible with all the lights reflecting up into the atmosphere. It reminded her of New York, and for the first time, she felt a twinge of homesickness.

"Forget it," Giovanna sighed. "She's not going to tell us. She has kept it a secret this long. She didn't even tell us she was having sex with him."

"What if I wasn't?" Chyna asked, turning back around. She crossed one bare leg over the other and watched the shimmer of her nude dress play off the dim lighting in the room.

All three girls laughed and shook their head in disbelief.

"You were," Ravenna insisted. "The man is too obvious."

"Well, we did work in his apartment," Chyna said, licking her lips.

"Yeah, I bet you used his camera." Giovanna winked.

Chyna couldn't hold back her laugh at that comment. It was too true for her to even begin to deny it. Marco was obsessed with his camera, and he liked to capture everything behind his lens.

"Oh my God! Did you make a sex tape?" Brigitte cried, standing from her chaise when the thought hit her.

Chyna bit her bottom lip and raised an eyebrow as she tried to hold onto her sense of mystery.

"You did! That's so hot! Can I see it?"

"Brigitte!" Giovanna yelled.

At the same time, Ravenna cried, "Me too!"

"I'm not showing it to you!" Chyna shouted, also standing in her excitement.

"So, you did make one!" everyone cried at once.

Chyna covered her mouth. She was laughing so hard. It hadn't seemed so funny at the time when they were making it, or when they had watched it after, or when they had immediately jumped right in between the sheets again because they were so hot from watching it. Now, standing there with Brigitte, Ravenna, and Giovanna, the idea that she had made a sex tape seemed utterly hilarious.

Ravenna put her hand against the wall to steady herself. "So, really, can we see it?"

"No!" Chyna cried. "I'm not showing anyone else."

"Ugh," Brigitte muttered. "At least tell us if he's good or not."

"He's better than good," Chyna finally relented.

"Natasha told me he was kind of kinky," Ravenna said, straightening and eyeing Chyna more closely.

Natasha? Chyna didn't know a Natasha. They had worked with more than two dozen other girls this summer, but Natasha didn't sound familiar. "Who?"

"She was selected as Marco's centerpiece two years ago," Ravenna told her. "I was a favorite, but Natasha was selected before me. I'm not really sure why. She wasn't all that spectacular."

Chyna had never thought about whether or not this had happened with another girl before. To be perfectly honest, she hadn't cared whether or not he had been sleeping with other models while they had been together, let alone whom he had slept with before her. She was still getting the personal attention, and as. As long as she was still getting what she wanted—the modeling and the man—then she didn't care if he diddled half of Milan. He still came back to her either way, so it hadn't mattered. But, she was curious about this Natasha character.

"And, she said he was kinky?" Chyna asked, desperate to ask a different question.

"Yeah. I wasn't that close with her, but a friend of mine said that she'd tell her stories about getting tied up to some kind of furniture. I wanted all the dirty details, but Natasha was pretty tight-lipped, kind of like you. So, tell me," Ravenna said with a curious expression, "does he tie you up? And, what kind of sex furniture does he have? I've been dying to know!"

"This conversation is getting a little out of hand," Giovanna said, pulling Ravenna back.

Desperate to have answers, Ravenna had moved forward until she was mere inches from Chyna's face.

Ravenna swept her hand through her long red locks and walked around the room.

"She's a bit nuts," Brigitte said, pointing her thumb at Ravenna. "Running for two years off of hearsay."

Chyna managed to laugh through her hammering heart. She wasn't sure why she was so worked up at the moment. It wasn't like it meant anything that Marco had tied up another woman to a sex toy. He had to have had them for a reason, but it was something in Ravenna's eyes that had made her uneasy. She couldn't even place it, but now, all she wanted to know about was Natasha. Whatever happened to Natasha?

"What..." Chyna cleared her throat. She couldn't ask that question. "What was she like? Natasha. To catch Marco's eye? If she wasn't that talented."

"Oh, she's talented enough," Ravenna said, waving her hand. "Just took her a long time. Marco was obsessed with her, like he is with you. She was a bubbly blonde with short curly hair. An American. Guess you have that in common, too. Actually, I think the centerpiece was American last year, too. Don't remember her name."

"What happened to Natasha? After they were together, I mean."

Ravenna smiled, looking more and more true to the animal form her name was a derivative of. "Modeling still, I think. I remember my friend saying she was pretty devastated when Marco left her."

"Why did she get attached?" Chyna asked with a flippant air about her. She had been wondering that about herself for the past couple of weeks. She didn't care if he fucked someone else, but she cared about him keeping her. Not even keeping her in the sense of a girlfriend by any means, but she wanted him to finger her irreplaceable. He needed her.

"How could you not?" Brigitte asked softly from a corner of the room.

"Yeah, I mean, I'm attached," Giovanna whispered into the silence that followed.

Chyna looked over to Ravenna. Ravenna was too strong, too abrasive. No way would she feel attached, too.

Ravenna sighed, her eyes softening. "That's the reason I'm back, isn't it?"

Chyna stared around at the three beautiful faces in front of her. Had she been in her own world so much the past two months that she hadn't even noticed everyone else's reaction to Marco? They didn't talk about it. It had never come up. Yet, here they were all feeling the same thing in varying degrees of obsession.

And then, there was Natasha.

Chyna didn't know what to make about her or that scenario. She hated the feelings running through her body. All she wanted to do was push them away, stomp on them in her high heels, and bury them six feet under. Was it terrible that she had thought she was special? Was it worse that she was disappointed?

The only time she had ever felt completely and singularly special was with Adam. Look at what she had done with that! Stupid Adam! Why was she even thinking about him today? That was the second time.

"I think I should get back to the party," Chyna said, her strength returning. "I have an Italian designer I need to speak with."

"Just one thing," Ravenna said, grabbing her arm before she passed through the door, "was there kink?"

Chyna smiled at her like she was a child. "If you think tying me to a chair is the kinkiest thing Marco is interested in, you should think again."

10

———

PRESENT

With that, she brushed past Ravenna and walked back into the ballroom. The room had started to clear out, but there were still plenty of stranglers binging on the free booze. Her radar went off as soon as she entered, and she spotted Marco with the same reporter from earlier. He was blatantly flirting with her at this point. Guess he wasn't coming for her after all.

She passed a drunk couple who started discussing her dress behind their hands. When she looked over at them, they straightened as best they could and turned away. Apparently, whatever they had been saying wasn't pleasant. Even better.

She just wanted to go home—not back to her penthouse but back to New York. Her Italian tour was basically over, and she wanted out before she was completely jaded to everything that had happened. She preferred to look back on what had happened here with a smile, knowing it was her first real modeling gig.

A passing waiter offered her a drink, and she graciously took it. She was being melodramatic about the whole affair. She had gotten nothing out of it she hadn't asked for herself. Who was she to think that Marco wouldn't discard her with a passing fancy?

The champagne swirled around in her glass as she stared down at it, contemplating her predicament. Maybe she should just leave with someone else. She smiled up at the cute waiter who had given her the drink, and he smiled back. His cheeks turned crimson as her heated gaze landed on him. He would do just fine, if she had any interest at all, but she didn't. She hated knowing she could do better, and she let that small fact dictate who she took home. It never had before, but she had gotten even pickier since Adam. God, that man was stuck in her thoughts! They had broken up! Who cared what he was doing now or that Alexa had said he was hurting? It had been mutual, and he had delivered the final blow anyway.

"Whatever," she mumbled, breaking eye contact with the cute waiter. She didn't even bother to acknowledge happiness that his face fell when he realized she wasn't going to approach him.

Chyna took another sip off of the expensive imported champagne and turned her attention back to Marco. He better fuck her right tonight. If she was being discarded, she damn well wanted a consolation prize. But, she didn't see him. Had he left with the reporter already? No, she zeroed in on the reporter who now looked sullen in his absence. That bitch had been trying for some Italian ass all night, and it was kind of comical that he had likely turned her down. What a tease. Guess Ms. Cupcake didn't cut it.

But then, where was Marco? Her eyes darted around the room for her man. Usually, she could spot him in an instant, but he wasn't there. If he wasn't' at Glam Ball, where was he and why had he left her?

Not finding him, Chyna's frustration got the best of her, and she left the main ballroom. The party was basically over. If Marco had, in fact, left the building, then it was officially over.

Everyone else in that room didn't matter to her. If she wanted, she could get another job with any one of them without the proper introduction. But, she wanted the best, and she was going to fucking get it.

She stomped back to the director's office where her clothes had been discarded. When she walked in and saw that big fucking desk sitting in the middle of the room, her body warmed all over, and her body clenched up at the dirty thoughts running through her mind. He should have fucked her on that desk. That way she wouldn't be so horny and desperate for him to be inside of her now.

"Asshole," she grumbled, coming around the backside of the desk. She reached out for her pile of neatly folded clothing, and on top of her clothes, she found a small envelope with her name scribbled on the front. She would recognize that handwriting anywhere. Her lower half pulsed as her imagination took off, but her heart also constricted in fear that this was the end. Would he leave her with just a note?

She opened the crisp white envelope and pulled out the gold-trimmed card stamped with Marco's logo on the front. Her shaky hands flipped it over and read the short message on the back.

Backstage entrance. Blue Bugatti. Don't think about taking off that dress.

Chyna wasn't sure she had ever moved that fast. She left her clothes, sitting discarded on the desk, and rushed out of the director's office. She turned away from the party and down the empty hallway, following the signs to the stage. A stray janitor gave her a suspicious look as she bolted past him, but he didn't do anything to stop her. Soon enough, she found the stage and the big sign indicating the exit. Without a backward glance, she pushed the heavy door open and walked into the back alley of the theatre.

As promised, a shiny blue Bugatti revved in the narrow street. The car was fucking gorgeous. Panty-dropping hot car! She licked her lips and cautiously approached the passenger side. The windows were tinted so dark that she couldn't make out an outline of the driver, but she could hazard a guess.

Slowly, the passenger door lifted upward, rather than out, as it turned a hundred-and-eighty degrees vertically, displaying the cream leather interior. Chyna picked up the train of her dress and slid into the car without a second thought. The door closed behind her automatically, and she turned to face the man sitting in the driver's seat.

"About fucking time," Marco said, shifting into gear and pressing on the acceleration.

He turned around the corner and onto the main street. He looked over at her and smirked. That was all the warning she was given before he punched the accelerator, going zero to sixty in just over two seconds, throwing Chyna backward into the seat.

"Holy shit," she muttered, quickly buckling her seat belt. This thing was fast!

He merged into traffic, out pacing every other car by a long shot. Other cars mercifully got out of his way as he flew past them. The images blurred in her vision and made her stomach twist. She looked up at the sky to ground her. How fast were they going anyway? She turned her head to the speedometer and saw the top speed written as four-hundred-thirty kilometers. They were sitting at just over half that. Her head spun. How fast was that? She couldn't do conversions in her head.

"How fast can this thing go?" she asked as he veered around another car.

God, we were so close to that thing. One wrong move...

But, Marco hadn't made a single wrong move. He was a

natural behind the wheel, handling the beautiful car with the ease of a race car driver. Why had they never gone driving before if he had this thing?

"Four-hundred-thirty kilometers," he responded, not taking his eyes off the road.

She was thankful for that. "In miles?" she prompted.

He chuckled softly, darting his eyes toward hers briefly. "Two-hundred-sixty-seven miles per hour."

"Fuck. We're going one-thirty to one-forty?" she asked as she pressed herself back against the seat, trying not to think about it.

"Is that too slow for you? I know you like it fast," he said, hitting the gas harder.

Chyna gripped the left handle to steady herself as they went shooting down the highway. Normally, it didn't take long to get back to his place. It would have been even shorter, punching it at one-hundred and sixty miles per hour, but it seemed that Marco just wanted to show off. He made a sweep of the city before circling back in the direction of his apartment. If she didn't know Milan so well, she probably would have missed the majority of what they were driving by. She had never driven it before, of course, but she had ridden around the city enough for various shoots.

. She could tell immediately that the ride in his Bugatti had sent a rush of adrenaline through him, and she would be lying if she said that she didn't feel it, too.

A few blocks from his place, he pulled up fast and turned sharply into an alleyway.

"What are you doing?" Chyna asked, sitting up a little straighter.

"I want to show you something first," he said with a sly smile.

"Will I like it?"

"You'll love it."

Chyna chose to trust him because really she had no other choice. As he took a few more sharp turns around the winding street, Chyna stopped keeping track. She was totally lost, and even if they were spit out on a street she knew, she wouldn't be able to tell you which one or on what end.

At long last, Marco came to a stop overlooking the Naviglio Grande canal, which joined the Ticino River to the Darsena dock. The canal used to be part of a series of navigational waterways connecting the entire city, but over time, it had been destroyed or covered up. Along the gorgeous flat waterway, much of the area had been converted into shops, bars, and tourist traps.

Tonight, however, the area seemed tame. It was late, but that hardly stopped the youth of the city from traversing the paths and bars hidden around the water. From their vantage point, they could see down the long stretch of water, but were blocked them from view.

Marco cut the ignition, removing even the hum of the powerful engine. She swallowed and looked out across the expansive display before her. Her heart was thumping a sharp tattoo in her chest as her anticipation grew. The tension was practically palpable between them, and Marco's hands twitched on the steering wheel.

"Well, do you like it?" he asked, turning to examine her face.

She continued staring out toward the city view, but she felt his eyes travel up and down her very visible body under the nude gown. "You can see the stars," she mused. She hadn't been able to see them from the windows of La Scala Theatre.

"I'm looking at mine."

With that, she turned her face back to Marco's and found herself examining him as well. He was so fucking powerful in every aspect of his face. He had a strong jaw, chiseled cheekbones, and ever-aware keen eyes. His entire physique just screamed at her. He had warmed her up with a glance. Before she knew it, her body was on fire all over again. As if she hadn't gone hours without his hand on her backside, she felt like she was transported back to that room, bent over that big fucking desk with his cock pressed against her ass. . This time he wasn't getting off the hook.

His hand reached across the car, grasping the back of her head and pulling her toward him as he deftly unbuckled her seat belt. Their lips crashed together, igniting the spark that had been burning low all night. God, she wanted him desperately. She wanted him for every handprint on her ass, for every time he left her in the dark, for every fondling of Ms. Cupcake the reporter, for every dirty and nasty thought he'd had about her, for every mention of the word *star*. She wanted to fuck his brains out. She wanted him to really feel her anger, passion, and frustration, and she wanted to take it out on him in the best way they knew how.

Chyna fumbled for his belt. She made quick work on pulling it open before unbuttoning his pants and yanking the zipper down. He untucked his shirt and slid his pants and boxer briefs off in one fluid motion. She had already kicked off her shoes and was soon throwing her underwear onto the spotless carpeted floor.

"Get back over here," he said, reaching for her lips again.

He grabbed her left leg, pulling it across the seat, and across his body. She ducked her head to avoid hitting the low ceiling, so she could straddle him. His dick was hot and hard in her hand when she reached for him, and his head dropped back when she worked her way up and down the shaft. She hadn't even needed to touch him really. He was already so turned on. At least she wasn't the only one who had been left wanting earlier.

"I'm going to fuck you now," she whispered into his ear.

She sat up a little higher so that she could adjust his dick underneath her. When the tip touched her wetness, she shivered all over at the feel of him. This was what she wanted. This was exactly what she wanted. Nothing else mattered but this, this moment.

Her sex slowly licked across the head, swirling teasingly against him. Marco growled deep in his throat at her taunting behavior, reaching out to grip her hips forcefully between his hands. He shoved her down on top of him, and she gave out a short yelp as her walls expanded to fit him. When he filled her completely, she dropped her head forward onto his shoulder, a moan of pleasure escaping her lips.

"God, you feel good," she whispered.

"I've been waiting for this for far too long."

"You and me both."

She slowly lifted herself up, feeling his hands tighten on her hips again. She eased back down on him before straightening up to look into his handsome face. Resting her hands on his shoulders, she began a quick bouncing movement—up and down, up and down. His hands kept the rhythm smooth, giving her some added force. When she rocked backward, he pushed up inside of her.

Her climax was already fast approaching. She had been impressively turned on from the spanking earlier, and now, finally having him inside of her was more than exhilarating. It was euphoric. She didn't know if she could think of a better place to be than inside a multimillion-dollar car with her designer forcing her down on top of him over and over again.

"Marco," she groaned. "Oh fuck!"

"My star," he murmured, pressing his lips to her collarbone. "You're going to come for me."

"Make me," she demanded, moving their bodies together faster. All she wanted was to hit climax. Her body was quivering on top of him with the impending release.

"When you do, I'm going to make you do it again," he

growled, pushing himself as deep as he could go. "You're going to come until I tell you to stop."

"Please, God, yes!" she cried, her body clenching demandingly around him as an orgasm ripped through her body.

He slammed her down twice more on top of him as her body shook uncontrollably, and then he grunted, reaching climax with her. He shuddered underneath her before they both went still, the only movement coming from her trembling legs. He kissed a light trail across her shoulder and up her neck.

"You're magnificent," he whispered softly against the light beading of sweat at the nape of her neck.

Chyna just sighed into his embrace.

"I'm going to keep my promise to you."

"What's that?" she whispered. Her stomach constricted, wondering which one he could be referring to.

He chuckled against her shoulder, nibbling softly on the soft skin. "I'm not done with you yet tonight."

11

PAST

"Are you sure this is the place?" Adam asked, looking up at the black building with a large overhang and patio.

Under warmer conditions, it would probably be full of black café tables and chairs. A large purple neon sign displayed the name, Sulgaana Hookah Lounge, in big swirly letters. Otherwise, the only decoration outside came from fake candles lighting the way to the entrance.

"Yeah. It's new," she said, pushing him forward. "A friend told me about it. Used to be a club or something, but it's been renovated."

He poked her playfully in the side. "It doesn't have a line out the door. Are you sure you're actually interested?"

"I'm not stuffy," she said, dodging his attempts to tickle her.

He stopped and raised his eyebrows. "Really?"

"Hey, you! Shut the fuck up!" She wrapped her arms around his waist and pulled him close to her.

He smiled and slung his arm across her shoulders.

"There she is!" he said, kissing her temple as he reached out for the door.

She jabbed him the ribs twice as he swung the door open. "You're gonna get it tonight," she said.

"You got me," he said, doubling over like she had actually wounded him.

Strutting forward purposefully into the hookah bar, she said, "And, stay down."

She could feel his eyes on her ass as she walked a catwalk to the host's station.

She felt better and more confident tonight. Last night had shaken her a little, and she had called it an early night. Well, early for her. She had even pulled out some of Alexa's double chocolate, chocolate chip ice cream from her freezer to see if that helped. It hadn't. She had just felt fat on top of everything else.

No, she couldn't think about last night—not about the pool, not about the bar, not about the club, not about leaving.

She refused to think about his body soaking wet in nothing but swim shorts. Her mind wouldn't even let her think about being at the bar with him afterward when he had bought all the right drinks and said all the right things. No way was she going to consider his charming personality, the way his hand found the small of her back when he leaned in to ask her a question, or those too smart hazel eyes that always focused on her face. If she wasn't thinking about those things, she certainly wouldn't go back to the feel of his body pressed tight against hers as they danced in the center of the nightclub. Nope, she wouldn't think about any of those things.

All she would let herself think about was that she had ended it. They'd had a nice time, and then she had ended it.

Yep, that was the only important part.

Adam was out with her tonight, and John had plans until later. Frederick was hanging out boyfriendless at some gay bar in Manhattan, and she was considering going to hang out with him later in the evening. If Alexa were in town, she would have already been with her.

The woman behind the desk was dressed in a traditional Indian sari in deep purple and orange silk. Her long dark hair was pulled back off of her face, showing the bright red bindi at the center of her forehead. "How many?" the woman asked, smiling with eyes veiled by thick black lashes.

"Two," Chyna told her.

Adam approached the podium and poked her in the side once more for payback. She turned and glared at him.

He smiled brightly at the woman with that ever-present grin on his face. "We don't need food though. Can we just go to the bar?"

"Of course, sir," she said demurely, directing them to follow her.

They passed three large rooms with low tables and chairs topped with cushions that matched the host's sari. Food was served in circular aluminum bowls in the center of the table, and the guests were scooping directly out of the communal pots or adding food to a separate plate. The whole place smelled sweet and fragrant like flowers mixed with honey. The host took a turn to her right and pulled back a deep crimson curtain.

"Here you are," she said, allowing them access to the bar area.

They both thanked her as they passed through the curtain into a different world.

The hookah lounge itself was made up of several adjoining rooms separated by sheer curtains. The perimeter had cushioned alcoves with curtains that closed around the area, allowing a bit more privacy. All over the room, pillows and chaises in deep burgundy, navy, purple, and orange were pressed together for couples to lounge on. Hookahs in various colors were sitting atop white tables. A faint fog already clouded the room, and Chyna realized the aroma she had smelled before was the mixture of all the various hookah flavors blending together.

"Come on. Let's head to the back," Adam said, taking her hand and walking through the already crowded room.

They found an empty alcove and took over the space. It was bigger than she had expected with room enough for five or six people rather than the two she had been anticipating. Adam deposited her there and then went in search of the bar. He returned a couple minutes later with her martini and a beer in hand.

"I ordered our hookah, too. They should be bringing it over."

"What flavor did you get?" she asked.

"Apple," he said with a shrug. "The guy said it was popular. We can try something else if you want."

"No, apple is fine," she said, reaching for her martini hungrily.

Alcohol was such a good idea. It made her forget things, and tonight, she really wanted to forget things.

A few minutes later, a waiter showed up with a bright green hookah and their apple selection. Adam tipped the guy and then went about his business setting up the shisha for them. When he finished, Chyna leaned forward, her navy spaghetti-strap dress revealing ample amounts of cleavage. She took a drag off of the hookah, winking at Adam. She breathed out the smoke and then licked her lips, surprised by how refreshing the faint hint of apple was. Adam followed suit, breathing the smoke out.

Then, he started digging into his pocket. "I'm going to take this," he said, taking a sip of his beer before he pressed the phone to his ear. "Hello?" he yelled over the music and people talking in the establishment. "I can't really hear you!"

"Yeah, that's better!" he yelled back into the phone.

Chyna looked over at him expectantly, enjoying the mixture of the tobacco and vodka in her stomach.

"Sure. You're finished already?"

Chyna's ears perked up. Excuse me? Who was done early?

"Yeah, come on over. We just got a hookah."

Who was he talking to?

"I don't remember. Hold on," he said into the phone before glancing back up at Chyna. "What's the name of this place again?"

Her throat constricted when she went to answer, and she had to take another sip of her martini. It didn't help much because her throat wasn't reacting to the smoke. "Sulgaana Hookah Lounge."

Adam repeated that into the phone and then hung up. "John is on his way over," he told her. "He said his dinner plans ended early, and he would rather hang out with us tonight."

With a shiver running down her spine, Chyna swallowed again, her throat tight. She slurped down her martini like it was her life force. "I...uh...think I need another," she said, standing.

"Where do you think you're going?" he asked.

He was in such a good mood from their evening together, and now, his brother was on his way. Chyna had never met anyone who liked his sibling so much.

"There's a waiter." He called the guy over and ordered another round of drinks for them, not letting her leave their little niche. He rested backward into the cushioned seat.

"So," Adam began, taking another pull from the hookah, "you have fun last night?"

"Yeah." Chyna shrugged.

"I was surprised you were in before me. I didn't finish the project until two, but I wasn't expecting you until at least three or four," he said with an easy smile.

Nonchalantly, she said, "Just an early night, I guess."

"I didn't know you had those," he said innocently.

"Sometimes."

"Thank you for dragging John out with you." Adam crossed his leg over his knee at his ankle and slung one arm across the back of the booth. "I know he's my older brother, but we're only two years apart. I guess I took care of him for long enough that it's kind of natural."

"Why did you have to take care of him? He seems like a big boy," Chyna said.

"Too smart for his own good. He always thought he could get away with murder." Adam laughed.

"He probably could," Chyna said under her breath.

"Anyway, he was a party animal in high school and college. He's cut back drastically since taking this job. I probably shouldn't try to keep taking care of him. He has a good head on his shoulders."

"You're a good brother." Chyna swallowed.

Adam chuckled softly. "Thanks. I know John didn't always deserve it, but I love him. It's kind of like how you are with Lexi."

"Yeah, she's basically my sister," Chyna said, doing anything to grasp on to a new line of conversation. "Bitch needs some serious therapy, but I'd do anything for her."

Both of them started laughing because, really, no one could deny that.

"There you guys are," John said, rounding the corner unexpectedly. "What's so funny?"

"Hey," Adam said, standing and making room for his brother.

Chyna's eyes went to John. He was in crisp, black dress pants and a white button-up shirt with the top button undone for a more casual look. When he glanced in her direction, she diverted her eyes.

"We were just talking about Chyna's friend, Lexi."

"The one who left for the week?" he asked with a curious glance in her direction.

Chyna nodded and tried not to look at him. "Yeah."

"You made it over here fast," Adam mused, moving closer to Chyna to give John room to sit down.

"Yeah, there's not that much traffic yet tonight. I hope you don't mind, but I brought some friends along. After I told them where we were going, they insisted," John said with a smile as his friends walked into the nook. "This is Nitya, Trey, and Darius. Trey and Darius work with me at Global."

He volunteered the information for those two but left out an explanation for the woman that was with him. That immediately drew Chyna's eyes to her. She was Indian with gorgeous dark-caramel skin, thick, long black hair with natural body, and almost unnatural blue eyes. She was exotically beautiful and clothed in an eye-catching red dress. Nitya smiled at them before taking a seat next to Adam.

"No problem at all. Nice to meet you," Adam said, promptly standing and shaking the two guys' hands. "I'm Adam, John's brother. This is my girlfriend, Chyna."

Chyna just smiled at them. Trey was a medium build guy with short blonde hair, and he was wearing a navy suit. He was everything she expected from a Global employee. In fact, he looked like he had the superiority complex to boot. Or, is it a Napoleonic complex? The guy next him, Darius, was a tall, skinny African American man with a perfect smile that was contagious.

They all filed into the booth. The room was already filling up, and they now had a party of five when she had been expecting just the two of them. She couldn't help noticing how close John sat next to Nitya when they all sat down.

"So, how do you know each other?" Chyna asked. She couldn't believe she had even opened her mouth.

"Nitya was at Harvard when I was getting my MBA," John told Chyna with a smirk.

Nitya rolled her eyes. "Don't make it sound so amazing," she said. "I was just getting an art history degree. It wasn't a big deal."

"Harvard is a big deal," Trey said, shaking his head.

"Not to someone who went there," Darius said, elbowing him in the side with a big full-watt smile.

"All right, guys," she said, rolling her eyes. "It's not like I'm the MET curator or anything. I still sell shitty paintings every day."

"They're not shitty," John said, his hand touching her arm in a way that Chyna was all too familiar with.

She narrowed her eyes at the movement. Then, he caught her looking at him, so she turned her attention to Adam, who was too busy with the hookah to pay attention.

"Do you...paint?" Chyna asked, breaking the private moment.

"Some, but I'm shit. And, don't you say otherwise," she said, pointing at John. "I work for a small art gallery as a viewer doing appraisals for their collection."

"That's pretty cool actually," Chyna said disappointed. That was actually really cool.

She hated these moments. She didn't regret not going to college because she got more partying done in New York, and she didn't have to deal with the whole school aspect. But, she had never had anything she could really call hers like this Nitya chick.

"And, your paintings aren't shit. I've seen the inside of your studio," John said with a smirk.

Nitya giggled and leaned into him like they were sharing a private joke. When, in fact, their joke wasn't all that private. It was obvious what he was saying.

Trey, obviously not picking up on what John was saying,

spoke up. "Yeah, I agree. I've seen some of your work. I'd love to see your studio though."

Was this guy that dense? The only one seeing *inside her studio* was fucking her, and Trey certainly wasn't.

The subject switched to business, and Chyna pulled back from the conversation. She didn't want to be involved, and she didn't want to have to think. Adam ordered her another drink, and the table got a round of tequila shots. She veered away from the alcohol. She'd had too good of a time last night, and she didn't want to make herself look worse by imbibing way more than she could handle.

Instead of taking the shot, she checked her phone to see if Frederick had ever responded to her text messages. Just when she was about to get up to give him a call, he texted back.

Dallas called. Sorry, chicky.

Chyna groaned, throwing her phone back into her purse. She took a drag on the hookah and could feel a slight buzz from both the alcohol and tobacco already. The sweet aroma was deceiving because it was already making her tingly in a way that alcohol never did anymore. It was nice.

"Are you still meeting up with Frederick?" Adam asked, standing. He was completely confident on his feet.

Had he even been drinking that much? Chyna hadn't really been paying that much attention.

"He cancelled," she told him, resting her head back against the cushion.

Adam bent down and kissed her forehead. "Maybe you should take it easy."

"I'm fine!" she said defensively, sitting up straight. She hadn't had *that* much after all. "Will you get another hookah while you're up?"

Adam sighed with a nod. "Anyone else need anything?"

Trey and Darius nodded. "We'll come with you." The three guys walked away to get more drinks for the table.

"Ah! Two wonderful, beautiful women," John said, his speech showing the signs of alcohol. He smiled that devious smile in Chyna's direction and crawled over Nitya to sit in between the two women.

"John! Watch it!" Nitya cried as he caught her leg when he scooted across her.

"Come here," he said, beckoning Nitya with his finger.

She glanced over at Chyna and then moved closer to him. He threw his arm across her shoulders and kissed her temple. Chyna watched him whisper something into her ear, and Nitya giggled, her eyes flickering to Chyna again.

Despite everything, her stomach was clenching in anger and frustration. This was a fucking ridiculous display and she wanted it to stop. She wasn't thinking coherently. She knew that he'd had his hands on her last night and now they were running up and down this bitch. It hadn't been right...even if they had just been dancing, but come on!

"Are you sure?" Nitya asked.

John nodded and trailed his finger across her bottom lip where she was biting it. Nitya sighed pleasantly before turning her attention back to Chyna. She crooked her finger at her.

Chyna furrowed her eyebrows together, but she was too jealous not to find out what she wanted. How did John have this much pull over her? She couldn't explain it, but she scooted across the chaise anyway.

Her body pressed almost completely into John. The warmth radiating off of him mixed with her curiosity was intoxicating. Nitya leaned forward, pressing her hand into John's thigh, as she moved only an inch away from Chyna's face.

Chyna sat very still, realizing where this was going. This was probably a bad idea. She should move, but her eyes couldn't even break away from Nitya's, who was holding

Chyna's gaze with such intensity that it was hard to even think about pulling back to see what John was thinking. She had a damn good guess.

Then, John's hand landed on the small of her back, and she froze in place. She couldn't have moved even if she had wanted to. It was like a magnetic force was in the air, holding them all at his touch. Her mind rushed back to the night before, and her eyes fluttered closed. His fingers moved softly against her skin, easing any apprehension she might have had.

She couldn't even fight it when Nitya's lips landed on hers. She felt soft and foreign against her own. She tasted like the apple hookah and lip gloss. Nitya wasn't the first girl Chyna had ever kissed, but this felt different. Her tongue flicked out and trailed across her bottom lip. She heard a groan come from John, and something about the pure sensuality of it made her want to continue. Chyna opened her mouth and allowed Nitya to deepen the kiss, finding her tongue and running along it. Almost as soon as it started, they broke apart.

Chyna's heart was pounding out of her chest, and she realized how turned on she was. She didn't even think it was from the kiss either. It was because he was watching, and he was still touching her.

"Fuck," she whispered, staring into Nitya's blue eyes.

The girl giggled and ducked her head.

"Fuck is right," John said in a strained whisper.

12

PAST

At the sound of John's voice, Chyna felt like she had woken up from a dream. Her eyes moved from Nitya to John, and she clenched her jaw. What the fuck was she doing? And why was she always thinking that when she was around him?

She slowly scooted away from them, unable to believe what she had just done. What had possessed her to kiss that girl? She seriously felt like she had been possessed because she wasn't even that drunk.

John laughed into Nitya's hair when Chyna moved away from them, and Nitya shared in his humor as he nuzzled her neck. Chyna felt feral at that point. She was fighting her own instincts. On one hand, she wanted to push Nitya out of the way and have her way with John. On the other hand, she wanted to punch him in the face for playing with her. He was teasing her purposely, and he was damn good at it. She was furious, horny, jealous, and frustrated. Goddamn man!

Adam returned a minute later with the other guys, complaining about long lines at the bar and shitty service.

Chyna had a hard time paying attention. She had too much else on her mind.

The night dragged on with John keeping up practically the entirety of the conversation. It was like a light had been switched on, and his full charm had taken over. She didn't know if it was the amount of alcohol in his system or if her kiss with Nitya had something to do with it. Whatever it was, Adam seemed to ease into the change, which made Chyna think that the switch was his normal personality—the guy that Adam had talked about before Global came into his life.

Even she ended up relaxing as he took over. She just wanted to erase whatever had happened while Adam had been gone, accept his brother for the charmer he was, and have a good time. Yet, as much as she wanted them to, the events that had transpired last night and what had just happened with Nitya couldn't just go away. She needed to tell Adam. She hadn't really done anything wrong, but he needed to know.

"Ugh," Nitya cried, swiping at her eyes. "Is it really one-thirty in the morning? I have to work in a couple of hours."

"Fuck, me, too," Trey said, elbowing Darius to get out of the booth.

"I have to work, too," Darius said, sloppily standing and reaching for something to steady himself.

"You guys should take a cab," Adam told them. He was hardly even tipsy.

How had she not noticed that he wasn't drinking that much? Or was he was just holding his liquor better than everyone else at the table? She was tipsy, but she didn't think she was over the edge. She had yet to stand up though.

Nitya stood, wavered, and then crumpled back onto the edge of the booth. She started giggling uncontrollably. "I can't stand up. Oh my God!"

"Do you need help?" John asked, standing and then immediately sitting back down.

"Yes!" she muttered, her head flopping backward. "I can't feel my lips."

Adam shook his head as if he knew that this would happen all along. "Come on. I'll help you guys to the cab," he said, scooting around John to help Nitya up. "Chyna, are we taking your town car?"

She nodded, her eyes heavy. It had been a long night, and she couldn't wait to get back to her apartment, even if she did have to talk to Adam.

"Great. Can you manage here until I get them in the cab?" he asked desperately.

Chyna bit her lip, debating with herself. She really shouldn't be alone with John at the moment. Probably not a good idea. But, she wasn't that drunk, so she could handle herself. She nodded again, hoping she appeared confident.

"Great. Hopefully, this won't take long."

Adam put an arm around Nitya's waist and helped her to her feet. Trey and Darius leaned on each other, putting a hand on Adam's shoulder to get through the darkened hookah lounge. As they exited the enclave, Trey laughed and closed the burgundy curtain to their area. The only light now came from a single covered bulb in the ceiling.

"Chyna," John whispered into the darkness.

She tensed and tried not to look at him. She knew she should have gone with Adam.

"Chyna," he whispered again.

She swallowed hard, wishing she had a drink so she had something to do with her hands.

He said her name one more time in the most seductive voice.

She couldn't help but turn to face him. "Yes?" she murmured.

"Why did you leave last night?"

"You know why I left," she replied, resting her head backward.

She heard him move closer to her and could feel the heat coming off of him. "Tell me why you left."

"No," she said softly, barely audible. "You know why."

"Chyna," he said, pushing her dark hair out of her face.

She sighed. The feel of his hand touching her face ignited a fire in her. "John, please."

"Please, what?"

"Don't make me answer. You know why I left. It was time to go. Simple enough," she whispered.

"It's a simple question, and I don't think that's the answer."

She could hear her breath coming out unevenly as she debated on how to answer him. "What do your tattoos say?"

"What?" he asked, clearly surprised by the question.

"You answer, and I will."

He didn't even think about it. "Deal," he said, standing and untucking his shirt.

"What are you doing?" she demanded, glancing anxiously at the curtain.

"Answering your question." He unbuttoned the top two buttons and pulled his shirt clean over his head.

Chyna just stared. Holy fuck! That body literally killed her. If she had thought she was on fire before, she had been all sorts of wrong.

"This one," he said, sitting very close to her and pulling up his left bicep, "says 'to define is to limit.'"

Her hand came up and lightly traced the words on the inside of his arm with her fingertips. "You've said that to me before," she told him.

"You remembered," he said with a smirk.

"And the other one?" she demanded, ignoring her manners.

He turned and showed her the inscription on his right ribs.

"This one says 'What does it profit a man if he gain the whole world and lose his own soul?'"

"Wow. That's deep," she said, resting her hand on his leg. She reached across his body and traced the other tattoo as well.

His breathing hitched as she pressed herself up against him while her fingers trailed across the sensitive skin.

"They're Oscar Wilde quotes. Just a personal reminder," he said, lifting his hand and running it through her dark hair.

She moaned softly, her eyes closing as his hand pulled through the long strands. She felt him stiffen beneath her hand that still held on to his leg.

"That feels good," she mused.

"Your turn," he told her. With both hands, he pulled back her black hair, making her face him.

Her eyes fluttered open, staring into those gorgeous hazel eyes that were mere inches away from her.

"My turn for what?" she asked, her feeling his body heat at his nearness.

"Why did you leave last night?" he reminded her.

Looking down at his lips, she finally told him, "I thought you were going to kiss me."

He beamed that gorgeous smile and leaned forward, bridging the distance, and he pressed his lips to hers.

It was like the floodgates were opened. The sexual tension that riddled both of them cracked and then crashed apart. John pushed her backward, his mouth hot and demanding on hers. His body forced her back into the soft-cushioned chaise, covering her. His hands ran down her body.

Chyna gasped against his mouth. In that moment, she wanted nothing more than to dig her hands into his dark hair and have him fuck her, but all sorts of warning signs were blasting through her conscious. This was so fucking wrong. So, so, so fucking wrong.

"Stop," she said, breaking their lip lock and rolling away

from him. Her chest was heaving up and down as she wiped the back of her hand against her mouth. "What the fuck were you thinking?"

John didn't look much better, except he was still distractingly shirtless. "What do you mean what was I thinking?"

"You kissed me!"

"You told me to!" he yelled back.

"Fuck that! I said I left last night because I thought you were going to kiss me," she told him.

"Chyna, I don't fucking get you."

"What is there to get? I'm dating your brother, and you have your hands all over me!"

"You don't even love him."

Chyna came up short, her mouth hanging open. Who was he to tell her what she felt? How would he even know if it was true? He didn't know her!

"If you didn't notice, you've been a fucking cock tease all weekend. How many times have you thrown yourself at me since we've been around each other? How many times have you eye-fucked me? How many times have you leaned forward, licking your fucking lips and pressing your fucking boobs in my face? Huh?" he asked, grabbing his dress shirt and throwing it back on over his head. "Don't have an answer? Yeah, let's not even bring up you fucking kissing Nitya and looking at me like you wanted to have me for dessert. Do you want me to keep going?"

"You don't know what the fuck you're talking about!" she cried, wishing he was wrong. "I'm dating your brother, and you don't even care about that. Who does that?"

"Tell me that you don't want to fuck me."

"I don't want to fuck you," she said, placing her hand on her hip.

"Liar."

"What part of 'I'm dating your brother' don't you understand?" she demanded, narrowing her eyes.

"The part where you got all wet at my pool. The part where you pressed your ass against my dick when we were dancing. The part where you kissed me back."

"Shut the fuck up! Gah! Just shut up!" she yelled at him.

"Cock. Tease."

"Fuck off."

"That's all you want to do with me anyway," he said.

"Don't flatter yourself, asshole."

John laughed and shook his head. "I hope you make Adam very happy," he said, walking over to the curtain and pushing it open.

"You'll make no one happy but yourself...if *you* are even happy," she said, glaring at him.

He smiled. "I'll let you think on that one," he said before turning and leaving.

13

Chyna watched him walk out of the room, and as soon as he was gone, she crumbled on to the cushion. She shook desperately, unable to believe the argument they had just gotten into and everything that had just happened. She couldn't get his words or his hands or his mouth out of her head. What had she done?

All she knew was that she needed to get it together before Adam got back. He would know something was up if she was shaking and near tears. He would want to know what had happened, and she couldn't tell him yet, not like this. It wasn't fair to him. Nothing she had done was fair to him.

She took a few deep, healing breaths, trying to calm her pounding heart, as she pushed back the oncoming tears. This was ridiculous. This was why she didn't date people. She liked to fuck around, and it had always been okay in the past because she hadn't been attached.

No matter what happened tonight, all she knew was that she didn't deserve Adam, not by a long shot.

She was composed by the time Adam walked back into the room.

"Hey, John already left. He hopped in the cab with Nitya. It took forever because there were so many other people. He was blessed with perfect timing. You ready to leave?"

Chyna was amazed that her facial expression didn't even flicker when he told her that John went with Nitya. Of course, he would go somewhere to get laid. "Yeah, let's get out of here."

"I think Carl is waiting outside," he said with a smile, putting his arm around her waist as they walked out.

"Great," she said, hating what she knew lay ahead.

Carl drove them back across town, and soon, they were parked out front of her building. Chyna slid out of the car, and Adam followed. Her doorman, Bernard, opened the door, greeting them warmly despite the late hour.

"Man, I'm beat," Adam said when the elevator deposited them on the top floor. "Working last night really wiped me out."

"I'm a little tipsy," she murmured in response, pulling her gold key out of her purse as she walked down the hallway.

"Yes, you are. Maybe a little more than tipsy," he said with a smile, deftly extracting the key out of her hand and opening the door. "You should try to sleep it off."

She walked through the foyer and kicked off her heels before padding across the clean white carpet. Chyna sighed, looking at the floor, and then she glanced back up at Adam. Here goes nothing. "Adam."

He followed her, yawning wide when he made it to the end of the foyer. "Yeah, sweetheart?"

God, she did not want to do this, but she couldn't lie. He was too good for her, and she knew it. He might as well be clued in.

"John kissed me."

The silence was excruciating. It was like the anticipation of the roller coaster ticking slowly up to the top of the hill before plummeting down the other side. She didn't know if she should speak and try to explain. Instead, all she did was stand there, staring at him.

"Come on, Chyna," he said, shaking his head. "It's too late for this."

Of all the reactions, that had not been the one she was expecting. "What?"

"John didn't kiss you."

"Yes, he did," she insisted. "When you took the others to the cab, he kissed me! He tried to take advantage of me."

Adam sighed heavily. "Do you really expect me to believe that?" he asked, glancing up at her finally.

"I do," she murmured.

"This is my brother we're talking about."

"Don't you think I know that?" she asked, flabbergasted by his refusal to believe her. She thought he deserved the truth, and he wouldn't even listen to it.

"No, you're not thinking, and you clearly don't know anything. Nothing," he said, enunciating the word very clearly. "John is my brother. He would never do that. In fact, I can't even believe I have to justify his behavior. I know him. I've known him my entire life, and he would *never* in a million years do this. Not to me."

"So, what? I'm a liar?" she asked, her anger rising quickly. "I'm just your lying girlfriend?"

"I take a lot of shit from you, Chyna. You get away with a lot of shit, all right?" he said, a bite cutting through his voice that she had never heard. "But, I would be the liar if I didn't say that you're making this a bigger deal than it really is. You blow *everything* out of proportion. I don't get it, but I've endured it because I care about you. You can't bring this shit up when you're drunk this late and expect me to take you seriously."

"I'm not drunk!" she cried back, infuriated. She was tipsy.

She'd had a few drinks, but that was it. She hadn't done anything wrong, and Adam wouldn't even believe her.

"Please, Chyna, I know when you're drunk. Stop being a drama queen."

"A drama queen?" she all but shouted at him. "Are you fucking serious? I come to you with this, and you call me a drama queen?"

"Yes! God, how do you think people see you?" he asked, slamming his fist in the foyer wall. "You're a big fucking drama queen! All John had to do was look at you for you to think he wanted to get with you, Chyna. That's how you treat everyone else."

"I don't know if you haven't noticed, but your girlfriend *is* wanted by every fucking guy who looks at her!"

"See!" he said, clenching his fists at his sides, restraining himself. "Drama queen! You take the cake! This is my brother!"

"Then, why do you think I brought it up?" she yelled back. "You think I wanted to hurt you with this?"

"I don't know what you wanted," he yelled, barely holding it together. "You probably just misinterpreted whatever happened. You drank enough to blackout tonight. Do you even remember the night?"

"I can't believe this shit!" she cried. She was shaking from her anger. "I am not drunk! I know my limits. I try to tell you the truth. I try to be honest, and you throw it all back in my face!"

"Well, imagine how I feel!" he cried. "I do everything for you, and you know I worship John. Yet, you still tell me that he —what? He tried to take advantage of you? Are you fucking kidding?"

"Fucking ridiculous! You can't even trust your own girl-friend to tell you the truth."

"From how it sounds, I shouldn't trust you farther than I can throw you!" he yelled back at her angrily.

"What the hell is that supposed to mean?" she demanded, crossing her arms over her chest.

"You know what? Fuck it! Just fuck it!" he said, throwing up his hands. He ran a hand back through his hair in frustration. "Find someone else to deal with all the drama, Chyna! I'm done! This shit is out of control. You had to bring him into this." He pointed his finger at her like he was going to say something else, but then he just shook his head and walked out of the door.

He walked out and left her. He left her all alone. Who does that?

Chyna grabbed her cell phone out of her bag. She was furious. Who the hell did he think he was? He couldn't just walk out on her. She chewed on her lips, her hands shaking, as she searched for Alexa's number. She wanted him to come back. She wanted him to fix this.

She had been the one to mess things up, but John had been the instigator. She hadn't even really done anything wrong. She just had bad thoughts, but who didn't have those?

By the time she found Lexi's number, her heart was racing, her palms were sweaty, and tears were streaming from her eyes. How could he handle all this so callously? Why wouldn't he believe her? She clicked *Call* on the phone and placed it to her ear, slumping down into her leather sofa.

"Hello?" Lexi answered.

"Lexi..." Chyna cried. She never called her Lexi, but she just wasn't thinking clearly tonight. Hysterics were taking over, and she couldn't calm herself down. She needed her best friend.

"Chyna, are you okay?" Lexi asked.

"No, oh my God, no, I'm not," Chyna told her, not able to stop the tears.

"What happened? Chyna, calm down. It'll be okay. Just tell me what happened," Lexi said reassuringly.

"I don't know. I just...I don't know where to begin," Chyna

said, wondering how she had gotten to this point. Had she really been all that wrong? She had told Adam everything.

"Just start wherever, C. Tell me from the beginning. Are you safe? Are you hurt? Did someone hurt you? Do I need to call someone to come get you?" Lexi asked, nearing hysterics herself.

"No, no, I'm not hurt...not physically. It's just...Adam. Alexa, it's Adam," she whispered into the phone. It was physically painful for her to utter the words.

"Adam?" Lexi asked anxiously. "Is he all right? Did something happen?"

Chyna chewed her bottom lip and wiped her eyes with the back of her hand, begging the tears to stop. She needed to tell Alexa. She needed her to know, and she needed her to understand what had happened. She couldn't keep it all bottled up, and Adam hadn't believed her. Alexa *needed* to believe her.

"Chyna, what happened?" Lexi demanded.

As much as she wanted to tell Lexi, her stomach twisted at the thought, and her heart hammered in her chest wildly. "Oh, God, Alexa. I can't talk about it. It's awful. We got into a horrible argument, absolutely horrible argument. My chest hurts unlike anything I've ever imagined," Chyna whispered, her voice pained. "He was so calm at first, and then the floodgates opened. We both just screamed at each other. I don't know what I'm doing!"

"Oh, Chyna," Lexi murmured softly. "I'm so sorry. Did you guys break up?"

Chyna stopped to consider the question. Oh my God, had they broken up? Was that what had just happened? "I don't know. Yes. No," she moaned, wishing she knew the answer. "Maybe. He was so mean to me. I don't know what we are anymore..."

"Maybe it was just a misunderstanding," Lexi reasoned. "Tell me what happened."

Chyna sniffled a few times into the phone. She might as well start from the beginning. Here goes nothing. "Adam's brother, John, lives in the city, but he's a businessman who travels all over the world. He's not here much, so I've never met him." Chyna began setting the scene for Lexi. She wanted her to understand. She wanted her to see what she had gone through—how he had been her type and how it had all gone horribly wrong.

"Well, he was in town for the weekend, and Adam wanted to introduce me to him. I thought it was a big step." Her tears renewed, and she broke down on the phone.

It had been a big step. Adam adored John, and he had wanted them to be around each other. He had forced them around each other, but John had taken it too far. Chyna sniffled a few more times before continuing.

"The three of us went out and had a few drinks. I tried to be low-key and handle my liquor. I wanted to make an impression," Chyna said, summarizing the weekend for Lexi in one swoop.

It didn't matter how much time they had spent together because she had tried to be smart about it. She had tried to be smart about John, but she had found out that he hadn't wanted that from the start. She had certainly made an impression on him, but now, it was clear that it wasn't the right one.

Chyna took a breath before speaking again. "John turned out to be very similar to Adam. I mean they're brothers, what was I expecting? Well, you know Adam. He's just a really nice guy. And well, his brother was exceptionally charming that night." God, he was so charming all weekend. "I mean...not that Adam isn't charming, but—" She broke off, not wanting to finish that train of thought. Adam was gone. He had walked out on her.

"No, I get it," Lexi told her.

Chyna's thoughts fluttered back to John and the kind of

person he had been when in Chyna's presence. Lexi needed to understand that. Chyna hadn't meant for it to go as far as it did.

"Anyway, John knew the right thing to say about everything. He was an accomplished businessman. He'd traveled the world. His family adored him. He's such a smooth talker, and by the end of the night, he had me eating out of his hands."

She had been eating out of his hands all along, but tonight had been the worst. The kiss with Nitya...the tattoos...when he kissed her. She shuddered, not wanting to think about it, but she knew she had to continue.

"Oh, Chyna, you didn't...do anything with him, did you?" Lexi asked, clearly terrified of the answer.

"What?" Chyna snapped, knowing how offended she sounded. She hadn't done anything! John had done everything! She had done the right thing by stopping it before it went any further. She had told Adam, yet he had still left her! "No! I wouldn't do that to Adam! That's the point. Argh! That's the whole fucking point, chica!"

"Sorry, C, I had to ask," Lexi apologized quickly.

"No, I know," she grumbled. She was being defensive. It was all still too fresh. "Just angry, and with everything else tonight... I can't." Tears stung her eyes, and she wished Alexa were there to hug her. "Lexi, you have to know it wasn't me. John's the kind of guy who gets whatever he wants, takes what he wants. You know those kind of guys!"

They were the kind of guys she had always gone for. They were the ones she had let take her home. Lexi certainly knew what kind of guys she was talking about. She had seen Chyna with them far too often. Lexi had been with them herself. Wasn't her Jack just the type?

"Well, it soon became apparent that I was what John wanted," Chyna told her, thinking back to the pool with his eyes roaming her body, the club with his hands on her body, and tonight, with his tongue down her throat. It should have been apparent what was coming. She should have fought against it harder. "I should have seen it coming from a mile away. And when I did see it, it was too late. Adam didn't believe me. He refused to see it. He loves his brother so much that he was blind to him—blind to his arrogance and fucking stupidity.

"I think if he actually knew his brother, he would have never left me alone with him. But he did leave us alone. John was smooth, but it wasn't anything I hadn't seen before. Before Adam, I would have gone for him any day of the week." She figured that went without saying, but she had to say it. She needed to see the contrast. "But I'm different now! John had his hands all over me as soon as Adam left the room, but I turned him down. Alexa, I turned him down."

Chyna paused for a moment, pushing her hair off of her face. She sat up a little straighter. It felt good admitting it. She might have had terrible intentions, but when push came to shove, she had done the right thing.

"When I turned him down, he got furious. He didn't understand why I didn't want this to continue, as if me dating his brother didn't matter," Chyna told her, remembering John's anger at her rejection and everything that had followed. "I felt like Adam should know what happened, so told him, and he wouldn't believe me. He said I was being a drama queen, and I had probably misinterpreted what had gone on." She still couldn't believe the things he had said. Where had her understanding boyfriend gone in that moment? Her anger returned with that thought.

"But I didn't misinterpret anything! I swear I didn't. Tell me you believe me!" Chyna said, breaking down at the thought of Adam leaving. "God, someone has to fucking believe me!"

"Chyna, I believe you. Of course, I believe you. If you wanted another guy, then you could have them every night of the week. Why would you make up something about his brother?"

"Right! Ugh! Why didn't he see that? We got in a terrible argument about it. He wouldn't believe anything I said," Chyna cried, feeling a fresh wave of tears coming on. "We stood there yelling at each other until he got so angry; he just stormed out on me. He left me standing there all alone. Who leaves me? Who does that?" Chyna just kept repeating that to herself. She didn't understand it.

"I'm so sorry. I think you'll need to give him some time, then it'll work out. He really cares for you. I know he does. He's going to want to work things out. I don't know his brother or anything, but the way you talk about him makes it seem that Adam idealizes him. He probably doesn't want to believe those things about John. He just took it out on you, which is wrong, but I think he'll realize he was wrong. Once he sees how much of an idiot he was, he"ll come around," Lexi said.

"You think so?" Chyna asked, hope in her voice for the first time. She really wanted to believe that Adam would come around.

"Yeah, I do," Lexi told her.

Chyna really wanted to believe her, but sitting all alone in her living room after Adam had just left her made that really hard. "Alexa, I still don't know. I don't know how to handle any of this. I wish you were here. I need you."

"I can come home if you need me to. You know I'll always be here for you," Lexi told her soothingly.

"You'd end your vacation early for me?" she asked, her voice in awe. She seriously could not ask for a better friend. "I know you don't get to see him all that often."

"You're my best friend," Lexi told her as if that solved every-thing. "Let me talk to him, and I'll see what I can do."

"Thanks...I'm so sorry. I hate taking you away," she said, the sniffles coming back.

"No need to be sorry. You had no idea this was going to

happen. Hopefully, I'll be with you soon, girl," Lexi said. She said her good-byes and then hung up.

Chyna hung up the phone after her. Alexa couldn't get here fast enough. Chyna didn't know what to do in the meantime, so she just curled up into a ball on her couch and kept repeating the same thing over and over again.

He left her all alone. Who would leave her? Who does that?

Chyna was still in Marco's one-of-a-kind dress when they finally made it back to his apartment. It was immaculately clean and well designed. Marco had a taste for antiques and furnished his apartment in ancient old relics from centuries past. Above all, Chyna coveted the priceless artwork gilded in large gold frames, depicting far-off countrysides, sky-high cathedrals, and the elegance and poise of beautiful women. The whole place was gorgeous and tasteful as if you were walking into a Duke's parlor from the seventeenth century rather than a fashion designer's home in the twenty-first century.

She trailed her hand along the grand piano in the living room, her fingers skimming across the white and black–tiled keys. The noise drew Marco's attention, and she happened to glance in his direction. When their eyes met, he walked over to her. He leaned her backward against the keys, releasing a cacophony from the beautiful instrument.

"Are we going to have a *Pretty Woman* moment?" she asked, not holding in her giggle.

"Hmm?" he asked against her neck as his knee spread her legs.

"The movie," she said. When he didn't acknowledge it, she explained, "I'm your hooker, and you take me across the piano at the hotel?"

"Sounds appealing. I've never been with a hooker."

"Or, against a piano?"

"I wouldn't go that far," he said, grasping her jaw firmly in his hand. "If you're my hooker, do I have to pay you?"

She shrugged her shoulders. "Aren't you already?"

"Not for sex."

"You'll never have to. I'd do whatever you want anyway."

"Good," he said, running his hand down between her legs as he pressed against her. "Was the car enough for you?"

She slowly shook her head. She already knew he wasn't done with her, and she was desperate for more. "No."

Marco loosened his tie, pulling the knot out, and slipping it from beneath his collar. "That's right. You'll have enough when I say you have."

Adrenaline pumped through her body at the sound of that. She was aching for him already, and they had just finished in the car. In that instant, she was able to forget everything that had happened earlier in the night. She could forget about the other models, about Natasha, who was the old American centerpiece Marco had thrown aside, about the Corsa job offer, about her addiction to powerful men, and she could even forget about missing Adam. All she was thinking about was the easiest way to get him inside of her again.

He placed his tie across her eyes to obscure her vision, submitting her into darkness. She felt him wrap it around her head, tying it into a perfect knot in the back. Her body was working in overdrive from the loss of one of her senses. She slowly reached out and touched the front of his button-up shirt to ground herself.

"I love when you're blindfolded, star," he whispered into her ear, causing her to jump at his nearness. He laughed softly, trailing a hand over her exposed collarbone down to the curve of her breasts that peeked out from the sweetheart neck of his gorgeous dress.

Gripping behind her knees, he hoisted her legs around his waist. The piano chorused a new round of music as she pressed down on the keys to steady herself. She never knew what to expect, and the debilitating effects of the blindfold only intensified her anticipation. He placed his hands on her ass, lifting her up into his arms, and she gently wrapped her hands around his neck.

"Where are we going?" she whispered into his ear.

"Now, now, hold your questions until after the movie."

She tried to judge where they were headed in the massive apartment, but since she wasn't walking and she couldn't see a thing, she lost all sense of direction. They could have been anywhere, and she resigned herself to the fact that she would have to wait and see.

Her back landed on a soft comforter, and she immediately wondered if they had reached the master suite. She loved his room with its big dark wooden furniture, including a larger-than-life bed draped in the finest gold silk sheets hidden under an embroidered navy comforter stuffed with the softest goose feathers. She had spent many a nights thrown about in that gorgeous bed, yet something about this one was different. Despite not being able to see, she could still *feel* the difference. Unless he had replaced the mattress recently, this one was not the master bed.

God, she had so many questions, but she remained tight-lipped, wanting nothing more than to find out what was going on.

"Without disturbing that blindfold, move up until your head hits a pillow," Marco directed authoritatively.

Chyna did as he commanded, trying to make it up the bed without messing up her million-dollar dress. When her head found purchase, she sighed, falling backward into the pillow. It was comforting and reassuring, and she needed that for whatever Marco had in store.

She heard a soft beep, and then Marco's footsteps moved from the foot of the bed up to the top. He reached out and stroked her dark hair, back across her breasts, down her stomach that was still thinly covered by the sheer material, across the exposed sensitive skin between her legs, and back again. Her body was pulsing with desire. She wished he would just take her already, but she knew the waiting—him drawing it out like this—would only make it better.

A soft leather cuff encircled her small wrist. When she pulled on it, it didn't give, and she realized she was trapped. For a second, she felt immobilized and terrified. With this amount of power, he could do whatever he wanted with her. He could terrorize her. He could tease her endlessly. Whatever he was thinking in his twisted mind, he could enact on her body for his own pleasure.

Yet, as she felt the second and third cuffs circle her ankles, the terror began to fade as her desire heightened. She wanted this. She didn't know exactly what he would do, but that was all the fun. He was in control, and she wanted what he was going to give her. By the time the final cuff wrapped around her left wrist, she was wet and needy.

"And, I thought I liked the blindfold," he said. His voice came from the end of the bed as if he were standing there, admiring his handiwork. "Now, don't move."

He chuckled to himself softly. She heard his footsteps growing fainter, and then she couldn't hear them at all. *What the fuck?!* Had he just tied her up here and left her? She wiggled against her bonds in frustration, but as she had felt with the first wrist, they wouldn't budge. She was trapped somewhere in

Marco's apartment, wearing a goddamn expensive dress, hand-cuffed and blindfolded to a bed she didn't recognize...and Marco disappeared.

Fuck!

She didn't know how long he was gone. She couldn't judge time very well when she was tied to a bed and blindfolded, but sitting there, each excruciatingly painful minute ticked by like an hour. After a couple of minutes or hours, whichever, his footsteps returned, and she had never been more thankful. He had tied her up before but never in a strange place, and he had never left her. It made her feel unsettled, and it was amazing how soothing it was to have him return after she had been so terrified of his presence.

What she did recognize was a very familiar click, flash, and whir. "Are you photographing me?" she demanded, shaking her body and pulling against her bonds.

"I said to leave the questions until later," he said, his voice turning to ice. "I also thought I told you not to move."

Chyna stilled her body reluctantly. "I must look fucking perfect if you're photographing me like this."

"I've never seen anything more perfect," he said, snapping another round of pictures. "Plant your feet on the bed and lift your ass into the air."

She was used to taking orders from him when he had a camera in his hands, and she found her body listening to him without complaint. Even though she was all but nude from the waist down, leaving her completely exposed, she still reveled in the fact that he found her perfect. Who was the twisted one?

The familiar sounds of a photo shoot filled the room, and she wondered what exactly he was taking a picture of. Was it a good shot? God, she couldn't believe these were the thoughts crossing her mind right now. And, somehow, she was still incredibly turned on, maybe even more so than before.

She felt his weight shift the bed as he crawled on top of her.

His skin brushed up against her, and she realized he had removed his pants. His hand softly rested on her stomach, pressing it back into the mattress. He straddled her and took a series of pictures from his new vantage point. His thumb flickered over her breast, causing her to arch her back. She pulled against her bonds, wanting nothing more than to take control, but he wouldn't allow it. Her mouth opened with desire as he pinched the other nipple between his fingers. He took the opportunity to trail his thumb across her body to her lip. He slipped his thumb into her mouth. She closed her lips around it, swirling her tongue and sucking on it greedily. The camera went off again as she teased his thumb the way she wanted to tease his dick.

He groaned and pulled it out of her mouth. He then reached behind himself and placed his now wet thumb directly on her clit. She moaned at the feel of him touching her, extracting heightened pleasure from her. The camera went off again, and this time she didn't even care. Two of his fingers had expertly inserted themselves into her, and they were working her pussy as his thumb swirled in circles on her clit. She could already feel her impending climax approaching, and she tightened and released around his fingers as she sought that release.

But, he would have none of it. As she lay there breathless and close to spent, he removed his fingers and hopped off the bed. Her body was humming. She had never wanted release more than in this moment.

"Panting is so damn sexy," he mused, his hand trailing up her calf, over her knee, and around her inner thighs.

She jumped at the first touch and prayed he would continue farther south.

"I'd like that to continue. Would you?" he asked.

"Touching me? Yes!"

"Panting," he said, running his fingers back up her thighs.

She groaned. Her body demanded more and more, but he wasn't giving it to her.

"I'll pant all night long if you get over here and fuck me," she said into the darkness.

"Oh yeah?" he asked, grabbing her thighs and pulling her down farther on the bed.

She yanked against her chains, causing a soft yelp to escape her lips as the cuffs chaffed against her wrists. Her shoulders were stretched as far as they could go.

"Is this how you want me?"

"Yes," she whispered, her voice hoarse as the pain in her shoulders and wrists eased.

"I didn't hear you," he said, pulling on her legs once more.

"Yes!" she yelled out. "God, yes!"

"Good. This is *exactly* how I want you, my little star, all tied up and helpless, begging for me," he said, He was careful with the dress, bunching the train up. He pushed it off to the side of the bed, so her body was laying more exposed to him. "Now, spread your legs," he commanded her.

She moved her legs apart hesitantly, testing the bonds with her movements.

"Farther!"

Without thinking, she moved her legs as far apart as she could manage, looking like a spread eagle with her legs bent at the knees.

"That's better," he murmured, dipping his fingers back into her unexpectedly. "God, you're so ready for me. It would be a shame to waste this."

Chyna whimpered as he stroked her wetness lovingly, riling her up further. It wouldn't take much more, and she prayed he wouldn't notice her heavy breathing or body tightening at his command. All she wanted at this point was to release...to finally release.

As if he could tell she was at a breaking point, she felt his weight at the foot of the bed again. Then, without warning, he pushed forward inside of her. She shook against her restraints, wanting nothing more than to push her hands up into his thick black hair, wrap her legs around his torso, and let her body fall in time with his. But, given the circumstances, she was just glad he had relented to being inside of her.

He grabbed her hips, raising her ass off the bed again so that he could rest on his knees. Then, he slowly eased out of her inch by inch. She whined at the feel of the head pulling out of her, and then he slammed back into her forcefully. Her body pushed back toward her shoulders, and she cried out in pleasure and pain. He repeated the movement—slow, slow, slow, followed by one fast shove into her—two or three times more. If she had thought that she was close before, the agonizing torture of this movement holding her just before the precipice of release was far, far worse. Her skin was tingling, her toes were curling, and her fingers were clawing up the bedspread. Stomach tightening, her body demanded with every fiber of her being to let her come.

And, when she did, *earth shattering* were the only words that came to mind.

Finally, releasing all control, Marco pushed into her as hard and fast as he could manage with three quick thrusts, and then he followed her. Chyna screamed at the top of her lungs as the orgasm cut through her body, bursting open like a firework. Her body was a volcano, and as her screams subsided, the stillness doused the burning running rampant throughout her body.

His breathing heavy, Marco collapsed on top of her with an air of satisfaction and victory. Her eyes closed beneath the blindfold, and she felt exhaustion turn into a desperate slumber.

15

———————

PRESENT

When she awoke next, her wrists and ankles had been released, and her blindfold was discarded along with her dress. She was lying completely naked on the same bed she had been tied to, and as she felt along the sheet that covered her, she discovered a figure lying next to her. No clocks were in the room, so she had no way of knowing what time it was. As the room had one window, she only knew that it was still dark outside.

She eased out of the bed, careful not to wake Marco, and she padded out of the room. Her stomach clenched painfully at what she had just done and what she was about to do.

Finding Marco's bedroom, she changed into a pair of jeans and a T-shirt that she had left behind from one of their shoots. She located a piece of paper and a pen, and after scribbling a short passage on the card, she tucked it into her pocket.

She swallowed hard as she quietly tiptoed back into Marco's photography studio where he still lay peacefully slumbering. The camera he had used sat undisturbed on a chair, looking harmless. She popped the memory card out of the back and placed it into her other pocket. When she turned back around, she almost cursed out loud. That son of a bitch!

A medium-size video camera on a tripod was set up in the corner of the room. That must have been what the beep was. He hadn't even told her he was going to be filming her. Why was she even surprised? Not wanting to take any chances, she figured out how to open the gadget. She slipped the tiny recording disc out of its slot and placed it in her jeans next to the memory card. No stone left unturned.

Glancing around the room, she bit her lip as she stared at the immobile man beneath the sheets. She blew him a kiss, wishing she could taste his lips one last time. As she turned to leave the room, something sparkled in her peripheral vision. She glanced at the distraction and saw her priceless dress hanging perfectly unharmed on a clothing rack. She couldn't help herself. She smirked, grabbing the dress off of the hanger, and then she slinked back out of the room. She would have giggled if she hadn't been trying to be silent. Walking back through the apartment and into the living room, she pulled the card out of her pocket and stared at it.

You thought I was the star, shining so bright, but you were wrong. You were the star, but you've burned out. Now, all I see when I look up into the sky are all my other options.

She took a deep breath and left the card on the piano. Then, she quickly darted out of the apartment.

She left without a kiss, without a good-bye—just with a million dollar dress, a sex tape, and nude photography from one of the best fashion designers in the world.

The sun was just peeking over the horizon when she made it to street level. She had managed to phone a taxi service when she had snuck into Marco's bedroom, and thankfully, she only had to wait a minute or two before it arrived. She gave the man her apartment address in Italian and was quickly whisked away from Marco's. Without knowing why, she swiveled in her seat and took one more forlorn look over her shoulder at the place of the man she had been with for the past month and a half. She wished she could have said that she saw the door open as he came running out after her, but no such thing happened. She turned back around, and with a deep sigh, she hugged her dress.

Her roommates were still sleeping when she returned. She wandered through her closet, wondering how the hell she was going to get all of this home. Coming here, she had traveled with nothing more than a carry-on suitcase, and she would leave for home with nothing more. The company was supposed to ship all of her stuff for her when she finished, but she wasn't sure if that would still happen under the circumstances. Grabbing only her most favorite clothing items, she stuffed them into her Louis Vuitton carry-on along with her star dress, Marco's sheer purple button-up shirt, her Christian Louboutin red lacquer–soled pumps, and three five-by-five black and white–framed photographs Marco had taken of Milan.

At her insistence, the taxi had waited for her to transport her to the airport. It wasn't a short drive nor would it be a cheap fair, but she really couldn't care less in the moment. She was waiting for her phone to blow up, for someone to notice she was gone, for Marco to pitch a fit about her disappearance. But, the hour-long drive out of the city produced nothing, just silence.

Her flight home was atrociously priced, but then again, so was her cab fare. Money hardly mattered at this point. She was just ready to be home.

She boarded her flight without any problems, and she checked her international cell phone one last time to see if anyone was going to contact her. She had expected at least some kind of snide remark from Marco, something to know that he had read her note. All she wanted to do was leave him before he had the chance to leave her.

It was easier that way.

Chyna dozed off on the flight. Eight hours later a flight attendant woke her her. She yawned and stretched her arms overhead, adjusting the kink in her neck from sleeping on the plane. She flagged down a stewardess as soon as she saw one.

"Yes, ma'am? Can I help you?"

"Can I get a Maker's on the rocks?" she asked, feeling a headache coming on.

"Ma'am, we're too close to landing for that," she said with a curt smile like she was used to dealing with bitches in first class.

"Are you serious? Alcohol. Anything. Thanks," Chyna said, throwing herself back in her chair and ignoring the woman's insistence that she couldn't provide alcohol at the moment.

A couple of minutes later, an older male flight attendant dropped off her drink while glowering at the other attendant. "Don't mind her. She's new," he said with a wink.

"Thanks," she muttered, taking a shot of the bourbon straight out of the first bottle before adding the second one to her glass. There—her headache was already going away. She sipped on her drink, thankful that someone had shown her some mercy.

The plane touched down at JFK Airport long after she finished her drink. She had another man help her pull her bag down. She hadn't eaten anything in nearly twenty-four hours, and the Maker's Mark was hitting her stomach stronger than it normally would have.

It was eight o'clock in the morning in New York, and her

stomach growled, ready for her afternoon lunch in Italy. The time change was going to be a real bitch to get used to. She had informed Carl that she would be arriving in New York that morning and was thankful when she saw his scruffy-bearded face appear among the individuals waiting with signs for their passengers. He ushered her out to the car, taking her carry-on in his hand. He didn't ask any questions as to why she was arriving two weeks ahead of schedule.

"To your apartment, Miss Chyna?" he asked as he veered into traffic.

"Alexa's apartment would be wonderful, Carl," she said, curling up into a ball in the back of her town car. Her phone had never gone off, except for the return message from Carl, and it died shortly after she landed. She felt sick, tired, hungry, and exhausted, and she wanted nothing more than to lounge around with her best friend.

"Of course," he said, swinging around traffic toward her apartment.

They arrived forty-five minutes later, having evaded most of the Sunday traffic.

"Want me to wait?"

"No, Carl. Thank you. I will catch a cab if I need a ride. Hopefully, I'll be here all day and night," she murmured the last part, not wanting to freak him out more than she already likely had.

"Are you all right, Miss Chyna?" he asked as she popped open her door.

"Fine, Carl. Go take your wife to church," Chyna added with a smile.

"Thank you. Hope you feel better," he told her, not believing her.

She slammed the door behind her and took the elevator to Alexa's floor. It was a rickety old thing that made her uneasy, but she didn't think she could manage the stairs in her state.

She traipsed down the hallway and knocked on the door. She had a key…somewhere. It was probably buried in her penthouse. Maybe Frederick knew where it was. He knew more about the design of the apartment than she ever would.

As she stood there, mulling over where she thought Alexa's spare key might be, the door swung open. Chyna's empty stomach plummeted, and she tried to hold back the rising bile. The day had been too long, the night too exhausting, the plane ride too burdensome, and the time change too weakening for her to have to deal with this right now.

At least to her credit, Adam looked just as shocked as she did.

"What are you doing here?" she demanded. Her voice came out angrier than she had intended. She was pretty sure it was ninety-five percent exhaustion speaking. The other five percent was blatant curiosity, considering the fact that he had continued to pop into her head yesterday after Alexa had brought him up.

"What are you doing here?" he asked right back. "Aren't you supposed to be in Milan?"

"Long story. What are you doing here?" she repeated,. He still looked the same. A month and a half hadn't changed him, except he had maybe lost a little weight. It didn't look bad on him. Damn those hazel eyes. They were more on the side of gold today than green, and she liked those days. What was she even thinking? She was clearly not in the right state of mind to be around him.

"I brought Lexi coffee," he said, holding up a bright white-and-orange coffee cup with big orange lettering that read Jittery Joe's.

"Where the hell is that from?" she asked because she had never seen it before.

"Uh…NYU off 45th," he said hesitantly.

"You went all the way to 45th to get Lexi coffee?" she asked, raising an eyebrow.

"Hold up with the third degree. Her coffee machine broke. Jittery Joe's is from Georgia. I just thought it would be nice." He shrugged and put on that goofy grin she had always loved.

No! No. No. She did not even think that word. She swallowed, unsure as to what the hell she was even doing at the moment.

"Who's at the door?" Chyna heard Alexa call from inside.

Adam turned around and called back. "Chyna."

"What the fuck? Are you fucking serious?" Lexi yelled, jogging to the doorway. When she saw Chyna, she threw her arms around her best friend like it had been centuries since she had seen her. "What the fuck are you doing home, chica?"

"Just wanted to surprise you," Chyna said, plastering on the smile Alexa was used to seeing.

"Well, come in! Oh my God, it is so good to see you." She turned back around after pulling Chyna into the apartment. "Thanks for the coffee, Adam. See you around," she said, smiling at him sweetly before all but slamming the door in his face. "I am *so* sorry about that." She waved her hand at the door.

"It's fine," Chyna told her, taking a seat on the uncomfortable, lumpy sofa.

"So...what the fuck are you doing here?" Lexi asked, grabbing her coffee and sitting down next to her friend.

"Time for a change," she said with a shrug, trying to remain lively.

"Yeah, but Milan!" Lexi's eyes went wide with the last word.

"Yeah...Milan," Chyna responded.

"You can't even pretend to be happy around me right now, and you're two weeks early! Spill!" Lexi commanded.

Chyna kicked off her shoes and pulled her knees up to her chest. "So...remember that fashion designer I mentioned?"

"Yeah," Lexi said slowly. "The fling?"

"Yeah, that one."

"What about him?"

"Well, I gave him up and came home, just like you told me to," Chyna told her.

"So, what's the problem?" Lexi asked, putting an arm around her shoulder.

"Nothing," she said, brushing it off. "I guess I was just in over my head. Time to come home."

Lexi looked at her like she didn't believe her, like she wanted to ask a million questions. Chyna seriously did not want to answer them. She didn't even want to think about how she had left. She had felt so strong when she had walked out of that apartment, choosing to leave him and actually making that move. Now, she just felt drained, and she didn't want to contemplate what that could mean, wondering if she had made the right choice.

"Actually, chica, can I borrow your cell? Mine managed to die on the drive over," Chyna said with a shrug.

"Of course," Lexi said. She stood and walked over to the counter. "You sure you don't want to talk some first? You look like you might kill whoever you're about to call."

Chyna took the phone when Lexi handed it to her with a smile. "I'll make it through."

"So...uh...who are you calling?" Lexi asked nosily.

Chyna sighed, hating what she was about to do almost as much as leaving this morning. "My mom."

16

———

PAST

Frederick smiled at Chyna, like a kid in a candy store. He was practically bouncing up and down on the balls of his feet. "Can you fucking believe this, hooker?" he whispered into her hair.

She shook her head. She was too anxious and excited to see this shit going down. "I've been waiting for this for far too long."

"And, to think we made the unveiling," Frederick said with mightier-than-thou pretenses.

"Of course, we made the unveiling," Chyna said, rolling her eyes. "Who do you think I am?"

"I would have started worshiping at your feet earlier if I'd known it would get me into Marco's fashion line grand opening on Madison Avenue!" he all but squealed.

"I'll remember that next time," she said with a catty smirk.

"How did you score this anyway?" he asked. "Not that I'm complaining."

"Just the right connections," she said with a shrug.

"Do you even *know*?" he asked, raising one perfectly groomed eyebrow.

"Of course I know!" Chyna turned back to face the gorgeous boutique on Madison Avenue.

Part of the street had been obstructed from public view for the cutting of the ribbon, and there was a private entrance for the viewing of the exclusive new clothing line. It was all hush-hush. So, of course, nearly half of the Upper East Side elite had scrambled for a chance to be present. The more exclusive, the more desirable it was to be in attendance.

Chyna hadn't really thought she would get access to the line. She had a name behind her, but she didn't model, she wasn't in the industry, and she wasn't a celebrity. The chance of finding the golden ticket had been slim.

When she had gotten back from her morning mani/pedi two days earlier, Bernard had stopped her at the door and handed her an envelope. He said someone had been asking around for her apartment or drop-box, but Bernard didn't know the guy. Since he wasn't with the postal service, Bernard had taken the letter and informed him that he would hand-deliver it to Chyna. She was surprised that whoever it was had given Bernard the letter.

Bernard had given her a fair warning about opening the contents. He was always looking out for her. She had reassured him that she would be careful, and then she had taken the elevator to her apartment. She had ripped open the envelope without care and stared in shock at the contents within—two gorgeous cards bordered in gold with the designer logo stamped on the front. She turned the stationary over and discovered that they were in fact invitations with her name on them.

She had phoned Frederick immediately. Alexa was too engrossed in finals for her last year of law school, and she probably wouldn't have been all that impressed with a grand opening for a boutique she couldn't spend money in. Frederick had squealed like a girl, asking her more questions than she had answers for. She had shut him up real quick by volunteering his pass to someone else.

How the hell the tickets had landed on her doorstep had crossed her mind several times since she had opened the package, but she didn't have an answer, and she didn't really care. She was exactly where she wanted to be.

Chyna turned her attention back to the building that was half covered in a white cloth to hide the completed boutique. An enormous red ribbon was held up in front of the entranceway, and a woman was holding a rather cumbersome pair of large gold scissors.

Another woman in an obnoxiously glittering dress with diamonds dripping from her neck, ears, and fingers smiled at the waiting crowd. She took a step forward and began speaking. "Thank you for being here for this very important moment in Marco's fashion line. I am Giselle, Marco's personal assistant, and I am happy to introduce you to the man himself."

The small crowd of people fell silent as an attractive man with a staggering confidence walked out in front of the store. He was every bit the man Chyna had read about—tall, dark-styled hair, deep penetrating eyes, and impeccable taste. What she hadn't read was the thing she couldn't describe even to herself. From where she was standing twenty feet away from him, some type of pull, a magnetic pull, drew her to him.

"Thank you all for coming," he said in crisp, clear English with the faint trace of a gorgeous Italian accent. "My name is Marco Moretti, owner and designer of Marco's Italian fashion merchandise. I am very pleased to have such a warm welcome in the States at the grand opening of my newest boutique. Thanks to my wonderful business associates, I have had a very easy transition onto your Madison Avenue. I am happy to call it home."

Frederick squeezed Chyna's hand. "He's looking at you," he whispered.

Chyna was already well aware. She hadn't taken her eyes off of him since he had walked in front of his new building. To say her pull to him was magnetic was beginning to become an understatement. She didn't believe in love at first sight. She didn't even know if she believed in love at all. All she knew was that she knew it when she felt it—desire. She was sure she was dishing out her fair share in his direction, but his eyes hardly portrayed otherwise.

The second or two he spent staring at her during the pause in his speech were breathtakingly long. She was thinking of a thousand places in the nearby vicinity where she would let him take her. How much effort would it take to convince him?

"After much anticipation, I am here to announce the opening of Marco's on Madison, the freshest Italian line to cross the Atlantic." He smiled like a true charmer and took the giant scissors from the woman holding them. She offered them up enthusiastically. With a gorgeous smile on his face that really lit up the camera, Marco leaned forward and cut the red ribbon into two.

As the ribbon fluttered to the ground, the white curtain followed, revealing live models posing in the all-glass storefront. The crowd applauded at the castle-like building's completion. The gold Marco's sign overhead was the perfect finishing touch on the classic design. Everything at eye-level rested on mahogany shelves. Plush red pillows with gold tassels and antique-looking clothing racks completed the display, portraying an overall feel of lavish royalty.

Chyna caught the eye of the young Italian designer once more before he turned away from the crowd, pushing the front doors open for the first time. A chill ran up her spine from his earlier gaze, and her mind traveled far away again. She needed to reel it in.

She had plans later, and she couldn't let this interfere. It was just an opening for a boutique. She wanted to go shopping, say she was one of the first to get a Marco design off Madison, and then leave. She wasn't afraid to drag Frederick out of there, if need be.

Following the surge of people moving forward into the store, Frederick grabbed her arm and pulled her out of the crowd. They wandered the perimeter of the store. She was almost as interested in the amazing craftsmanship of the interior design, admiring its difference from the modern stores she was used to. Frederick kept a continual conversation going, yammering in her ear about the layout, the state of the furniture, the cost of the upholstery, and on and on.

She couldn't deny the exquisite taste of Marco's designs. His lines were even, colors perfectly integrated, and style replete with both unique pieces and mix-and-match options. She didn't even know him, but she could feel his touch on every item, which was a hard thing to manage.

As she fingered a turquoise silk button-up, she felt a presence behind her. All she wanted to do was turn around and confront whoever was having such a profound effect on her. Instead, she continued to stare down at the beautiful piece of work, ignoring the person now hovering behind her.

"I think you would look better in something like this," Marco said, holding out a purple shirt with gold accents in a similar style. "Matches your skin tone and complements your green eyes."

"My best friend wears a lot of purple," she said with a shrug. "It's all right." She tried to sound indifferent. She had never needed fashion advice before. But, this wasn't advice. This was the designer.

He smiled, seeing through her attitude. "Hardly," he said, turning her around to face a mirror. He placed the shirt in front of her body. "See."

Chyna stared at her reflection in the mirror. The colors really did work for her in just the way he had said they would.

She should have trusted him, but sometimes she just liked what she liked. "You're right. It's better," she told him.

"I know," he said, taking a step back. "Marco Moretti."

He offered her his hand, and she placed hers in his gently. He leaned forward and kissed both of her cheeks softly. She knew it was just a greeting, but her heart leapt at the contact.

"Chyna Van der Wal," she said, licking her lips when he pulled back. "You have a very impressive store."

"Thank you. I like it." He smiled at her and drew her away from some of the other customers. "These. This and this," he said, grabbing a pair of dark skinny denim pants, a gold tank, and light brown boots. "Go!" he commanded, pushing her off into the dressing room.

She barely had time to process before she was following his order. She took the outfit out of his hands and quickly stripped down behind the dark wooden dressing room door. When she reemerged in the outfit he had picked, she could hardly believe the man's taste. Honestly, he was almost *too* good.

"*Perfetto!*" he said, examining her outfit. "You'll wear it out."

"Mr. Moretti, would you like me to ring that up for her?" a gorgeous woman with slick blonde hair hanging down to her waist asked. She was dressed in black from head to toe with some faint gold accents in between.

"That won't be necessary, Lydia," he said with a smile. "I believe Giselle might need some more help up front." The woman nodded curtly and left the dressing room, understanding his need for privacy.

Chyna wondered where Frederick was at that moment. Had he noticed her leaving with Mr. Moretti...with, the owner of Marco's fashion line? Why did she even care right now? He was gorgeous and alone with her in a dressing room. Oh, the possibilities!

This was much better than thinking about her meeting later. She had been putting it off for far too long already. She didn't know what to think about everything that had happened. All week, Alexa had been convincing her, convincing both of them, to just talk it out, but Adam hadn't relented, and it had hardened her fortitude. At this point, she would rather be alone with a fashion designer in his dressing room while a crowd waited outside. Who was she to care if anyone heard her?

All right! All right! She cared. A little. A lot. She needed to figure out what she was doing anyway. At least she could enjoy her time with this handsome Italian designer.

"So, Miss Van der Wal—" he said with a charming smile.

"Please, call me Chyna," she corrected.

"Chyna," he said as if he were tasting her name on his tongue. "That outfit looks better on you than any of my models."

"Thank you," she said with a self-satisfied smile.

"Have you ever been photographed before?"

"No," she said, narrowing her eyes cautiously.

"Would you like to be?"

She scoffed. "Is that your best pick-up line?"

Marco laughed at her catty remark. He didn't look like a man used to hearing rejection. Not that she had necessarily rejected him. She was still pretty open to the idea. She just hoped he would be a bit more creative. She could make him work for it—of that, she was sure.

"So, is that a yes?"

"I mean, I'm not opposed to it," she said with a smile. "Would I be wearing this?" She trailed her hand down the side of her sheer purple blouse. The gold tank under it shimmered in the dressing room lighting. She liked the way his eyes followed her hand, taking her in.

He took a step toward her, closing the distance. "In that," he agreed. "Just that."

Her eyebrows rose at his blunt answer. She had expected him to be coy, flirting around his true meaning. She had expected cat and mouse even. Looking into his dark brown eyes, she was wondering why she'd had expectations at all… and where they had come from.

This man didn't need to play games. He won them without entering.

A chill ran down her spine at his heated gaze, and she felt a familiar stirring in her body. He reminded her of someone… someone she was trying to forget ever existed…someone she wanted to stomp into oblivion. His very presence was dangerous, and all she wanted to do was revel in it. But, she had been there with this type of guy before, and she knew the road that laid ahead.

She tried to push those thoughts away, focusing on the present. A very important fashion designer had just asked to photograph her nude. How often did these kinds of things happen?

"I'm sure your fashion line would skyrocket to the top with that ad," she said with a wink.

"Hasn't it already?" he asked with a cocky tilt to his head.

"Are you saying that I wouldn't improve it?"

"If anything could improve it, you wearing this blouse would do the trick," he told her.

Chyna laughed. She ducked her chin and looked up at him through her dark curved lashes. "Thank you. Though, I do have to get going. I was very happy to see your line opening on Madison Avenue, and I'm thankful that you provided me with an invitation."

"Did I?" he asked, tilting his head slightly to the left as if he was trying to place her.

"Did you not?" She bit down on her bottom lip, not sure how else she would have come across the invitation. It didn't make sense that Marco would have delivered it to her directly. He didn't know her at all. Still, how else would it have gotten there?

"I didn't make the list, but it's possible. When did you receive the invite?" he asked.

Chyna wasn't sure how that would have anything to do with it, but she told him anyway.

"Two days ago."

"No, that can't be right," he told her with a conniving smile. "Unless your envelope was lost, I sent them out three weeks prior."

Chyna stood there in silence, contemplating all over again how the invitation had landed on her doorstep. Bernard had sworn that it wasn't someone with the postal service, and if Marco had sent them through the mail, then something was really off. She just didn't know what was off about it.

"I guess mine got lost then," she said with an uneasy smile.

This was not the conversation she wanted to be having with him right now. She would rather be talking about him undressing her again. In fact, she would rather have him undress her right now. After all, he owned the place, so he could keep the dressing room clear long enough to bend her over this settee.

"How unfortunate. You could have missed it had it not arrived in time."

"And, how fortunate I am that it did then."

"I feel quite fortunate as well," he said, unexpectedly taking her hand in his.

His hand was warm and soft, and she wanted nothing more than to let him hold it all day. She was such a sucker for powerful, seductive men. He was enticing like the gorgeous exterior to a poisonous flower. She could see how easily she could get lost in him, if she didn't have somewhere else to be.

"I guess I should go pay for this. Not going to find a better outfit than the one the designer has chosen for me," she said, pulling out of his grasp.

"Please," he said reassuringly, "it's on me."

"I couldn't—"

"You already did."

Chyna nodded, knowing that glint in his eye meant there was no reasoning with him. She could afford the outfit, but it wasn't about that at this point. He was picturing her in nothing but the sheer top with a camera. How could she deny him the pleasure of her taking it home?

"Thank you," she said, grabbing her purse and the dress she had been wearing earlier out of the dressing room. She walked past him, heading toward the exit, as he nodded at her in acknowledgment.

He called out to her when she reached the curtain to the dressing room. "Chyna?"

She stopped, her hand poised on the drawstring curtain. She turned around and faced him, wondering if this was going to be her movie moment. Would he come forward, kiss her, and beg her not to go? All she wanted to do was giggle at the thought. He didn't seem like the Prince Charming type.

He traversed the length of the dressing room, stopping in front of her. He pulled out his dark leather wallet and extracted a white-and-gold card. "When you change your mind," he said, handing the card to her, "give me a call."

"What makes you think I'll change my mind?" she asked, reaching forward and taking it out of his hand.

He smirked. "Because you just took my card."

17

PAST

Chyna flipped her hair over her shoulder and pushed past the curtain, refusing to acknowledge his statement. She wondered if he was laughing at her as she exited the room, but she wouldn't look over her shoulder to find out.

Frederick found her on the other side as she walked out of the dressing room, holding her old clothes. "You slut! I'm so jealous!" he cried when she approached.

"Jesus, Frederick! Will you shut up much?" she asked as eyes followed her around the room.

"Okay, my little twatwaffle," he said, grabbing her elbow and ushering her out of the building like a high schooler desperate for the latest gossip.

"Seriously?" she asked, rolling her eyes at him. "Can we please go have sex now?"

"Threesome with Dallas? Neither of us do chicks, but you could...you know, watch," he said with a shrug. "Or, maybe bring another dude and make it a party?"

"You amaze me," she said, peering into traffic before exiting onto the sidewalk.

"No, three dudes would amaze you."

Her head was spinning. "I have to go. I can't right now."

"No fucking way! You were alone with Marco Moretti, *the* Marco Moretti, for what like twenty to thirty minutes? Don't think you can just pull the I-have-to-go line on me!"

"Nothing happened."

"Well, why the fuck not? I'd bang Marco Moretti in a dirty alleyway in front of a dumpster when it was raining with a football stadium full of people watching."

Chyna arched an eyebrow. "You've really thought about this, haven't you?"

"Not the point, whore! What happened back there?" Frederick demanded.

"He came on to me, offered to take some pictures of me, put on the charm real thick, and nothing else," she told him, stuffing her clothing into her oversized hobo bag.

His eyes bugged out. "He wants to photograph you? And, you said no?"

"I didn't say anything, fucker, so calm your ass down," she said, stopping at the intersection.

"Well, let's turn right back around and fix that." He grabbed her elbow again and started pulling her back in the direction from which they had come.

"No! Quit it! I'm not going to go back to him groveling!" she cried, slapping his hand.

"Grovel for the man! It's worth it."

"Frederick, I can't today," she said, swishing her long hair over to one shoulder. "I can't...today." She sighed heavily and glanced away from him.

"Are you all right, baby?" he asked, wrapping his arms around her waist and pulling her into a hug.

"Just not ready for this...this thing with Adam today. I can't concentrate on anything. I'm all over the place. I'm scattered." She fanned her face when she pulled back from Frederick. "God, now I'm leaking."

Frederick smiled, wiping away the tears welling in her eyes. "You're too strong for this, sugar. Adam's a great guy, but then again, so is that hot ass Italian fashion designer. And, he's just as interested in you. No use worrying your pretty little head over a guy who hurt you. If Dallas pulled half the shit that Adam's pulled on you, I'd cut off his dick and feed it to a blender."

Chyna cringed. "Bad, bad imagery!"

"All I'm saying," he said over her cries of protest, "is that you can do better. All right? I'm only saying it once. I hate sappy."

"Thanks," she said, kissing his cheeks before pulling away. "Wish me luck."

"You don't need it. You're a fucking goddess," Frederick said, smacking her ass as she walked away.

She laughed as she veered through traffic to her waiting town car. Carl whisked her across town to a quaint restaurant that Adam adored. It was all Americana food, which meant she could eat hardly anything on the menu, but he loved it, so she obliged him. Dieting wasn't really necessary, but she just hated greasy food like that. It made her feel disgusting and unhealthy. Guess her mom's supermodel lifestyle had rubbed off on her in certain ways.

When she walked into the restaurant, the bell jingling overhead, she saw Adam sitting in their normal spot in a bright red booth in the back. His eyes found her across the room, and he almost smiled before he looked back down at his plastic menu. She frowned and crossed the tiled floor to where he was seated.

"Okay if I sit down?" she asked, hating how her voice sounded. Hadn't she just been seduced by a multimillion-dollar fashion designer? Wasn't she a strong desirable woman?

He put his hand out, gesturing for her to sit, but he said nothing. She plopped down and picked up a menu, staring at it. Her appetite evaded her now that she was sitting in front of him, and everything on the menu suddenly sounded unappetizing.

"Thanks for meeting me," she said, biting on her bottom lip. She wished she had something else to do besides stare at the stupid menu.

He didn't glance back up from his menu, and for a second, she thought he wasn't going to respond. "Well, you have the most annoying best friend in the world."

Chyna laughed and then coughed, trying to cover it up.

"She certainly doesn't give up on the people she cares about," he said, looking up at her then, "like ever."

"Sounds like her," Chyna said, holding back a smile. That sounded *way* too much like Alexa.

The waitress came over, wearing a red and white–striped old-fashioned dress with ruffled socks in white Keds. Her hair was pulled up into pigtails with scrunchies. She looked utterly ridiculous. Chyna could never get over the outfits here. Just dress them in normal clothes!

"What'll ya have?" she asked, smacking away on her bubble gum, not even looking at them as she held her notepad poised and ready.

Adam ordered a double cheeseburger with bacon and a fried egg on top with onion rings, instead of French fries, and a root beer. He burned calories like a maniac. Lucky fast metabolism. Chyna just asked for a strawberry milkshake, happily handing over her dirty menu. The waitress walked off with a grunt, flipping her pad back to the front, and slipped the menus under her arm.

"Charming," Chyna grumbled.

"Judgy."

"With reason," she said, pointing at the woman. "She was plain rude."

"She's probably just had a long day."

Chyna hmphed, not wanting to talk about the unfortunate waitress.

With nowhere else to look, Adam returned her gaze with a sigh. "You wanted to meet, so we're meeting. I only have an hour lunch. What did you want to talk about?"

Chyna swallowed and steeled herself for this. She was pleasantly sober. She hadn't even been drinking the night before in anticipation of this conversation. "I...wanted to apologize," she said meekly, wanting to break eye contact but not allowing herself, "for what happened."

"Apologize?" he asked suspiciously.

She paused, wishing she didn't have to do this. Why did it have to be this way? The one guy who she had agreed to actually give it a go with had ended up leaving her. She didn't know how to do what she was about to do.

"I can understand why you were pissed and why you left," she said, her voice breaking. God, she had wanted to keep it together! "I shouldn't have gone behind your back. I probably could have picked a better time to tell you about it, and I could have handled everything that happened afterward better. So... I'm sorry. I was a shit, and I'm admitting that."

"You were a shit," Adam agreed, "but..."

Chyna froze in place at that word. She had not been expecting that word.

"I was a shit, too. You were drunk, and I got pissed. Instead of working things out, I just left and let them simmer all week. That wasn't fair to either of us," he said, sighing. "I talked to John."

She felt her blood boil at the name. That son of a bitch! He had used her drunk ass for his own amusement. She had thought she was attracted to him, but really, it was one big façade. He was as charming as a con artist, slippery as a snake, and tricky as a thief. He had thought he could get an easy lay out of her, and when she had pushed him back, he had freaked out on her. She knew guys like him. From now on, she hated them, too. No one should be able to be that manipulative. He was a certified douche.

"He owned up to what happened. Told a slightly different tale than the one you fed me, but I don't think anyone will know what happened unless they were in the room that night. Frankly, I don't want to know. What happened, happened. It's over now. I can't continue to dwell on it."

"I know what you mean," she said softly as their food arrived.

Adam took the opportunity to fill his mouth, so he didn't have to talk. She could see he was brooding behind those big hazel eyes, but she didn't ask a question. She wanted to soak up the fact that he had apologized as well. No way had she thought he would do that. She had been in the wrong, not him. Chyna sucked on her strawberry milkshake, mulling over the situation in silence. He had more to say, and she knew it. They weren't finished with the conversation after not talking all week.

Adam tore through his burger, and then he started picking at his onion rings. She waited for him to speak. He looked like he wanted to lead the conversation. When he finally spoke up, she almost wished he hadn't.

"Why my brother?"

It was a question she didn't have an answer for. She hadn't kissed John. He had kissed her. But, that wasn't good enough. As cruel as John had been that night when she had stopped the kiss, he did have a fair point. She had been thinking about the kiss and worse since she had met him. Her intentions had been anything but honorable, and it made her feel worse. She didn't even want to fight him on this. She didn't feel like she had a right to.

"I don't know," she finally answered.

"Really?" he asked, dipping an onion ring in ketchup.

Chyna sighed, wishing she could go back and fix it. Fix her

attraction to John. Fix her reaction to his advances. Fix the way she had confronted Adam. "It was a mistake. Plain and simple. I don't have an excuse, not even a reason. It happened, and it was a mistake."

"You knew I looked up to him."

She nodded. She sucked harder on her milkshake, hoping he wouldn't drag this out.

"I asked you to hang out with him."

"I know," she whispered, staring down at her milkshake, frustrated. What more did he want her to say? Did he want her to beg? She wouldn't beg. "It was a mistake, Adam."

It was the first time she had said his name, and at the sound of it, he seemed to soften.

"For a while, I thought you were a mistake," he admitted.

Chyna's heart clenched painfully. She felt like she had been shot or punched or some other terrible thing. All the air was gone from her lungs, and she felt sick at the same time. How could he even say that to her? It was so cruel.

"But, if you were a mistake, I wouldn't want you back...and I do."

18

———————

PRESENT

Chyna crossed through Central Park, passing the far side of the MET, as she walked back out onto 5th Avenue. She veered north against traffic toward the entrance to the colossal building. She had always thought that when she grew up she would be the president of the board at the MET. It had been a strange childhood aspiration as far as dreams went for little kids, but she had thought it ordinary then. After realizing how much charity work she would have to do to even fathom getting on the board, she had quickly given up the thought. She didn't want to be forced to do charity work. She would rather do it all on her own. However, she still enjoyed the opera and ballets that graced the stage.

Staring up at the enormous stone building made her feel at home. In that moment, she realized how much she had missed New York City while she had been in Milan. She adored Milan, and it would always have a special place in her heart, but nothing could compare to New York.

She couldn't believe that only yesterday she had been the centerpiece for a major fashion show. Her reaction regarding

Marco had been rash, but that was usually how she worked. Act now and think later. It wasn't always the best approach.

She was miffed that she hadn't received so much as a *fuck off, bitch* text from Marco. Not to mention, she hadn't heard a single word from her three bitchy roommates. How could they see that she was gone and not even ask if she was alive? What great friends! Alexa would be worried sick. Well, Alexa was worried sick, but Chyna didn't really want to share what had happened. She already knew what she would say anyway, and she had been chastising herself enough.

In all honesty, she was just ready to get back to her life. She wanted to leave Milan and Marco behind and start fresh here. Fashion was huge in New York, and she was sure she could top fashion here as easily as she had in Italy. Plus, she had all of her favorite places back, and tons of men that had probably missed her in the clubs. She hadn't been available in a while, so it would be fun to get back into it.

She smiled faintly and took a seat on the south side of the MET stairs. That was all she wanted anyway, right? Modeling and men. She could live on that.

Leaning her elbows back on the step behind her, she waited, watching the tourists pass her by. A few stared at her as they passed, whispering to each other excitedly. Another openly ogled her, nearly running into the person in front of her. When a third group took out their cameras to snap a photo of her, she started getting confused. What was going on? She knew that she was pretty, but total strangers didn't normally pull out their cameras.

"Excuse me?" a giggly teenage girl said as she approached while handing her camera to her friend.

Chyna's eyes narrowed. "Yes?"

"Can I take a picture with you? My friends will *never* believe that I met a supermodel!" she cried, nearly jumping up and down.

Chyna had the good sense not to let her mouth fall open or show her surprise on her face. She took the picture, and the girl thanked her before scurrying off.

What. The. Fuck. Was. Going. On?

She stood up and walked up a couple more steps to get out of the direct line of sight of the people passing by. She needed to uncover the truth of what was happening. How had four separate groups of people known who she was? Why had that girl called her a supermodel? It wasn't a term she took lightly. Her mother was a supermodel. She resembled her mother, but come on, it was pretty obvious Chyna was twenty years younger!

Speaking of her mother...

"There you are, darling," Andrea said, walking briskly up the MET steps in her characteristic white pea coat and over-sized black sunglasses. She kissed both of her cheeks in greeting.

"Do you know what's going on?" Chyna demanded, skipping the introduction.

"What do you mean?" she asked coyly.

"Someone just called me a supermodel. Last I checked, the bill didn't fit," Chyna told her.

"Let's go inside. It's a bit chilly out here. I assume you wanted to ask me something else also," she said, linking arms with Chyna and dragging her along.

Chyna relented to follow her up the stairs and inside.

"Let's walk," Andrea suggested.

"Can we just sit?" Chyna asked, not looking forward to this conversation. She looked forward to very few conversations with her mother. It was only the second or third time Chyna had seen her in the past couple of years, and she didn't do family time for no reason.

Andrea sighed dramatically before answering, "Well, all right."

They walked toward an empty bench in the main entranceway and took a seat next to each other. Chyna saw a woman glance in her direction, but she kept walking. She suddenly wished she had a hooded jacket. She normally enjoyed the attention, but this felt very different.

"So, how did you manage it?" Andrea finally asked.

"Manage what? Do you know why all these people are staring at me?" Chyna asked.

"They went up this morning all over the city."

"What did?" she demanded.

"Are you certain you don't know? I'd be shocked if you didn't," Andrea said, narrowing her eyes as if she didn't believe her daughter.

Her disbelief wasn't really out of the ordinary though.

"Would I be asking you if I knew what was going on?"

"Marco's new advertisement went up all over the city. You're the cover of his boutique. You're at every bus stop, and you have a full-page spread in the *New York Times*. Darling, you're everywhere."

Chyna saw stars. No. No. No. No. No. This could not be happening to her. "Wha-what does it look like?" she managed to get out.

"Stunning. You're wearing a purple mermaid dress, full sequins, perfect lines. You look like you're ready to crawl through the camera," she told her, eyeing her warily. Clearly, her reaction wasn't what Andrea had been expecting.

"I'm sure someone has a *New York Times* around here."

"That's all right," she said. Her hand dropped to the bench. She gripped it, trying to hold the nausea back. How had she fucked-up this badly?

"Didn't he tell you?" Andrea asked suspiciously. "They always tell you."

"It doesn't matter," Chyna said, swallowing. This was going

to be much more difficult now. That damn man! "I came to talk to you about something else."

"You look sick, darling. Should I get you something?" She waited for Chyna to respond, but Chyna said nothing. "Chyna, am I missing something?"

"Besides six years of my life, no," Chyna spat back coldly, shutting Andrea up real quick. "Please stop trying to mother me. I don't need a mother right now."

"Fine, what do you want then?" she asked, crossing her leg and tapping her foot in the air impatiently.

"You know Cassandra Corsa?" Chyna asked straight out. She didn't want to beat around the bush with this. She just needed answers, and she intended to get them.

"What the hell do you know about Cassandra Corsa?" Andrea asked, planting both feet on the ground as she turned to face her daughter.

Chyna shrugged. "I know enough."

"Why are you even asking about Corsa? You have Marco's line at your feet. You're plastered on every corner. I've been there," she said wistfully. "Now, why would someone like that need Cassandra Corsa?"

"It's really none of your business."

"It is if you are asking me about her. Marco knows Cassandra Corsa. You could have asked him," Andrea said as if seeing a chink in the armor. "So, why haven't you asked him?"

"It really doesn't matter whether or not I'm talking to Marco about Cassandra Corsa. I just asked you about her," Chyna said, hating her mother's perverse logic. She had been married to Chyna's father for too long.

"Marco won't let you near her, you know?"

"Mother!" she cried, raising her voice, drawing unnecessary attention her way. "Can we not do this?"

"Oh, now you want a mother," she said, narrowing her eyes.

"I just want you to give me her phone number," Chyna countered, ignoring her previous statement.

"Why should I do that?" Andrea asked her point blank.

Chyna sighed and stared at the ground. She knew where this was going. She couldn't be hard, edgy Chyna in this situation. Her mother knew her too well. She had, kind of, raised her, and Chyna had gotten a lot of her bite and attitude from the person sitting next to her. Everything else she had was from her father, and Andrea knew how to get around him better than anyone. Andrea also hated it more than anyone, so Chyna needed to be someone else.

"Because I need it," she finally said. "I need her number because Marco won't give it to me. He doesn't want me near another designer. He thinks he owns me."

It was mostly the truth, and it sounded like something her mother could sympathize with. It wasn't like she was going to go around telling Andrea what had *really* gone down.

"Sounds like a typical male designer," Andrea said with a snort at the end for extra emphasis. "Self-indulgent, egotistical, demanding, self-righteous...assholes. I'd love to eliminate the whole lot of them."

Chyna laughed at her mom's perfect description of Marco. It was like she had experience with these types of men or something. Well, she probably did.

"Fine," Andrea finally said. "Just because I know the situation you're in." She pulled out her phone and handed the number over to her. "I'm still in contact with her some. Sweet girl. So much like her mother. I bet she'll be in New York for her line reveal in two weeks," she threw out offhand.

"Thank you," Chyna said, grateful for the shred of mercy her mother had shown her. It was the most she had seen since she and her father had given Chyna her penthouse.

19

Hiding from the constant stares the next four days was harder than Chyna had thought possible. It was a strange feeling to go from being well known to being an overnight celebrity in her hometown. Alexa had the decency not to bring it up. She was laid back enough to not care that her best friend's face was plastered around the city. In fact, the only time it had come up, Alexa had just shrugged her little shoulders and told her she had assumed that was why Chyna was in Milan in the first place. Alexa certainly had more faith in her newfound supermodel status than Chyna did.

She hadn't ever realized it would be that different, but she had lost all anonymity with Marco's cover spread. It was infuriating. She just wanted to move on; she wanted to forget. But, her face was everywhere. And she couldn't avoid the heated fuck-me eyes she was sending Marco's way or the dress he had originally created for her to wear to Glam Ball.

When she had seen the photo that Marco had chosen, she'd had to grab onto the bus stop for support. She knew that picture. Marco hadn't been satisfied with the quality of the photo shoot one day, so they had played around with lighting and camera angles back at his apartment all afternoon. The picture plastered all over New York was her seduction. It had never been meant for anyone else's eyes. No wonder everyone was eating it up.

At least, Cassandra Corsa was interested. She had seen the spread—everyone in the fashion world had at this point—and was willing to meet with her. She was still in Italy on business after the Glam Ball. She sounded surprised that Chyna had already returned to New York since most of Marco's girls usually spent the final two weeks of the summer at the beach together, finalizing deals for modeling jobs in the fall. Thankfully, Cassandra hadn't asked any questions.

Chyna was hoping that her offer was still on the table. Cassandra had made it seem that way at Glam Ball, but that had been a different time. Chyna couldn't even let herself worry about that. Remaining positive was key.

In fact, she was just ready to get back to her old life. She was pretty sure she was already beginning to fool Alexa. That was all she needed right now. She would get this new modeling job, exactly what she deserved, and things would go back to normal. She was sure of it.

As soon as Chyna made it up to the VIP area in her favorite club, she took her dark Ray-Bans off and pulled her long black hair down from the loose ponytail at the base of her neck. Recently, it had been easier to hide behind her glasses. No one in VIP would say anything though. She was secure in her identity here.

The club was packed, and she had to fight her way through the club, even in the VIP section. It was much more crowded than normal for a Thursday night, but she appreciated the cover that gave her. Plus, it meant it was more likely that she didn't know everyone. She was ready for some normal. She wanted to prove Alexa right.

The bartender had two shots of tequila waiting for her

when he saw her approaching the bar. God, she loved him! She had been gone for two months, and he still knew exactly what she wanted. At least one man did.

She took one after the other, appreciating the never-failing bite as it burned its way down her throat. The lime that she chased it with had never tasted so refreshing. She took the martini from the bartender and left the bar to scope out the scene. A group of girls in the corner waved her over. She recognized one or two from the private school she had attended during middle and high school. They weren't her favorite people in the world, but she was looking for normal after all.

"Chyna Van der Wal," the first one said, standing uneasily with her drink in hand. She threw her other arm around Chyna's shoulders. She was nearly as tall as Chyna with long, wavy blonde hair and a snooty upturned nose. Her parents had old, old money, and she let everyone know it. "It has been too long."

"Totes true," the second one chimed in. She had a round face with a short chin-length brown bob and dimpled cheeks. She looked like she had put on a few pounds since high school and was hiding it behind her boob job.

"Good to see you, Layla," she said to the blonde. Then, she turned to the brunette. "You, too, Amy."

The two girls scooted their friends over to give Chyna room to join their group. Feeling obligated, she sat down. Layla introduced Chyna to the rest of the girls, but she wasn't planning to be around for much longer, so she didn't pay attention. In fact, she had other things on her mind, like getting wasted, dancing away the rest of the night, and stumbling home to try and forget the rest of the week.

"So, what have you been up to?" Chyna had seen Layla at the MET sometime last year. She had tried to avoid her, but Layla had somehow cornered her on the way out. She had just graduated from Yale with her bachelor's in interior design or fashion or something Chyna knew Layla was likely never use as a stay-at-home mom.

Layla thrust her left hand out, revealing the massive diamond on her finger. "I got married!"

"Nice," Chyna said unenthusiastically. Marriage was pretty low on her list of priorities. Actually, it might not be on the list. Sex sounded nice though. Nice, straight, rough, vanilla sex.

"And, I'm engaged!" Amy followed it up by showing off her own rock.

"Great," Chyna said, barely glancing at their rings.

"And, you..." Layla said wide-eyed. "You're all over New York. Following in mommy's footsteps, I see."

God, she remembered why she hadn't been friends with these bitches in high school. The bite of jealousy in Layla's voice was so unbecoming.

"How did you get to model for Marco's anyway? I'm still trying to get him to return my calls. I heard he designs wedding dresses, and hubby said I could get whatever I wanted," Amy crooned.

Chyna clutched the armrest at the mention of his name. She couldn't escape him. She just couldn't get away from any of it. She put her glass down on the table and stood. She hadn't even noticed that she hadn't taken a single sip from the drink. "I have to go."

"Wait!" Layla called. "Where are you going?"

"Away."

"What's wrong?" Amy cried, standing as well.

"Nothing. I just...you know what? It doesn't matter," Chyna said, turning away from them.

"Rude much?" She said heard Layla call at her as she walked away from their table.

She didn't stop or turn around. She made it to the center of the dance space and began grinding her body to the beat. She wasn't drunk enough to forget what had just happened, but she tried to fill her mind with the music, the dance, the grip of someone's hands on her hips. Still Marco weaseled his way into her thoughts even then.

She wasn't supposed to care about what she had done. It was no more than he deserved. He might have been about to surprise her with the cover spread of his new advertisement, but that didn't mean anything. How many other women had been cover models for him? How many others had he photographed in his studio? How many other models had he tossed aside for the next thing? And how many had left him?

She was sure that she was the only one.

The only one dumb enough.

"Hey, baby, what's your name?" the guy whispered into her ear while she pushed her ass against him.

"Doesn't matter," Chyna said, pushing her hands up around his neck and rolling her body back against his. Her name was too recognizable at the moment. Maybe he hadn't seen the advertisement. Maybe he hadn't seen her name written in shiny gold font at the bottom. But, she wasn't taking chances. Tonight, she was just some anonymous girl in the VIP lounge.

"I like that," he breathed into her ear. They danced for the next three songs before he leaned forward and spoke to her again. "You want to get out of here?"

She debated. He was cute and a good dancer. He definitely fell into the high school jock category as far as looks went. He was kind of built like a baseball player with shortish blonde hair and a cocky smile. She could dig that cocky smile. It usually meant good things in the bedroom...or it meant terrible things. Taking a second look at him, she guessed the former.

But, did she want to leave with some guy that she just thought was cute, even if he had a smile that she knew held promise? "I don't think so," she finally responded.

He didn't acknowledge her refusal as he continued to dance with her, his movements getting impassioned. His hands ran up her sides, and as she began to pull her hands down from around his neck, he reached up and locked them back in place. She obliged his forceful behavior and kept on dancing with him. That was good enough for now. He was a good enough distraction.

He took this as encouragement and moved his hands back down her arms. His hands got adventurous, rounding the curves of her breasts and then trailing down her flat stomach to the waistline of her black shorts. His fingers dipped under the material and fluttered lightly across the inside of the seam. She dropped her head backward onto his shoulder as his touch heated her body. Maybe this was the easiest way to forget.

They were pressed in on every side by a mass of bodies dancing in the darkness. She couldn't tell one person from the next, and it was giving him courage he likely wouldn't have had otherwise. His lips found the side of her neck, kissing up to her ear. She tilted her head sideways, giving him easier access, as she enjoyed the taste of pursuit.

She laughed at his boldness, but she didn't stop him as his hand moved farther into her shorts. His finger stroked her silk underwear in time with the music. She rolled her ass in circles against his hardening cock, teasing him despite her refusal.

"Tease," he growled into her ear. He pinched her clit through her panties. Her body arched backward into him, surprised by his forcefulness. She had clearly been right about her assessment of that smile. "Come home with me."

When she nodded, he released her and pulled his hand out of her shorts. She let him take her hand, and she followed him out of the club. See, back to normal.

They took a cab to his place, and she told Carl to tail them. She already knew she wasn't going to stay the night with this guy.

They reached his apartment building fifteen minutes later, and he practically dragged her up to the second floor. She followed, trying to get into the haste and enthusiasm that was radiating off of him. By this point, she was wishing that she had finished her martini earlier. Another drink would do her some good. He had clearly had a few more than her.

He jiggled the door open and pushed it with his hip. He grabbed her by the waist and pulled her into his apartment. Their lips crashed together before he even got the door closed behind him. He tasted like whiskey and cigarettes. He stumbled backward, trying to guide them to the bedroom in the dark, but he ran into an armchair and fell over the edge. He stood up laughing awkwardly.

"Sorry. Guess my roommate trashed the place," he said apologetically.

Chyna had no doubt that his roommate did not trash the place, or at least, he had something to do with the disaster she could see even in the dark. Men!

Once they finally made it into his bedroom, he scooted a pile of clothes off the bed. Chyna tried not to judge her surroundings, but she was really wondering how he had made it into the VIP section at all. This was why she had always brought people back to her place. It was really easier. But, under her present condition and the fact that her face was everywhere, she thought it best not to draw any more attention to herself.

His lips found hers again, and she tried to push energy into the kiss. He was demanding passion, and she wasn't feeling it. Normally, she didn't care as long as she got something out of it, but tonight just sucked.

She tried to push Marco and everything associated with him out of her head as she forced herself to concentrate on his kisses. His arms wrapped around her hips, pulling her into his body. She eased into him; she wanted this.

They fell backward against his bed, which creaked with their added body weight to the poor frame. His hands found the end of her shirt, and he awkwardly pushed it up to her throat. He flipped her bra up, rather than unsnapping it in the back, and he massaged both of her breasts between his hands. She tried to feel something, anything for this guy. God, he was caressing her breasts like he was surprised she had them rather than adoring their beauty!

He kissed around her right nipple before sucking it up between his lips. He pinched it gently between his teeth until it became a small peak. He worked on the other one until it matched, continuing to massage the right breast like he was playing with Play-Doh. Chyna closed her eyes and let her head fall back, wanting nothing more than to let herself feel the heat that had traveled through her body in the club.

One of his hands found her wrist lying limp on the bed. He grabbed it and placed her hand on his erection that was throbbing through his dress pants.

"Play with him," he told her, pressing her hand down harder.

Her eyes flew open, and she stared up at the ceiling. Had he just said *him*?

"Come on, baby. Play with him," he repeated. He helped her by unzipping his pants, shoving his boxers down over his dick, and showing *him* to her.

It was nicely sized but nothing to write home about.

In the split second she stared at it, hanging over the edge of his boxers with pre-cum dripping from the tip, she decided she was better than this. What the hell had she been thinking? How had she ever gotten to this point?

She went through life accepting the short end of the stick, thinking she deserved nothing more than what was handed to her. She fucked millionaires and busboys alike because she was gorgeous and rich and could get away with it. She could get away with not caring what anyone else thought, thinking she wasn't worth much more. It was easier not to get attached, not to allow anyone else to see that she wasn't worth their time.

But, this guy was clearly *not* worth her time.

"Sorry, I can't believe I'm doing this, but I can't sleep with you," Chyna said, sitting up and adjusting her top so it was no longer strangling her.

"What?" he asked, sitting up next to her.

"This just isn't working for me."

He hid *him* back in his boxers, and then he zipped up his pants. "You're joking?" he asked, glancing away from her.

"Yeah, I just..." she began, shrugging. What could she tell him? The thought of his pre-cum getting near her grossed her out? He had played with her breasts like a kindergartener? She wasn't at all interested in him? He would never live up to an Italian fashion designer? He would never live up to Adam? God, why was he still on her brain?! And, why did he have to be at Alexa's last weekend? Focus!

"I don't understand."

"What don't you understand?" she asked, standing. Placing a hand on her hip, she leaned into it and stared at him, raising her eyebrow. "This was a mistake, plain and simple."

"So, we're not going to fuck?" he asked, standing up from the bed to look at her.

"No," she said with a shudder, "definitely not."

"Whatever," he said as if he wasn't offended. "I just wanted to say I slept with a supermodel anyway."

Chyna felt like he had punched her in the face. She kept the shock off her face, but she couldn't keep her stomach from clenching like a vice grip.

Really? He knew who she had been all along. He had just wanted to fuck her, so he could tell all of his friends that he had slept with the girl in the *New York Times* advertisement. What an asshole!

Thank God she had made the right choice!

"I doubt you ever will," she said, stomping through his house.

"You were easy enough to get home," he called from the door of his bedroom.

"It's too bad you don't even know how to use your dick," she called over her shoulder, wrenching the door open.

"Cunt!"

She smiled. Now there was a compliment.

As she walked out of the door, she realized how much she could not wait to meet with Cassandra and get her life back on track. Because she was crumbling in her new existence.

20

PAST

Chyna heard the door click closed in the living room, and she jumped up from her closet floor. She had turned the place upside down, debating on what to bring for two months in Milan. She always packed heavy. Well, she had always had someone pack heavy for her. She and Adam had just returned from Alexa's graduation party in Atlanta, and her two biggest Louis Vuitton bags were still stuffed full of garments she had never worn. How could she possible decide what she was going to wear two months out?

Trying not to think about it anymore, she wandered out of her bedroom and down the hall. "Hey, you," she said, walking up to Adam and throwing her arms around him. "How was work?"

He bent down and kissed her on the mouth. "I'm glad it's over, and that my night belongs to you."

"Me, too," she said before she deepened the kiss.

"I wish all of my days belonged to you," he whispered against her lips.

"They do," she said, threading her fingers through his hair.

"Except for those two months when you go to Italy."

Chyna sighed, resting her head against his shoulder. "Are we having this conversation again?"

"Nothing wrong with me wanting you close."

"No, there's not," she agreed. "But, come on, Italy for a photo shoot for two months. It's a dream come true."

He held her tighter. "I didn't know it was your dream though."

"Well, it is," she said, breaking his hold. "I really don't want to talk about this again. I feel like we've had this same discussion a dozen times since I got the job offer." She shook her head and started walking back to her bedroom.

"Can we talk about how you got this job again?" Adam asked. "Seems kind of suspect."

"Is it suspicious because someone thought that I could perform a job well or because I want to go?" she demanded, her anger rising.

This was ridiculous. He just couldn't fathom why anyone would hire her. She had no prior experience, no references, and no in to the modeling world besides a mother who no longer spoke to her. Yet, she still managed to get this job. He didn't understand that she needed none of that. She still managed to get this job. She just needed a break, and she had found it.

"Why do you have to change the subject?" he asked, striding down the hallway after her.

"Because you make it seem like I can't do whatever I want to do," she said, pushing the door open with her hand.

"I never suggested that. I merely want to know how you ended up getting a modeling contract thousands of miles away from me without batting an eyelash."

"Oh, so you think I batted an eyelash?" She whirled in place. "Is that what you think?"

Adam walked slowly up to her, standing all tensed-up in the middle of her bedroom. He placed his hands on her arms and stared down into her eyes. "No," he said with a wry smile. "That's not what I think."

She stared up into his hazel eyes that were looking so intently down on her, and she felt bad for getting so riled up. She was leaving in twenty-four hours and didn't need this bickering. Why did she have to get like this? He only had her best intentions at heart.

"I was merely curious about the circumstances surrounding a job that you didn't apply for or know anything about. I don't want you walking into some kind of scam," he told her reassuringly.

"I've told you about how I got the job," she said, not breaking eye contact. "It's not a scam."

"Tell me one more time," he requested, running his hands down her arms.

"I met Marco," she began.

He raised his eyebrows.

"Mr. Moretti," she corrected, "the fashion designer for Marco's clothing line, at his grand opening."

"And, you got those tickets..." he prompted.

She shrugged. "I don't know. They showed up at my front door."

"Right. They showed up at your front door," he said, his voice disbelieving.

Chyna soldiered on. She was telling him the truth, even if he was refusing to believe her. She didn't know how she got the tickets, and frankly, she didn't care because those tickets led her to get the job. "Mr. Moretti offered to do a photo shoot with me when we met at the opening."

"Just like that. For no reason. No other offer," he said snidely.

Chyna swallowed. "No. No other offer." Okay, so she fibbed a bit, but he didn't need to know that. "I told him I would think about it, and then I took his card and left."

"And, you thought about it and decided you wanted to go to Italy for two months."

"I didn't *know* he would want me to go to Italy for two months when I agreed to model for him," she told him exasperated.

"Well, what *did* he tell you?"

"That he would meet me in Central Park since he was still in town. We took a few pictures. He offered me the job and told me some information about the shoot. I accepted. I found out about the extent of the modeling job after I'd already agreed to go. I couldn't back out!"

"I know," he said, running his hands across her waist and pulling her in close. "I know how you feel about it all. I'm just going to miss you." He whispered that last line into her ear.

She nearly lost it. He would miss her. He hadn't said that before. No one had ever missed her. Not really. Not like that. Not heartbreakingly so.

She grabbed at the back of his button-up shirt, fisting it in her hands, and she pulled it loose from his pants. She needed him right now like she had never needed anything else.

"What are you doing?" he asked softly.

She looked up at him with a devious smile. "What does it look like I'm doing?"

Once his shirt was untucked, she ran her hands up the front and began unfastening each button individually.

"Why the sudden shift in mood?"

"You're going to miss me," she whispered, biting on her bottom lip.

"Of course I am," he said, reaching up and running his thumb across her jawline before he captured her lips.

"No one ever misses me," she admitted, pushing her hands underneath his shirt and sliding it over his shoulders.

He shrugged out of the shirt, letting it fall to the ground.

She felt so vulnerable, but this was Adam. She could do this with him.

He seemed to respond to her declaration with vigor, pressing his lips desperately against hers. Their mouths locked together in an emotional feverish embrace, speaking volumes more than either of them had ever been able to say about their affection. He broke contact to kiss her neck, lowering the spaghetti straps of her dress so that he could kiss across her exposed collarbone. It was a helpless longing of two souls craving nothing more than the other.

Chyna's hands went to work, unbuckling his belt and then shoving his pants to the ground. She wanted him, needed him. It was something more than desire pushing through her, but she couldn't place it. All she knew was that this needed to happen, and it needed to happen now. Everything else could wait.

His hands found the hem of her dress, and he pulled it over her head. She smiled up at him confidently. She was so unbelievably ready for him. He stripped out of his boxers while she unclasped her bra and stepped out of her pink thong.

"You look so pretty," he said, brushing his lips against her.

"Pretty?" she asked with a giggle. Pretty was for girls. She was accustomed to being called gorgeous and sexy...not pretty.

"Yeah, Chyna. You are so unbelievably pretty. The prettiest thing I've ever laid eyes on," he said, slowly walking her backward toward the bed. His right hand came up, tucking a strand of black hair behind her ear.

"Ever?" she asked. She felt giddy. Pretty didn't sound so bad coming out of his mouth. He was breaking all the rules, and she liked it.

His hands ran down her naked body, gripping her hips. "Ever."

The backs of her knees hit the footboard of the bed, stopping her in her tracks.

"Just see yourself through my eyes for one day," he pleaded, pulling her into a soft, sensual kiss.

When they broke apart, she stared up at him breathless, uncertain how to take that last statement. "How do you see me?" she asked, seeing her reflection in his hazel eyes. She looked the same as always.

"As so much more than a pretty face," he whispered, brushing his nose against hers lightly. "So much more."

She placed both of her hands on his cheeks, leaned forward, and kissed him with all the promise of what was to come. He pressed her backward toward the mattress, and they eased into the plush down comforter together. His hands roamed her body, and sparks ignited at his touch. As their kiss heated, warmth spread through her lower half, and she had the sudden realization that she never wanted this to stop.

It was somehow...more than anything else she had ever experienced. She didn't know what that meant or what she was feeling. Her stomach was clenching up, her heart was beating erratically, and her palms were clammy. Every sensation seemed heightened, and she felt lost in his every touch.

As he pulled back from their passionate kiss, Adam's hand came up and stroked her dark hair. All went silent. It was just the two of them. She wanted him for everything he had said and more, so much more.

He eased into her without another word, and she was so ready for him. She was ready to feel all of him. She needed to know that he was hers—only hers. That was all that she wanted in that moment. She was glad that someone finally wanted her exactly as she was.

She wrapped her legs around his hips, meeting him stroke for stroke. They moved together effortlessly, working up a sweat as their desire mounted. Her back arched off the bed as his movements quickened, and her impending climax awakened her body.

"Chyna," he groaned, resting one of his elbows next to her head while thrusting into her.

She moaned louder than before as he slid into her again faster.

"I'm getting close."

"Me, too," she moaned, her hands digging into his slick back.

"Will you look at me?"

She breathed heavily, letting her back fall down to the bed. He was moving faster on top of her, slamming into her body at irregular intervals, and she was on the brink. Her head tilted toward him, and her eyes slowly fluttered open.

"That's exactly how I want to remember you."

"Remember me?" she asked through her deep breaths.

"Every time I think about you," he said with a smirk.

"Fuck!" she cried, orgasm ripping through her body at his sweet words.

He doubled over on top of her, grunting as he came inside of her. She shuddered, clenching around him and holding him tight. She didn't want to let him go. She wanted to stay like this forever.

But, forever wasn't meant to be forever.

21

PAST

Adam kissed Chyna lightly on her nose. He slowly rolled off of her, grabbed his boxers, and headed for the bathroom. She watched him go with a wonderful satisfaction settling in her stomach. She had never experienced sex in quite the same way. Her heart was open, laying bare on the bed, and she felt light and free. She was...happy.

He returned a moment later, resting his shoulder against the doorframe as he looked down at the floor. Chyna sat up on her elbows and turned her head to face him. She had his typical goofy grin on her face for once.

"Don't go," he whispered so softly that she barely heard him.

"Go where?" she asked, having already forgotten their earlier conversation.

"To Italy. Don't go to Italy."

She dropped her head back onto the pillow and smiled up at the ceiling. Why was he even bringing this up again? She was leaving in twenty-four hours. It was settled. "I have to go," she said with a yawn, stretching her arms over her head.

"No. You don't," he said, his voice clearly restrained.

She kept her hands overhead and rolled to face him, lying on her right arm. "Adam, come back to bed. I want you to hold me."

"Chyna, aren't you listening?" he asked. He still hadn't looked up from the carpet.

She studied him standing there, bathed in the bathroom light. He was tense, which didn't make any sense given the circumstances, and he wouldn't look at her.

"I guess not," she said softly, her heart picking up speed.

"Don't go to Italy."

"Adam, we've already talked about this," she whined. Sitting up cautiously in bed, she wrapped the comforter around her.

"And, you don't seem to hear what I'm saying."

"I get that you don't want me to go."

"Do you?" he asked, looking up at her finally.

"Y-yes," she said uncertainly.

She had thought that she got what he was saying. He didn't want her to go. He would miss her. They had just had unbelievable sex. Did she mention he would miss her? Well, she would miss him, too, but it didn't make any sense why he was bringing this up again.

"Then, why are you going?" he asked.

"Adam, I didn't think you were serious," she said, tilting her head and assessing him. "I mean, I know that you wanted me to stay, but I thought that was just because you were going to miss me. I didn't think that you actually didn't want me to pursue modeling."

"You didn't think I was serious? You thought I wanted my girlfriend on the other side of the planet?" he asked in disbelief.

"Well, no, but—"

"But, you were going to do it anyway."

"I don't understand," she said, shaking her head. Her post-coital bliss was disappearing with every word he uttered. "Why are you doing this?"

"Chyna, I want you to understand. I don't want you to go. Stay with me here in New York," he said, walking forward out of the bathroom. He sat down on the side of the bed and took her hands in his, pleading with her. "Why would you want to leave New York? Why would you want to leave me?"

"I'm not leaving you, Adam," she reassured him. "I'll only be gone for two months. I'll be back before you know it."

He shook his head. "At what cost?"

"What are you getting at?" she asked, staring down at where he was still holding her hands.

"After what happened here…" he trailed off.

"After what happened?" she asked, her eyes narrowing.

He glanced away from her but answered, "With John."

"You think I'll cheat on you?" she hissed. After everything that had just happened and their perfect relationship since that incident, he still thought so poorly of her. He still thought that she wouldn't be the girlfriend that he deserved.

Her chest expanded, and her breathing suddenly became very heavy. It was like she was sucking air in and breathing it out, but none of it was happening fast enough. Her hands began trembling lightly in his. She couldn't believe this. She couldn't believe him. After the best sex of her life…he had to go and…she couldn't even think it.

"I don't know, Chyna. No."

"Well, which is it?" she asked slowly, trying to make sure she kept breathing.

"No. No, I don't think that. I just…don't know."

"Now, you're not making sense," she whispered, clutching onto his hands to keep hers from shaking.

"I just don't want you to go. You don't need the money!" he insisted. "Why are you going? Why are you leaving me?"

"Adam, I'm not leaving you," she reassured him again helplessly. Why did he keep saying that? "And, it's not about the money. I don't care about the money. I want to prove that I can do something right, but apparently, even the right thing is wrong.”

“You don't need to go to Italy to prove that you can do something right, Chyna,” he told her. “You can do something right by staying here in New York! Don't you see?”

“No, I don't. Can't *you* see that I need this? Aren't you supposed to see that?” she pleaded.

“Chyna, but we're happy. Right?”

“Yeah, Adam, we're happy. I'm not unhappy with you. I just need...my own life. You have a job that you love, and you want to work late nights because you love it so goddamn much. I don't have *anything* like that! I just have...me,” she whispered. “I want something that's mine.”

“I'm yours,” he told her.

“Then, let me do this!”

“Okay,” he said, standing and dropping her hands.

She breathed out a sigh of relief. He was finally coming around. He was finally seeing that she needed this.

“Then, you should be able to do this your way,” he whispered softly.

“I agree.”

“Good.”

“I'm glad we're finally on the same page.”

“Me too,” he said, nodding. “I can't do long distance.”

Chyna snapped her head around to look at him. She ground her teeth to keep from showing the shock that she was sure, if he just looked at her, registered in her eyes. “You...can't do long distance?”

“No. You want this. Then, you should have it. I'm glad we agree on that.”

“Is this about Christina?” she asked him desperately.

It was the only thing that explained how this was coming so far out of left field. His last girlfriend had left him because they couldn't do long distance. Why did he assume that she was the same way? She wished he would just talk to her!

"What?" he asked, showing the shock that she had on her face only seconds ago. "No! This is not about Christina. This is about you wanting to go off and find something of your own. This is about you following your dreams. This is about you, Chyna. This is *not* about me."

"Adam," she breathed, begging him to look at her.

"I have to go," he said, pulling his clothes back on. "This is a mutual thing. We agreed."

He made the last part sound like a death sentence. A mutual agreement had never felt so one-sided.

"Have a safe trip," he said, glancing at her one last time over his shoulder before making a break for the door.

She pulled her knees up to her chest and rested her chin on them. Her heart felt like it had been run over by a bulldozer. If she had thought her breathing was bad before, she wasn't even sure if she was breathing now.

Her normal reaction would have been to immediately call Alexa or even Frederick and talk out this ridiculous turn of affairs. But, she didn't even have it in her heart to give either of them a call. What would they say to her that she couldn't tell herself?

The fact that Adam would have the audacity to leave her not once but now twice was unbelievable. He claimed it was mutual, and maybe it was to an extent. She had agreed with him after all. She needed to go. She needed to do this to prove to herself, if no one else, that she could do something great.

He had every right to leave her. He had every right to want to have a stable girlfriend. He had every right to find someone better.

She didn't deserve the heartache. If he didn't want her, then she shouldn't want him. She could have another guy in a second.

All true.

None of it mattered now.

She brought her hand up to her eyes and pressed against them hard. God, she was a mess! Why did he have to leave? For once, why couldn't things be as wonderful and perfect as everyone thought her life was?

They were happy. They were so happy. Yet, she still wasn't good enough for him. She still wasn't good enough to keep around. She was going to be gone for two months, not six months, not a year. They could have worked through it. Other people did it! What made them so different?

Was it just a way out? Did he want to be rid of her? This would be the easiest way for him to do that, if that was what he wanted. But, that didn't explain his behavior. He didn't have to come to Atlanta with her for Alexa's graduation. He didn't have to be so sweet and caring. He didn't have to have beautiful, passionate sex with her.

He had done all those things and left her anyway. So, maybe the reasoning in the long run didn't matter. Regardless, he had come to the same conclusion. He had struck the final blow.

She pulled her hands away from her eyes and saw that they were wet. A sob escaped her, and she bent forward over her knees, tears streaming down her face. She hiccupped, pain racking her body as she shook with the force of her despair.

Why was she crying? Why was she crying? Why the hell was she crying?

She couldn't cry over him. She didn't cry over boys. This was ridiculous. She hadn't cried the last time they had broken up...well, not until she had called Lexi and realized the extent of the situation. Why couldn't this be like last time?

Why couldn't she find the anger instead of this pain that had locked itself away in her heart and was slowly eating away at it from the inside out?

PRESENT

 wo weeks.
Two whole weeks.
That's how long it took before Marco pulled the advertise-ment with her picture on it. It was long enough to make her truly feel the weight of what she had done, but it wasn't long enough to make it look like a mistake on his end.

It was strange walking the streets of her home again. She had already gotten used to people staring at her, trying to place her face, or pointing out an advertisement as she walked by. The ad had made her an overnight celebrity, a constant reminder of what she had left behind in Milan. Whatever Marco's original intentions were, the display was now only laced with regret.

She turned the corner toward Barneys and came face to face with Ravenna. She looked exquisite in painted on black pants, an olive button-up shirt, and black peep-toe heels. Her red hair was pulled off of one side of her face, and she managed to wear blood red lipstick perfectly.

Chyna knew that the picture wasn't as good as her own. Ravenna was second best, a backup, and it showed. Probably not to most eyes, but Chyna knew. She had been there when this picture was taken in the middle of the summer at a mock studio outside of the city. Marco had been in a foul mood, yelling at everyone. He hadn't liked a single picture that day. Guess he had changed his mind.

She knew what he was getting at. She was replaceable. He didn't need her. Even on his worst day when nothing was going right, he could capture something fitting enough to plaster all over New York City...without her.

She heard him loud and clear. Loud. And. Clear.

Asshole.

Chyna passed the sign, ignoring the woman who commented on how pretty the model was, and walked down the street toward Madison Avenue. Tourists flitted around outside of Barneys. Some were walking purposefully with their cell phone plastered to their ear while others were moseying along, occasionally snapping photos. Why they were taking a picture of a department store was beyond her. Didn't people have department stores at home? Granted this was Barney's, but still.

She pushed past a crowd of people debating whether or not to go inside and she walked through the doors toward the elevator. The elevator deposited her on the ninth floor, and she strolled into Fred's for her afternoon luncheon.

The hostess asked for her name, and Chyna was thankful that she had a reservation. The restaurant was packed. She never came here on Saturday afternoons, but some exceptions could be warranted. This was definitely one of them.

She followed the hostess to her table and took a seat. The past two weeks had gone by painfully slow, and she was ready to get back to modeling. She had gone to Milan to prove to herself that she could do something great, and she had done it. Modeling was something she was great at. She had never known how much she would *love* it though.

She tried to act like she was going to move on and do some other mindless activity like she always did. Alexa was seeing through her act though. She was thankful that she had a friend who would give her space and let her deal with her problems on her own. After Chyna had landed on her doorstep when she returned from Milan, Alexa had been giving her the time she needed. She wanted to help, but they had known each other long enough to know that Alexa needed the push, and Chyna rejected it.

She shrugged the thoughts away, wanting to concentrate on the present. What mattered now was moving forward. She couldn't change what had happened with Marco—that she had left him...and that note.

How could she have left that? No. She wouldn't regret it. That note was perfection. It was something he needed to hear, and it was something she needed him to know. She wasn't going to be tossed aside. Even though he was playing his card by pulling down her picture, it was the only card he had.

She had left *him*, after all.

Her thoughts vanished as her quarry walked through the restaurant entrance. Cassandra Corsa was a slight woman with more style than anyone Chyna had ever met. A brown dress tied around her neck, cinching in her dangerously slim waist, and pleated slightly into a perfect A-line just past her knees. She wore white peep-toe heels and a white signature Corsa purse. Her hair was parted on the right and pulled back into a low bun at the nape of her neck, and she wore accentuating makeup. Chyna couldn't have guessed her age if she had tried.

Cassandra was a woman who knew the inside and outside of beauty. She could take something ordinary and create something beyond what you could have ever expected. Her family line was made of designers, and she had been in Corsa designs since she was an infant. The Corsa name carried weight and power in the world that Chyna wanted back into, and Chyna wanted nothing more than to use that to her advantage. Plus, she liked Cassandra.

The hostess smiled at Cassandra and walked her back to Chyna's table. Chyna stood gracefully, leaning forward, as she kissed both of Cassandra's cheeks.

"Good to see you, dear," Cassandra said with a smile.

"And, you as well. I'm fortunate that you are in New York this weekend," Chyna said, mirroring her smile.

"Ah, yes. Business calls," she said, taking a seat across from her.

A waiter arrived promptly. They both requested water and salads, the customary model diet. Cassandra started haggling the waiter about their variety of wine, and she ended up ordering a bottle of some vintage import. Chyna was hoping that the conversation would be shorter than a bottle of wine. She hadn't really been drinking much the past two weeks and couldn't afford a slip up.

"I was surprised to hear from your mother," Cassandra mused aloud. "I wasn't even aware that you were related at first."

Chyna smiled, sitting up straighter in her chair. "Well, I'm glad she was able to reach you."

"Your Marco wouldn't give you the number?" she asked, her face giving away nothing.

Chyna breathed in sharply, not wanting to have this conversation. She wanted the modeling job. That was all she was here for. She wasn't here for Marco. Forget about Marco. He put her on the map, and she damn well was going to keep herself there.

"It didn't come up," she answered honestly in as vague a manner as she could muster.

"I saw your spread," Cassandra noted.

"I think everyone saw it," Chyna said. "Isn't he extraordinary?" She wasn't sure why she was using the same phrasing Cassandra had used at the Glam Ball, but it seemed fitting. She wanted to stay in comfortable conversation.

"He's young," she said with a shrug.

She had probably seen many talented young men come and go. Chyna doubted many of them had Marco's flare. She needed to stop thinking about him. She was obsessed with an imaginary dream, and she needed to let it go!

"A young visionary. I think many have started as such," Chyna said as Cassandra's wine arrived.

The waiter popped open the bottle and poured each of them a full glass of red wine. It was truly incredible—sweet but not too sweet and as smooth as butter. She could have drunk the whole bottle herself. Probably not the best idea under the circumstances.

Cassandra sipped from her glass and sighed. "If only it was Italian," she purred, her face a mask with a smile that didn't seem to fit her.

"I miss Italian wine," Chyna agreed. But, this shit was fantastic.

"I always miss my home when I'm away," she said, swirling the wine around in her glass before taking another sip.

"I can understand that. I'm back in New York after all."

"This is your home?" she asked, studying her face.

Chyna nodded.

"I would have thought...well, it doesn't matter."

"You would have thought what?" Chyna prompted.

"Just something...more. I can't explain it," Cassandra said, flourishing her hand to close the conversation. "Well, let's get down to it. I've been up to my ears with meetings since I've been here. Why did you call this one?"

Chyna set her glass of wine down on the table and looked back up at Cassandra. She wore the strangest smile on her face. In a way, Chyna wasn't even sure if you could call it a smile. It was just her face.

"I wanted to talk to you about that job offer. You mentioned that you were looking to add me to your collection, and I just needed to contact you. So is that spot still available?" Chyna asked, finding that she was rambling more than she had thought. Why was she so nervous?

Cassandra reached forward across the table and touched Chyna's hand. Chyna looked down at it. She was a little surprised that Cassandra would touch her. It seemed out of place.

"What happened?" she asked.

"What are you talking about?" Chyna responded. She was getting irritated for no reason. It seemed like Cassandra was trying to sympathize with her...or pity her. Not only did she have no idea why Cassandra would do that, but it also wasn't the appropriate response when asking about a job offer.

"With Marco. You were at the height. You were the center."

"You offered me a job, and he didn't. Plain and simple," she said. Nothing about it was plain and simple, but it was the truth. She hadn't given Marco the opportunity to get that far.

"But, why? What happened? He should have offered you that job. I saw the spread," Cassandra reminded her.

Why was she reminding her though? Why was she digging? *Everyone* had seen the spread! Every fashion designer in the world knew what her picture looked like at this point. What did that have to do with anything?

"I don't know," she spoke flatly. "He just didn't."

"Huh," Cassandra said, releasing her hand and leaning back in her chair. "You don't know?"

"No," Chyna lied. She knew damn well what had happened. She had walked out on him. She had ruined it. "But, Marco doesn't have anything to do with this meeting. I just came to talk to you about the job you offered me."

"I know, but unfortunately, Marco Moretti has a whole hell

of a lot to do with this meeting," Cassandra said, tipping her glass back and finishing off her first glass of wine.

Oh, no! Oh, no, no, no! This could not be happening. What did Marco have to do with this? What had he done? She could feel the vibrations on the train tracks, but she couldn't move. The train was coming whether she wanted it to or not, and she couldn't stop it or slow it down.

"Why?" was the only thing she managed to get out. She was pretty sure that she looked shocked.

"You really don't know," Cassandra muttered softly. "Interesting."

"Care to enlighten me?" she asked dryly.

"You've been blacklisted across all design markets. You're unhirable."

23

PRESENT

Unhirable.

Chyna's head swam, and she rested her hand on the table to keep herself from spinning. Blacklisted. All markets. Her throat ceased. She didn't understand those words, especially not all together in relation to her. She...she couldn't be. She just couldn't be.

He wouldn't do that. She had been on top. She had been everything. Then, one fuck up—leaving him—and that was the end? That couldn't be the end!

This was what she wanted! He couldn't steal the one thing that she wanted. It's not like she had taken anything from him except the break up. She would gladly go back to Italy and let him end it if it meant that he would change this.

She didn't even know that he could do this. How could he blacklist her? What did he have on her that would justify murdering her career before it had even officially begun?

And, Cassandra was somehow going along with it. After offering her the position at the Glam Ball, Cassandra was now... retracting her offer. Was a blacklist so disruptive that even someone who had already made her an offer could recant the statement?

"So…he didn't tell you," Cassandra said.

That was pretty fucking clear!

"Did you come to this meeting just to find out if he had?" Chyna asked her desperately, surprised she still could form words.

"To be perfectly honest, I assumed that you would try to talk me out of it. I thought it might be worth a shot to hear you try. I didn't expect to be the one to break the news to you," she said plainly.

She was a plain woman. So plain. Why was she fortunate enough to not be on a blacklist? How did one even get on there?

Chyna was pissed. She had given up so much to go, wanting to find her piece of greatness. And, she *still* managed to lose it. She lost everything that ever mattered to her.

"Did he say…why?" she asked, clenching her teeth to keep herself together. She was ping-ponging between uncontrollable, fierce anger—the rip-your-throat-out kind—to hyperventilating, soul-crushing depression—with big, fat ugly tears.

"You don't want to do this," she told her warningly. "If it were me, I'd let it go and find a new profession. No one in this town or the next is going to hire you."

"So, he said why," she muttered, wondering how far he had dragged her name through the dirt to make her unhirable. What did it take?

"He did," Cassandra confirmed. "But, it might be best if you—"

"What were his reasons?" she snapped, cutting Cassandra off. She could never work for the woman. Who cared what manners looked like when she needed nothing from her? What was she going to do…keep her from a job? Oh, wait…

"Breaking-and-entering and theft mainly, but also, you apparently quit the modeling contract two weeks early without a word, causing him to have to rework his entire layout and lose money," Cassandra told her flatly. "I don't know what to think about the first two, but losing money in our business, in any business, will be a good enough reason for most designers. You must have done a real number on him."

"He's totally fucked-up!" she told her.

Of course! It all made sense now. Theft—she had a one-of-a-kind million-dollar dress tucked away in her closet as they spoke right now. Not to mention, she had confiscated the sex tape and *modeling* pictures from his apartment before departing. And, she had ended her contract early. The breaking-and-entering was just icing on the cake, but everything else he had said was true. He was trying to make her out to be the worst kind of scum.

What was worse...was that it was working.

"So, you're not going to hire me?" Chyna asked, just wanting to clarify.

"I'm afraid not."

"Seriously? Because of one man?" Chyna scrunched her eyebrows together.

"It's more than that. You don't understand how the blacklist works."

"But, I certainly know that you're following a wolf in sheep's clothing," Chyna spat at her, furious with Marco for what he had done. "And, you'll regret it."

"Why would I regret it?" Cassandra asked plainly.

"Because I'm the best."

"Every model thinks that."

Chyna scoffed. "Go back and look at that spread. The only reason he put me on that list is because he can't have me," Chyna said, pushing her chair back, "and he doesn't want anyone else to either."

"That may be," Cassandra conceded. "But, in your position,

I would just be glad that he's not pressing charges," she said softly. She actually looked a bit sad.

"And, isn't that strange? I mean, all things considered," Chyna snapped, knowing it was a better defense than denying the charges.

"It is," Cassandra admitted.

"Right," she said, popping the *t* at the end of the word, as she rose from her chair. "I would think about what I said. You're the one letting him win."

Cassandra slowly stood, too. She extended her hand toward Chyna who reluctantly shook it. Chyna was surprised she was even receiving this much hospitality. It wasn't quite the warm welcome she had received at the Glam Ball.

"I'm sorry about Marco," Cassandra finally said.

"Don't be," Chyna said viciously, trying to pull her hand back.

"I think he was madly in love with you," she whispered, staring intently into Chyna's green eyes.

Chyna's mouth popped open in surprise. She was not expecting that. "Then, you don't know the first thing about love."

Cassandra sighed and shook her head, releasing her hand. "I wish *you* did."

She wrenched her hand back from Cassandra. How dare she! What a nosy little bitch! She had no right to presume anything about her or Marco. She certainly had no right to dash her dreams and then shove the stupid L-word down her throat. How would she even know if Marco loved her? He was a player, and she wanted to be played. When she didn't want to be played any longer, she left. There was no added complication and no secret devotion between them. They were just two people who wanted to be fucked as they tried to get ahead.

Chyna grabbed her purse off the ground, took one last fleeting glance at Cassandra Corsa, and then left the restaurant with her last shred of dignity. She was barely keeping it together.

By the time she made it out of Barneys, Chyna thought she was going to combust. Her hands were balled into fists and shaking. Her jaw was set, and she thought she might scream any second. Short angry bursts escaped her mouth, and people passing by glanced at her nervously. She let out a string of expletives, cursing everything under the sun for her existence today. More people stared, but she didn't care. She was seeing red.

She took a seat on an empty bench and pulled out her phone. Alexa would make it better. She would understand... except Chyna hadn't told her everything that had happened. They had breezed over the details when she had landed at her door. Of course, she knew about the cover spread, but that was what she had been in Milan for in the first place. Not that she was trying to hide it from Alexa. She had told her about Marco, but Alexa had assumed, as most people would, that it was a just a fling. Nothing more. She just hadn't gone into the details.

Plus, Alexa was leaving for Atlanta today. Another harebrained idea to deal with her men. Why couldn't either of them manage relationships?

Chyna figured that at least she had one person left whom she could always vent to. Pressing Frederick's number, she waited for him to answer.

"Sugar, it's been a while since I've heard your sweet voice," Frederick crooned into the phone.

"Hey," she said, her voice lacking her normal pep. "Can you talk?"

"I'm at work but sure," he said, kind of taken aback by her somber tone.

She usually took her lows to Alexa, but she couldn't right now. Maybe she just wanted him to call her a bitch and be done with it.

"I can't sugarcoat it," she said, swallowing. She had cried once before, and the crumbling of her dreams should have warranted the same emotional breakdown. But she would not cry over this. At least this time, she found her anger. "I really fucked up."

"What else is new? Tell me?" he said.

She could hear him adjusting the phone, likely holding it up against his shoulder while he reupholstered a couch or sewed a pillow or wherever his interior decorating skills took him.

"Where to start?" she grumbled. "I fucked Marco Moretti."

"Shut up!" he cried.

"He likes it kinky."

"Shut up!"

"I let him chain me to the bed naked, photograph me, and make a sex tape."

"Shut the fuck up, you dirty little slut! Can I have your life, please?!"

"Please take it," she told him, trying hard to keep breathing properly.

"What could *possibly* make you want to give that shit up?" he demanded.

"That's the thing...I did give it up. I stole a million-dollar dress, the pictures, the sex tape, left him, and came back to New York," she whispered the whole explanation. It sounded less and less believable every time. How had she actually gone through with that?

"You...what?" he asked, nearly dropping the phone.

"He's ruined it all. He's blacklisted me across the entire design market. I've been termed unhirable. I had a job offer for modeling in the fall, and they retracted it! They actually retracted the fucking offer!" she cried, unable to believe what she was saying. How could he be so cruel?

"I hate to say this," Frederick said, suddenly serious, "but... he didn't ruin it all. You did, baby girl."

"What?" she asked, standing straight up off of the park bench in astonishment.

"You walked out on him after all of that? Sweetheart, I'd do *way* worse!" he told her honestly. "If he's going through the effort to fuck you over so thoroughly, he had it for you, and he had it bad. I'd go through hell and high water to make sure you were miserable without me."

"Fuck!" she cried angrily. "Can't you just fucking sympathize with me? Why do you have to be so logical?"

"Look, bitch, if you can't take the heat, get out of the fucking kitchen!"

"Fine! I will!" she yelled through the phone.

"Whatever. You'll come crawling back for more. I'm the only man you ever keep coming back to."

She felt that like a slap to the face. She needed to remind herself never to fight with Frederick again. He fought dirty, and she was too sensitive right now. What he was saying hurt! And all she wanted to do was stop feeling.

"Just wait until you see what I do to my apartment," she growled into the phone.

"Find another designer to clean up your mess!" he snapped, the double meaning clear in his words. He hung up before she could get the last word in.

Of all the things she had been expecting from Frederick, anger and judgment were not among them.

Without him, whom else could she talk to about this? How could she make them understand that she had lost something special to her...something that had really mattered to her? People didn't think anything mattered to her besides drinking and random hook-ups. How could she prove them wrong now? The industry wouldn't let her stick with modeling, and it would all look like just another thing that Chyna quickly got tired of.

She sat back on the bench, her anger seeping out of her like sand through a sieve. There was one person. One person who would understand what she had given up to get to where she was in modeling. One person who would understand what she was losing by giving it up.

Her hands were trembling as suspense stole her stomach. This shouldn't be so difficult. She used to talk to him every day.

She waited for the line to click over to voicemail. He wasn't going to answer. Just another disappointment. She heard him clearing his voice before anything else. It was so familiar that she nearly smiled.

"Hey," he muttered into the phone. "Now really isn't a good time. Can I call you back?"

She sighed. "Can we talk?"

"I...uh, do you...think that's a good idea? We kind of..." he trailed off.

"Please," she begged. "I'm not asking for much, just some of your time."

He paused, releasing a sigh that said he was going to give in. "When you didn't call after you got back, I thought it was over," he said softly.

"Isn't that what you want?" she asked, her desperation palpable.

"How could you think I wanted that?"

"You ended it."

"You were leaving."

She sighed, thinking about everything that had happened since she left New York. A lot of it was pretty fucked-up, but a lot of it wasn't. She loved modeling. Wasn't it better to have loved and lost than to never have loved at all? Even if it hurt like hell?

"I'm glad I did," she finally responded softly, "but not that I lost you in the process."

There. She had admitted it.

Chyna watched Alexa walk away from her town car toward the airport. After her conversation with Adam earlier, she had felt a lot better about what had happened to her. She had wanted to tell Alexa about what had happened with Marco, Cassandra, Frederick—with all of them—but she had so much else to deal with right now.

Going to this wedding was a terrible idea, and as much as Chyna had tried to talk her out of it, she couldn't reason with Alexa. If Chyna had unloaded all of her problems on Alexa today, that would have been really bad for her friend. Chyna wanted to tell her, but timing was key. It could wait until she got back. It was just one week.

Plus, Alexa was hiding things from her anyway. She wouldn't tell her whom she had been secretly seeing. She thought she was so clever, but Chyna saw it all over her that she was into someone new. Eventually, she would get it out of her, but perhaps, that was a conversation for later as well. After that godforsaken wedding.

Adam would be off work soon, and he had promised to come over to talk. She was picking up Chinese food, his favorite take-out. It felt really normal, and she kind of liked it. She needed some normal in her life after the whirlwind that had taken over.

Carl drove her back to her place, and a weight seemed to settle on her shoulders as she took the elevator to the top floor. She'd had to keep it together for Alexa, but she couldn't keep the act up. What had happened was eating away at her slowly but surely.

She had officially hit rock bottom.

Before this, she had never really known what it felt like. She had lost Adam of her own volition. Hope still sprung up between them, but she didn't know what would happen once they started talking. Would the old feelings blossom again? Or, would he realize what she had known all along—that she wasn't good enough for him? It seemed fitting, considering everything else.

She had lost Marco. She had lost the Corsa contract. She had lost modeling all together. Frederick was mad at her, not that she thought that would last.

Chyna hated sounding like the poor, little rich girl, but she had never put herself out there before long enough to let everything fall apart. It was an eye-opening experience to...fail.

She heaved in a deep breath and entered her apartment. She stopped in her tracks at the living room. How had she forgotten that she was tearing the place apart? She and Frederick had gotten into a lover's spat last week, and the place was still only halfway back to normal. She had threatened to take it back to its earlier form of distaste, but now, it felt dramatic. Staring at her messy apartment only made all the fresh memories wash over her.

What had she been thinking?

She had a lot of work to do.

As she waited for Adam, she placed the take-out in the refrigerator and did something she should have done a long time ago. She walked through her living room and back into her massive closet. Hanging in the back, hidden behind hundreds of other garments, was the million-dollar dress.

She removed it from the hanger and carried it back into the living room. She grabbed an empty box from her latest purchase that was discarded on her floor and placed it on her black leather sofa. She smiled forlornly at the dress as she fingered the precious material. That part of her life was over, and it was time to let go of the past. She sighed heavily, letting it all out.

Carefully folding the dress, she placed it into the box, sealed it, and wrote Marco's address on the shipping label. Once she mailed it tomorrow, that would be the end of it.

Satisfied with her decision, she went about actually cleaning her apartment before Adam's arrival. It wasn't dirty. She still had housekeepers after all, but she was tired of the clutter in her life. She took the bamboo blinds and a few other random environmental pieces she had acquired on a whim and hid them in a side closet. She would get rid of them properly later. She grabbed a stack of old framed black-and-white photographs from the same closet, happy to place them back on the wall where they belonged.

The collage she had built over years from collecting pictures of obscure locals finally came back into shape. She hung up the next one, adjusting it to make sure it was straight, and then grabbed one of the last pictures. As she stood up and glanced at the picture, her breath caught, and she nearly dropped the picture.

She had completely forgotten that she had brought back framed photographs from Milan. When she had returned to New York, she had been furious for even using all that space in her suitcase for them, so she had hidden them in that closet. She was a collector, and even then, leaving the pictures had seemed like a waste.

But, staring at the pictures now was a reminder of what she had given up by leaving. She sighed, tracing the outline of the frame. Maybe she needed them now to remember how far she had come.

The first one that she was holding in her hand was of the Naviglio Grande canal. All she saw when she looked at it was a blue Bugatti. She placed it on a nail in the wall, wanting to cling on to the remaining happy memories of Milan. The second one was from the coast in Genoa. She didn't remember which day Marco had taken this one. She just remembered the happiness of spending time with people whose company she enjoyed. That one followed suit, and on the wall, it went. The final one she picked up was a photo shoot she would forever remember. It was taken from the window of Marco's bedroom with the city skyline captured perfectly. He had hated it because it blurred around the edges, but she loved it because it illuminated the stars.

She swallowed hard, deciding she couldn't hang that picture. It wouldn't be right. She had left her star in Italy, and now, she looked at a new night sky. Marco had made that as blatantly clear as her letter, and she was returning the dress. Her last link to him.

The picture was replaced back into its hiding place in the closet where it belonged, and she finished up the rest of the cleaning. When the doorbell rang an hour later, the place wasn't a hundred percent back to normal, but it was as close as it was going to get by herself. She had threatened to tear it apart to upset Frederick, but all she had done was put it back together herself. She needed to do that to the rest of her life now.

Chyna opened the door and immediately burst out laughing. It felt good. "Is that Chinese?"

Adam shrugged, clearly not understanding her laughter. "I thought you might be hungry."

She rolled her eyes with a smile on her face. "I am. Come on."

Adam followed behind her and placed the food on the island just as she pulled Chinese take-out from the refrigerator.

Seeing that they had ordered the same thing, Adam burst out laughing as well. "Guess we both wanted the same thing."

"Well, yours is still warm," she said, snatching a box of rice and some chicken concoction out of his hands. "So, I'm calling dibs."

"I assumed so," he said, taking a seat on a bar stool and popping open his own take-out boxes.

Chyna ripped open the chopsticks provided and dug into her meal. She was surprisingly hungry after such an exhausting day. Oh yeah, she hadn't actually eaten her salad during her meeting with Cassandra. No wonder. Had she had anything today?

They ate in silence for the most part. He chatted briefly about work, and she told him about Alexa's plan in Atlanta. They both laughed at that one, knowing how her plans normally went. It was nice. Normal. Comfortable.

She swallowed as much as she could eat, happy to be eating real food again. Her diet had been delicious but small, very small, and specific in Italy. Plus, they didn't have Chinese take-out like this.

Neither of them seemed ready to move on with the conversation. Even after they were both stuffed and Chyna had put the leftovers back into her refrigerator, they seemed hesitant as to where the conversation should go...where it should even begin.

"So..." he said, trailing off.

"Yeah. So..." she copied.

"How was Italy?" he finally asked.

Chyna chewed on her bottom lip and fiddled with her chopsticks. "A dream come true."

"Hey, it's just me," he said, reaching out and extracting the chopsticks from her grasp. "You can talk to me."

"No, really," she said, dropping her hands onto the island. "It was a dream come true. Everything I wanted and more. I was actually great at something...beyond great at something."

"Then, why do you seem so down? How could it be everything you wanted?" he asked softly.

She looked down and away from his probing eyes. She didn't want to tell him, but isn't that why she had asked to talk to him? She had been thinking about him before she even left Marco. And she had been an emotional wreck after they had broken up. At the time she couldn't even figure out why. She still didn't know why...not really. Nothing had ever hit her so hard. Except this. Maybe worse than this.

"Because I messed it all up... like I always do," she whispered the last part glancing up nervously into his hazel eyes.

"Why do you always say that? You don't mess everything up," he told her placing his hand on hers reassuringly.

"Well, I messed this up. I can't model anymore," she told him. The words felt tragic coming out of her mouth. And every time she thought about it, she felt like someone had punched her in the gut knocking the breath out of her.

"Why not? I thought you said you were great at it. Won't people notice that? I sure noticed your picture all over the city," he said with a fake cough to break eye contact.

"Because I...I, God!" she cried dropping her face into her hands. "That picture is the whole problem!"

Adam sighed, reaching across the island and raising her chin with his hand. "I wanted you to be happy when you left. You thought it was the right thing, and I wanted to believe you. I thought when that picture was up all over the city that it had all happened for a reason. Now, you're telling me that it didn't?" he asked, trying to put the pieces together.

Her bottom lip quivered as she stared up at him. How could

she make him understand what had happened? "It did until I left."

"Why did you leave?"

She closed her eyes. She didn't want to admit the truth. "Because I was scared."

His resolve crumbled at her admission. "What could scare *you*? You're fearless. You charge into every situation head on ready to conquer the world."

"You think so?" she asked feeling very small in that moment.

"I know so. You scare me sometimes with how you react to situations," he told her. "And sometimes—I want to be more like you."

"You do?" she asked her brows furrowing.

"Yes, Chyna. So what were you afraid of?"

She swallowed trying to absorb everything he had just told her. He thought she was fearless. He thought she conquered situations. She had always thought the opposite. It was easier not to get attached, not to have anything she obsessed over, not to feel *anything* really. That way, at least, she never felt this.

She turned her head away from him and looked out in her living room. Taking a deep breath, she finally answered him, "Failing."

"Everyone fails."

"Not me," she told him.

"Never?"

"No. Never," she said. "I've never put myself out there to fail. So I left, because I didn't want to face the alternative. Then when I got here and saw the ads, I started seeing how much I messed up by not giving it a chance. Now I can't model anymore. He blacklisted me," she whispered the last part.

"He?" Adam prompted.

"Marco," she said, meeting his probing gaze.

"Ah, the fashion designer," he said as if he knew where this was going.

She took a deep breath and plunged forward. "We were together in Italy."

He nodded, pursing his lips. "I figured."

She cringed slightly at his reaction. She knew it would be there. "And, I left him without a good-bye."

"But, you think you made the right choice?" he asked.

She bit her lip, thinking about the question. Leaving Marco, in the end, was the right thing, but the consequences...that was a different story. "I know I did."

"And, it's over?" he asked the loaded question but the easier one for her.

"Yes," she told him without hesitation. It was very over. "But, now I can't model. All because I left."

Adam sighed, standing and coming around the island to wrap his arms around her. She turned to face him, burying her face into his shoulder. He stroked her hair back as she nuzzled into him, and he gave her the moment she needed to just feel.

"Now," he said, keeping his arms around her but pulling back so that he could see her face, "you are not a failure. Even if you were, it would be okay because you're resilient. You bounce back. You are a beautiful, confident, accomplished young woman, and this one pitfall—because that's all it is—will not break you. I promise."

A smile slowly returned to her face. "You think I'm beautiful?"

"Was that ever a concern?" he asked, poking her in the sides playfully.

"Maybe."

He gave her *the look*, and she giggled.

"Fine. No."

"Are you feeling any better?" he asked.

"Yes," she admitted. She was actually feeling much better

with him around. He alleviated so much of the weight that had been on her shoulders. "I'm glad you're here."

"I'm glad you want me to be here...especially after the way I ended things," he said sheepishly.

"I thought you said it was...mutual," she said. She hated that word.

"You and I both know it wasn't," he admitted, dropping his arms from around her

PRESENT

Chyna followed Adam the living room. She was surprised at how easily he had admitted that it wasn't mutual.

She had been beating herself up about the break-up since it had happened. She had felt backed into a corner, having agreed with him accidentally. Yet, she couldn't have imagined being in Milan with Marco while dating Adam. Things would have been very different, and maybe she needed her time away to see how she felt about him.

The silence lingered between them. Chyna stood back and observed him before the photographs she had put up. Her heart ached as she watched him. Why had it taken her so long to see what was standing directly in front of her all this time?

"New additions," Adam mused, staring at the collection on her wall. "I'm guessing you got these in Italy."

She nodded. "Yeah, I did." She was prepared to tell him about them if he asked. She was ready to move on.

"They seem to fit the wall," he said, staring at them with his head cocked to the side. "The lines in Italian architecture are just stunning."

She chuckled softly. Of course, he would always bring it

back to architecture. It was his job and his life. When he looked at the pictures, he saw only well-constructed buildings, a beauty that few others could really appreciate. Where he saw the beauty of a well-crafted building, she saw only memories— memories of a past that she had left behind after boarding the plane to New York. Such a sharp, determined decision had changed everything.

"Hey, you," he said, turning to face her. "Come here."

She walked up to him, not hesitating for a second. "Yes?"

"I really am glad you're back," he said, his arms circling her waist as he pulled her into a hug.

"Me too," she whispered against his chest.

She loved the feel of his arms around her. It felt like home. It felt like the only home she had ever known…the only one she had ever chosen. It was comfortable and relaxing, and she could have laid her head against his shoulder, breathing in his familiar scent, all day.

Just when she was getting comfortable, he pulled back and stared down into her face, memorizing every inch of it like a blueprint. "So, why those two pictures?" he asked softly, bringing her out of her reverie.

She knew she had to answer him, and she figured she had a response. Taking a deep breath, she answered him, "Because they are the memories I *want* to remember from my time in Italy."

He nodded, not needing to ask anything further. She figured he could guess that they had something to do with Marco. He would forever be intrinsically linked with Milan to her. The memories were not something Adam would ever want to know about, and she was glad that he didn't push it.

"You know," he began, staring back up at the picture like he was trying to find the answers hidden within the still frames. "I found out how you got those tickets."

"What?" she asked, surprised by the change in direction. He

must be talking about the tickets to Marco's grand opening. She had never discovered their origin. "How did you find out? They were dropped off at my front door."

"I know. I didn't really believe you at the time, but I found out that you were right," he said, looking a bit sheepish.

"Of course, I was right. I wouldn't lie to you about something like that," she told him. Oh, those tickets were the key to her ending up in Italy!

"Sorry. It didn't seem very plausible at the time," he admitted.

"Well, who sent them, and how did you find out?" she demanded, curiosity getting the better of her.

"John," he said, glancing into her green eyes for the shock that immediately registered there.

Her stomach felt a bit queasy. She couldn't believe what he had just said. How? Why? What the...

"Apparently, the big deal that he had negotiated with Global was for Marco's clothing line to come to New York, and the designer gave him two complimentary tickets as a thank you of sorts."

That son of a bitch! She wasn't sure if she could form coherent sentences because she was so furious. Of all the fucking people to gain her access to Marco Moretti, it had to be the one person that she despised for his very existence in her life. Stupid, fucking hot, tattooed man! Why the hell did he send her tickets? Hadn't he done enough damage?

"He told me that he would have given them to you in person, but you were out, and he had a flight to catch. He wanted to apologize, and I guess this was the only way he knew how. Not sure how he knew you wanted to be at that opening."

Because she had told him...or at least told him about how she wanted to model. She couldn't believe this. She just couldn't.

She knew that she should be happy with John. He had

given her the means to model in Italy all through his supposed apology, but she just couldn't be happy with him. Not only had he *ruined* her relationship once by kissing her at the Hookah Lounge, he had then sent her the very tickets, introducing her to Marco, that forced the untimely destruction of her relationship a *second* time. Unforgivable!

She didn't care what his supposed intentions were. All she cared was what had happened because of his interference.

"Pretty nice thing for John to do to apologize. He didn't have to give those tickets to you and look at the direction it took your life. You got a job modeling in Italy," Adam said, trying to sound more excited than he had two months ago when she had suggested the opportunity.

Stop it! She didn't want to hear about how nice he was! He was disgusting, a pig, the scum of the universe! What kind of guy hits on his brother's girlfriend? Terrible kinds!

She wanted to hate him! She didn't want to think that... perhaps he was actually a nice guy who had made a mistake. She didn't want to think about him apologizing. Then, that would just be one more thing that she had gotten wrong and one more thing that she would have to change her perspective on.

No, she was determined that he was a bad guy. He saw what he wanted and took it. Plain and simple. None of this apologizing. Nothing more than a set up.

"At the time, he said to me, 'Every saint has a past, and every sinner has a future.' It's an Oscar Wilde quote. Kind of stuck with me."

Chyna shook her head. She didn't want to think about him or his Oscar Wilde quotes. She didn't care that they made sense.

"I don't want to talk about him," she said, knowing she was being short with Adam.

"All right. I just thought you would want to know."

She didn't, but she didn't say that. She didn't have to. It was written all over her face.

"Forget I said anything then," he said, drawing her close to him again.

She wanted to forget, but she knew she wouldn't, not now.

"I'm just happy to be here. Whatever that means," he said, finding her hand and circling his thumb against her palm.

"What does that mean?" she asked, looking up at him.

"Whatever you want. What do you want?"

So many things—a modeling career, for one. But, she couldn't have that now, and she realized the only other thing she had ever wanted that much was standing directly in front of her. She knew the answer to his question then.

"You. I just want you," she breathed, wrapping her arms up around his neck.

His smile was contagious, and she found herself mirroring his goofy grin.

"That's convenient."

"Why?" she asked, unable to drop her smile even if she had tried.

"Because I want you, too."

Her heart skipped a beat as everything came into focus. She had gone through a lot to get to this moment, and it was incredibly perfect just the way it was. She knew that there would be things that would linger with her—John, Marco, modeling— that she couldn't control. The only thing she could control was where she would go from here.

"I told you before you left that I would miss you, and I meant every word. It wasn't the same without you in my life. I'm sorry I pushed you out of it," he told her, staring down into her face.

"I'm sorry I let you," she whispered.

Adam bent forward, brushing his nose against hers before letting his lips fall on hers. His kiss was sweet and full of apologies for their time apart. She wanted to tell him that it was okay...that everything was okay now. She was back. She wished they could just pick up where they had left off, but maybe it was better that they couldn't. Leaving Italy had changed her, and she liked herself better for having done it. For having gone and done something great, and came back to find him still there.

Chyna's heart hadn't known what it wanted. It wasn't even been able to process what she was feeling.

She just kept finding herself repeating the same mistakes over and over again. But, it was going to stop. She couldn't keep avoiding intimacy with the one person she truly wanted it with. All the other guys had been temporary flings, forgettable. Even the ones who had stayed with her long after were only shadows of this feeling right now. She had pursued them out of a thought that they were the kind of guy she wanted or even needed, her *type*, but she had been wrong. They couldn't hold a flame to this.

Yet, what was she feeling? What had she felt that day that she and Adam had *mutually* broken up? Her world had been shattered, and she had been devastated. It felt like her like her life was imploding, and there was nothing she could do to fix it. It was like she was being held underwater, struggling to break free. She could think of a thousand different agonizing scenarios, and none of them were as bad as when her heart had broken.

And, none were as good as him sewing it back together.

"Adam," she said, curling her finger around the hairs at the nape of his neck.

"Yeah," he murmured, resting his forehead against hers.

Her heart hammered in her chest. She knew. She knew then.

"I love you," she told him.

It was the first time she had ever said it to anyone, and she meant every word. That was what she had been feeling all along, and she just had never stopped long enough to realize it. She had never felt it before, and when it had taken up foreign residence in her heart, she had been scared of the new emotions it elicited out of her. But, being with him now...she just knew.

"I knew that all along," he said with a smile. "I love you, too."

Their lips met, washing away the aches and pain of their past. They knew the road ahead would hold many more trials of their love. But today, they were content with their reunion—with the knowledge of reciprocated love.

Chyna knew then that although they had gone through much to reach their destination, the journey had only brought them closer. And, in the end, she had found him.

He was the one she had to go through all the jerks to find.

He was her end game.

THE END

ACKNOWLEDGMENTS

Avoiding Intimacy

Avoiding Intimacy is a book for the fans. The wonderful fans of the Avoiding Series have made it possible for me to be here writing something as fun as a story about Chyna. You supported me when I put Avoiding Commitment out, when I made you wait five months for the next book, when I left you without a happily ever after, and when I left you with one. These aren't typical books. They're not exactly a romance or a love story. They're stories about life. And I appreciate you supporting me when times were tough and people didn't believe in my voice.

Every book I write I should in part dedicate to and thank my wonderful boyfriend, Joel. He's the one putting up with the long hours, crazy hectic work schedule, insane ideas, rants over dinner about what some character was doing…yeah, he puts up with it all. But still he comes back to me with even better ideas about the story, and for that level of support, I can never thank him enough. Plus, he convinced me to get my new Italian Greyhound, Riker, and he and Lucy keep me company while writing!

As always, I couldn't have done any of this without my family. For every time my mom told me that she would never tell me I couldn't get a book at the store. You guys inspire me—my crazy active imagination and creativity. I wouldn't be here without the library of books at home and all the travels and experiences we had together.

My creative consultant, task master, insomniac, Jessica! You don't know how important your line by line feedback is to my writing process. I'm not sure I'll remember how to write without you around, up until 3am, searching pinterest, and telling me what's good and what sucks...even though you *swear* it doesn't suck. Thank you for all your time and enthusiasm!

Avoiding Betas! Yes, the name still makes me giggle. *Taryn* —Thank you for your honesty. I know it can be hard to say what you're really feeling, but your comments mean everything to me. I believe whole-heartedly that your concerns make my work better. You push me to be better. *Becky*—I think you might know my writing better than even I do! Some of the things that you suggested I'm pretty sure I would have never caught. You have the best eye for detail, and I love you for it. *Shannon*— Thanks for encouraging me to move forward and write about Chyna on my Seattle trip. You've always been there for me in my writing process, and I'm so glad we were finally able to meet! *Autumn*—I can't believe we finally were able to meet and hang out. I want you in my life more often! Thanks for loving the characters! *Lori*—Your help and encouragement throughout this whole process has been so helpful. You had great comments throughout and I'm lucky to have you to help me and my writing! *Mollie*—I know your new life has you all over the place recently, but thank you for the time that you were able to give. You're my favorite tough critic. *Jenny*— Congrats on all the success with your blog. I know it keeps your super busy, and I'm glad you were able to fit me in through everything. Your feedback is always much appreciated. <3 *all of you girls!*

My lovely cover designer and friend—Sarah @ okaycreations. We've come a long way from when we were messing around with Avoiding Commitment, shooting in the dark for something that fit together. Avoiding Intimacy just kind of fell together. It was almost too easy. You have a perfect eye, and I'll always appreciate your clear voice and style.

My editor—Jovana. I know I pushed my deadlines, put you on short notice, and asked you way too often if you were finished, but thanks to you I have a polished product. I love all your comments in the margins, and our late night conversations about German and Australian accents! Thank you for your help!

Thank you all the people I have met along the way that helped me and believed in me. I'm sure I'll leave someone out, but you're all appreciated—Bridget, Bekah Haters Club, Writer's Club, Rebecca Donovan, Colleen Hoover, Crystal Serowka, Maryse, Nicola, Denise, K. Anne Raines, Trish, Courtney, and Jillian Dodd.

Big thank you to the plethora of blogs that have supported me along this journey including TotallyBooked, My Secret Romance, Maryse @ maryse.net, TalkSupe, Flirty and Dirty Book Blog, Fiction & Fashion, C&C, Little Black Book, Angie's Dreamy Reads, Madison Says, Autumn Reviews, SubClub, The Boyfriend Bookmark, Brandee's Book Endings, A Bookish Escape.. Where would indie writers be without bloggers?

Avoiding Decisions

Thank you so much for everyone who encouraged me to write from the point of view of my two males leads. Ramsey's point of view came out of a fun contest I did with Mollie

Harper at Tough Critics Book Blog. I appreciate everyone who voted and participated in her contest that gave me the opportunity to write Ramsey's POV.

Also, I would like to thank Kallysten for allowing me to participate in the Shades of Pink anthology to raise money for breast cancer awareness. Without you and the urging of Madeline Sheehan, I wouldn't have ever written Jack's point of view.

Additionally I would like to thank early readers of each novella: Jessica, Bridget, Rebecca. And as always my boyfriend Joel, who suffered through me writing from a guy's point of view and making sure it sounded realistic.

ABOUT THE AUTHOR

K.A. Linde is the *USA Today* best-selling author of the more than thirty novels. She has a Masters degree in political science from the University of Georgia, was the head campaign worker for the 2012 presidential campaign at the University of North Carolina at Chapel Hill, and served as the head coach of the Duke University dance team.

She loves reading fantasy novels, binge-watching Supernatural, traveling to far off destination, baking insane desserts, and dancing in her spare time.

She currently lives in Lubbock, Texas, with her husband and two super-adorable puppies.

You can reach her online at her website:
www.kalinde.com

Or Facebook, Instagram, and Twitter:
@authorkalinde

For exclusive content, free books,
and giveaways every month.

www.kalinde.com/subscribe